RUTHLESS ACQUISITION

PIPER STONE

Published by Stormy Night Publications and Design, LLC.
www.StormyNightPublications.com

Stone, Piper
Ruthless Acquisition

Cover Design by Korey Mae Johnson
Images by Depositphotos/feedough and Shutterstock/tomertu

PROLOGUE

*S*ome women don't get just under your skin; they slide in so quietly that you have no idea they've managed to claw their way inside, digging at the armor wrapped around your psyche. She was that kind of woman, a stunning temptress with the most enigmatic green eyes and a body built to kill.

However, she was a barracuda in disguise, determined to bring down my empire. That would never happen. After I was finished with her, she would learn what happened to anyone who dared cross that line.

Or the man she'd defied more than once.

Soon, she would face the consequences.

Soon, she would surrender.

And soon, her company and every inch of her delicious body would become my possessions.

My father had once told me that there was a fine line between good and evil and that every man would be forced to face a choice at least once in their life. I had a feeling my father was right. Was I capable of doing something horrific?

The answer was easy.

Without a doubt.

- Randolph Worth

 *carlett*

"There is no trap so deadly as the trap you set for yourself."

Raymond Chandler

Run. Run! Keep moving.

I flew up the stone stairs, panting from the exertion, every muscle in my body aching. I had to get away. I had to survive. I'd never felt such a burst of adrenaline before, my heart thudding to the point sounds echoed in my ears, terror implanted in my mind. If I couldn't get away, they would kill me.

As my bare feet scraped across the rough stone, pain shifted into my legs, but I ignored it even though my skin was bloody and raw. I had to find a way out of the building. There was no other chance at survival. Panting, exhaustion powered through me, stealing my energy as well as my breath. I'd been confined in that dark, dingy place for far too long. Prickling sensations washed down the back of my legs as I tried to catch my breath.

The fuckers wouldn't capture me again. I refused to allow that to happen.

Even with my heightened determination, I knew escape was impossible. but I would not give in. No fucking way. They would have to kill me first.

Three fucking assholes.

Dangerous men.

All of them determined to break me. That just wasn't going to happen.

I'd been caught in a vicious trap, yet one I'd allowed myself to succumb to. I'd been stupid thinking I could win. Now I was about to lose everything.

Including my life.

My heart ached at the thought but not for that reason, but for the burning need that I'd allowed to overcome all rationality.

I willed myself to move, powering up the remainder of the steps, bursting onto the roof of the building and into the wonderful air. Joy filled my heart as I was finally able to take a deep breath. It seemed so long since I'd experienced anything but stale air, chains wrapped around my wrists in an attempt to keep me their prisoner. Now I was free.

If only for a little while.

As the light breeze filtered across my skin, I closed my eyes briefly, envisioning my life before the nightmare. Anger boiled deep inside, the kind that had allowed me to do the unthinkable. I'd escaped, nearly beating a man to death, but I felt no guilt, no remorse for doing so. After all, everything was fair in love and war.

The thought almost made me laugh as I raced toward the opposite side of the terrace, trying to find a place to hide. The monsters would attempt to find me soon, storming through the single door with weapons in their hands. Little did they know I'd secured one of my own, able and ready to use it when necessary. When I hid behind one of the air conditioning units, I said a silent prayer.

I couldn't imagine surviving this, but the bastards were never going to force me to submit to their vile, filthy needs, no matter the circumstances. I lowered my head, doing everything I could to steady my nerves.

I heard a noise only two minutes later. Steel slapping against steel.

They were coming for me.

They'd found me.

And they were never going to let me go.

All because of a game. The vicious game of revenge.

Suddenly, all was quiet, only the sound of the whipping wind echoing in my ears. My legs ached from the awkward angle, my rage only increasing. I gripped the gun with both hands, perspiration rolling down both sides of my face. I continued envisioning the last few days, wary of trusting anyone including myself. How could this have happened? Why had I fallen prey to such brutal monsters?

The questions wouldn't be easy to answer. Not now.

Maybe never.

I continued clutching the weapon, listening for any sounds.

Then I heard his voice, so dark and demanding that I shivered to my core.

"Oh, Scar-lett. We're here."

What a fucking son of a bitch. If he thought that he was going to encourage me to expose myself freely, the asshole was dead wrong.

"Come out, come out, wherever you are."

God, how I hated his singsong lilt, the deep, sensual baritone doing little but creating a wave of nausea.

I held my breath, doing everything I could to keep from making a single sound. Within seconds, I could tell the bastard was exasperated, huffing and puffing like some creature in the wild. I couldn't help but smile. The three assholes had underestimated me.

Another noise caught my attention, the scuffling of boots on the craggy stone surface. The men were covering all sides of the building, searching every hole and hiding spot. It was only a matter of time before I was found. At least the weapon I'd stolen from the man who'd dared try to accost me had enough ammunition I could defend myself for a little while.

Although I wasn't certain how much good that would do.

However, I was fully prepared to die instead of being taken again. My teeth were chattering as a chill rushed through me. I couldn't see where they were coming from, but I knew they were close.

Too close.

I rarely prayed but that's all I could think about, begging for forgiveness for my sins as well as my merciless nature. I'd learn to become a better woman, if only I could escape their tyranny, a horrible game I'd never intended on playing.

But I'd accepted the wager, never expecting the horrific turn of events. No one was coming to save me. There wouldn't be any heroes to keep me safe.

They were...

"Boys. It would seem our guest no longer wants to play with us."

His voice reverberated in my system, creating a wave of terror and jerking me out of the disparaging memories. The man was unhinged, drunk on his power. My body swayed, my legs cramping from the horrible position I was in.

Don't give in. Don't give in!

I had to listen to my inner voice. I had to keep fighting.

After another few seconds of silence, I dared to peek around the compressor unit. Seeing no one, I eyed the door that could still lead me to freedom. Maybe the fuckers had gone around to the other side of the terrace, thinking I might have attempted to jump to a building in close proximity. When I heard nothing for another ten seconds, I took the chance, easing into the shadows, shifting my fully extended arms from one side to the other.

No one was in sight. Very carefully, I padded toward the exterior door, remaining in a crouched position, my breathing ragged.

"Not so fast, sweet angel."

I yelped, immediately doing everything I could to bite back another sound, but it was too late. I'd failed. Every time the man spoke, he placed the fear of God into me. I rose to my full height, sucking in my breath.

Then another wave of fury tingled every one of my muscles. When I swung around, I made certain I had a smile on my face.

"You won't take me again," I said in a husky whisper.

"If you think that, you're a fool, which surprises me, Scarlett. I thought you were more intelligent than that." He took several steps in my direction, the weapon he carried firmly planted in one hand. Even in the slender light of the moon, I was able to catch his expression.

One of satisfaction.

One of evil determination.

And one of possession.

The fucker believed he'd won.

I raised the gun in my hand, doing everything I could to shut down my emotions until I was no longer shaking. "Don't come any closer. You won't like what I do."

He laughed at the fact I'd defied him.

"I have every intention of coming closer. All three of us do." He motioned to the other two who flanked his sides. "Then we're going to have a nice, long chat about your disobedience."

As the three men walked in my direction, all perfectly attired in their expensive Armani suits, I narrowed my eyes. There was no turning back. "I said stop. If you don't, I will shoot you."

Laughing, he threw out his arms, still swaggering toward me. "Sweet pet, you better be prepared to kill all three of us, which you don't have the talent to do. Anything less and you're going to spend the rest of your life in a cage."

"You don't get to call me your pet."

"We get to do anything we want, our sweet, beautiful Scarlett. You now belong to us."

When all three monsters converged, inching toward me with grins on their faces, I swallowed hard, ignoring all the things I'd been taught as a child. Right and wrong. Good and bad. None of that mattered.

Then I gave into my rage, jerking to my full height. "No!"

As I prepared to fire, all I could do was pray.

Boom!

Pop!

Pop! Pop! Pop!

CHAPTER 2

 *wo weeks earlier*

Randolph

Like father, like son.

The verbiage stuck in my mind even now, at a time when the company my father had spent his entire life building into a billion-dollar empire was ready to enter into another contract that would take us to an echelon few competitors could reach. I should be ecstatic, gloating as I usually did. Somehow, I knew the outcome wouldn't be as planned and that brought a kind of formidable rage that was crushing to my soul.

If I still had one.

Enemies.

My partners and I had crushed several like bugs, destroying not only their hopes and dreams, but the ability to regain any of their losses. In turn, Worth Dynamics, the company I served as CEO and the one started by my father years before had risen significantly in value as well as standings in the ranks of the robotics industry over the years. While I'd allowed two men that I trusted to purchase large amounts of stock, Alexander serving as CFO and Trent as VP, the company's reputation relied heavily on how I handled business transactions, following in my father's footsteps. That had led to all three of us becoming rich beyond our dreams.

But it hadn't been without personal sacrifice or heartache, the ugliness of the wretched incidents shutting down my emotions, both customers and competitors calling me a cold-hearted bastard. Some even used the term evil. I took pride in the terminology, feeding it by taking everything I wanted without hesitation.

My position allowed me that right. After all, money could buy anything. Cars. Yachts. Houses. Hell, I owned several villas in tropical locations that I hadn't been to in well over a year. Having billions even bought loyalty. However, being worth that kind of money hadn't secured the one thing I'd hungered to own for over two years.

Scarlett Prestwood.

I'd wanted nothing more than to take over her company, but that wasn't the only thing I craved.

I hungered for her luscious body writhing under mine, her sweet moans filtering into my ears. No one was going to stop me from getting what I deserved, even if I would have to use dark and demanding tactics. Snickering, I took a deep breath, still envisioning what I would do to her naked body.

I remained at the conference table, barely listening to my partners as they bantered on about the last movie they'd watched or perhaps a sports event, neither of which I cared about. All my attention was drawn to the oversized monitor and to Scarlett, the teleconference we'd both been asked to attend yet to start.

My mouth watered as I studied her body language, her attempt at acting as if she couldn't care less about the meeting. I knew better. We'd butted heads on more than once occasion since both our firms were vying for the same space. She was certainly a creature of beauty, able to capture any man's attention, which she often used to her advantage. I would never forget the first time I'd met her, a young woman determined to make mincemeat out of what had been an old boys club, suggesting a different way of doing business. She'd defied the odds, securing deal after deal as she'd clawed her way to the top, her actions almost as ruthless as mine. Maybe I should admire her.

Instead, I wanted to crush her.

Use her.

Own her.

And I always got what I wanted.

I was a keen observer of people. Her smugness meant she wholeheartedly believed she was going to win the contract. I found her search for power beguiling, although my desire had nothing to do with her business tactics.

My partners had expressed the same interest, which had led me to a decision, one that would alter our future.

What the stunning redhead didn't know was that she'd soon belong to the three men of Worth, a cherished pet to do with what we pleased.

My cock ached just thinking about the idea, something I'd envisioned far too many times over the last few months. Given the wait, I allowed my filthy visions to take over, if only for a few precious minutes.

"Why are we here?" Scarlett asked, her plump lower lip trembling as she glanced at the cold steel table positioned in the middle of the room.

"It's a surprise, my little pet," I said, keeping my tone husky and dark.

"You know I don't like surprises, sir."

I raked my finger back and forth across her stiff training collar before cupping her face, rubbing my thumb up and down her cheek. "And you know you're required to follow the rules. We've talked about this. Now, be a good little pet and undress."

"Here?"

"Right here. If I have to ask you again, I'll pull off my belt. I don't think you want me to spank you in front of the employees or my customers. Do you? Would you enjoy

being humiliated, your voluptuous body put on full display? I'm certain they would. I could make that happen with a single phone call."

"No, sir. No." Her lovely face turned bright red, matching the dress I'd insisted she wear. If she persisted, her bottom would match perfectly.

"Good girl."

I nodded toward the screen covering a small portion of the concrete room. When she slipped behind the partition, I glanced around at the space. While everything was sterile, something I'd insisted on, the cold bleakness was unappealing as fuck. Couldn't the asshole owner hang some colorful pictures? Sighing, I realized the tattoos were usually handled in another section of the building, this one meant for piercings only, but it appeared more as a prison clinic than a well-respected company. Nevertheless, the owner was being paid very well for his services, adhering to my specifications without question.

And I would enjoy every minute of watching the procedure.

Since she hadn't earned the right to wear panties, I didn't need to command her to remove them. When she finally appeared, holding her arms by her sides as required, I gave her a nod of approval. I approached slowly, indulging in a few precious seconds of gazing over her voluptuous body. My body. Every inch of her belonged to me.

"You are almost perfect, my little pet," I said in a tone as soft as the touch of her skin. When I cupped her breasts, she shuddered, her lower lip quivering. "Yes, almost. Soon you will be." I adored the way her lips pursed every time I touched her, the light sheen creating an almost translucent glow across every inch of her skin. I especially loved her rosy nipples and the way they remained fully aroused at all times.

"Yes, sir."

Chuckling, I flicked my fingers back and forth across her hardened buds before taking them between my thumbs and forefingers. I watched her carefully as I pinched and twisted them, enjoying the way her eyes reflected light from the nuance of pain. I couldn't wait to see the sterling silver chain that would always remain dangling from her nipple piercings. The thought was delicious as well as sinful.

Very slowly I lowered one hand, digging my nails into the skin of her stomach as I inched closer to 'my' pussy. She didn't like when I called her most intimate body parts mine. Her eyelids fluttered as I neared her slickened mound, her irregular breathing matching the hard thumping of my heart. When I eased my hand between her legs, her body reacted as it always did, her back arching as she pushed her rounded hips in my direction.

I took my time toying with her clit, swirling my finger in aimless circles. She was wet, hotter than usual, and a part of me wanted to bury my cock deep inside. To have her dripping with my cum just before the piercing was the ultimate in dominating her, but certainly wouldn't be allowed. I almost snorted at the thought. As if the owner of the shop could stop me from doing any damn thing I wanted. I thrust my finger deep inside, shoving past her swollen folds. The sound of her single moan was like sweet music to my ears.

"I suggest you go and stand in the corner while we're waiting. That will give you time to reflect on your need for obedience."

While she darted a look toward me, the single glance suggesting her rebellious side remained, she followed my orders. I took several deep breaths, glancing at my watch. If the man was even a minute late, I would refuse payment. He was well aware of my requirements as well and knew better than to cross me.

I slipped my finger inside my mouth, savoring her sweet flavor, my cock pushing hard against my trousers. I couldn't wait to fuck her like the savage I truly was.

As expected, he entered the room at precisely two in the afternoon.

"Mr. Worth. It's good to see you."

"And you as well, Andre. I assume everything is in order."

Andre chuckled. "Just as you requested. This must be Scarlett."

"Scarlett, come and meet Andre."

She held her head high as she shook his hand, fighting the embarrassment I could tell she was feeling. God, I did love the rose-colored tint on her sweet cheeks.

"Get on the table, my pet," I further instructed.

The way she was staring at the stirrups and shackles meant she knew exactly what she was about to face. I remained hard, my balls aching. I couldn't wait to see the finished results. She would look even more dazzling than she did wearing my collar.

When she hesitated, I reacted instantly, forcing her to lean over the edge of the table, swatting her naked bottom several times. Andre didn't say a word, nor did he make any sound. I moved from one side to the other, making certain I covered every inch of her rounded backside. She did her best to keep from whimpering, her nails clawing at the table.

"I'll be good, sir," she promised.

When I pulled her back to her feet, she blinked several times. "Then I suggest you climb onto the table."

I could almost taste her anger, which only excited me even more.

When she was in position, I backed away, watching as Andre placed her feet in stirrups, strapping her ankles in place. Then he moved to her arms, pulling them over her head, securing both wrists. Only when he repositioned her legs, altering the position of the stirrups until her glistening pussy and most of her buttocks were fully exposed, her legs open wide, did she make any sound.

"What's happening?" she finally asked Andre.

"I'm going to pierce your nipples as well as give you a VHS." When her eyes opened wide, he smiled. "I'm piercing your clit vertically. After that, I'm going to tattoo your inner thigh. Don't worry, the procedures will only hurt for a short period of time. First, I'm going to check your temperature to ensure that you're well enough to have the procedures."

As Andre pulled away, rolling a cart closer then sliding into a pair of gloves, she pursed her lips. When he slid a rectal thermometer into her asshole, she closed her eyes.

I moved to a chair, ready to observe the glorious moment. After this, she would completely belong to me.

Body and soul.

Yes, I was one evil man.

All three of us were powerhouses, the kind of men who controlled everything and everyone around us. Money was the key, influence a close second. We were wealthy beyond our means, relishing the kind of lives most people could only dream of. I enjoyed that power tremendously, which made me exactly like my hardhearted father.

Brutal.

Dominating.

Capable of destruction.

"Earth to Randolph."

I opened my eyes, shifting in my seat. The fantasy was the filthiest yet, delicious in every way. I turned my attention toward Alexander, a grin on the man's face. "What?"

"You were zoned," Alexander answered.

"Yeah, well, this is taking far too long."

"It's time you paid close attention, *partner*," he retorted.

"You should listen to him, Randolph. We might have issues," Trent said as he leaned over the table.

"What issues?" I huffed. Everything had to go perfectly. If not, I just might unleash my wrath. We'd worked far too hard on this particular deal. Anything less than success was unacceptable.

"I know you've been concentrating on making more money, but it appears someone is purchasing large portions of our stock," Alexander said as he kept his eyes on the monitor. His tone was full of disdain.

"What do you mean, *someone*? That's your portion of the business to watch out for as CFO, for Christ's sake." I heard the heavy contempt in my voice, something he didn't deserve, but at this point I didn't care. I had been paying attention, but more to my instincts. Something was brewing that could alter the course of our future and I had yet to find the reason why. That pissed me off almost as much as being forced to vie for this damn contract like amateurs.

"They were purchased under what appears to be a fictitious name."

"That's bullshit. A legitimate name of an entity or company must be on the paperwork, not some made-up company." We were set up as a typical corporation with publicly traded stock, although the three of us owned a significant majority of shares. While we had certain protections in place to avoid a hostile takeover, there were methods to make that happen. If a large enough portion was owned by someone else, that entity could cause issues within the company. Even the safety measures in place weren't effective one hundred percent of the time.

"Oh, it's a company, although I haven't been able to find out much about them. Does Southbound Industries ring a bell?" Alexander was a whizz at getting any kind of information we needed. His admittance surprised me.

I shifted my attention toward the monitor, leaning in. "No."

"Never heard of them either. Do you think Scarlett is behind this?" Trent asked.

"I certainly wouldn't put it past her. She is that cunning, but it would take time and extensive planning to create a company, an offshore account, and all the other items necessary to fool the Securities Exchange Commission." Alexander's answer didn't shock me. From what I knew about Scarlett, she was quite capable of doing anything she put her mind to.

I remembered something my father had told me years before.

"You have to be cautious around women even more than men. The reason? They are capable of seducing you in bed while destroying everything you've worked your entire life to achieve."

While he hadn't been talking about my mother, I could tell he'd had some personal experience with the scenario. Scarlett certainly had reason to hate me, but would she stoop this low? Southbound Industries. The name had no special meaning and it certainly wouldn't draw any attention in the robotics industry. "How much are they purchasing at a time?"

"Small increments, although the last purchase was more significant." Alexander inched closer. "So far they haven't contacted the other shareholders."

"But it's only a matter of time," Trent murmured.

"Exactly," Alexander said quietly.

I rubbed my jaw, my blood pressure rising. Maybe I should have acted on my desires regarding her months before. If she believed she could best us in such an underhanded method, then there were no holds barred as to what I would do to her.

Not one.

All three of us studied her. Finally, I shook my head. "Find out who is behind Southbound, Alexander. I don't give a shit what you have to do, or what favors you need to call in." Hell, I didn't care if he used extortion at this point. My instincts told me we were in for a rough ride and I couldn't allow that to happen.

"Don't worry, buddy. I will."

While I appreciated his confidence, I knew I'd have to formulate a plan B just in case. One way or the other, Scarlett Prestwood, her company and her soul, would belong to... all three of us. That's the *only* hostile takeover that was going to happen. The thought was even more enticing than the fantasy.

Ruthless.

That's another term I'd heard more than once to describe my tactics. Scarlett and all the others who sought to take Worth down a notch or two would soon learn the true meaning of the word.

Scarlett

"Be careful, Ms. Prestwood."

The caller had yet to identify himself, his husky tone one I'd never heard before.

"Who the hell are you?" I demanded, pulling the phone away from my face and staring at the screen. The 'unknown' caller had somehow managed to find my private number.

His laugh sent a shiver all the way down my spine to my legs.

"Let's just say someone you should listen to. Or else."

"Are you threatening me, asshole?"

"Don't worry, Ms. Prestwood. I never make threats. However, I do make promises. Stay away from Worth Dynamics. This is your final warning. You won't receive another. The sins of the fathers will be repaid."

What in God's name did that mean? The fucker ended the call, leaving my mouth dry and my pulse racing. I'd received two other similar threats, although both had been by email, the sender making certain I hadn't been able to track down the address.

"Prick." I tossed my phone, snarling under my breath. What kind of a terrible game was being played? I rubbed my eyes, refusing to allow it to bother me. I needed to focus. This was a very important day.

Ruthless.

I'd been called that several times in my career, including by a handful of my employees. I never made apologies for my actions, nor did I accept anything less than perfection from everyone on my team. In turn, my hard work had paid off, pushing what a been a small company into a multimillion-dollar successful venture. That had provided my employees with a substantial benefits package, including bonuses at the end of the year.

Every year.

However, the robotics industry was merciless by nature, smaller players shoved aside even if their products held merit.

I refused to be pushed aside by anyone, including the largest player in the field.

Worth Dynamics was an unscrupulous organization, the three men running the billion-dollar company true piranhas. However, they'd ignored the shark circling the deep waters surrounding them, pretending as if I didn't exist.

They would soon learn that in doing so, they'd lost their edge.

I had every reason to hate them, even if the prodigal son acted as if he didn't know why. That was horse-shit. He'd followed in his father's footsteps so much so that he even dressed like Sampson Worth had. Perfectly coiffed, not a hair out of place. Randolph Worth looked like he'd stepped out of a *GQ* maga-zine, for Christ's sake. I bit back the bitter memories of the meager beginnings of my company, deter-mined to shove aside my anger.

At least for now.

Revenge was best served cold after all.

What continued to be almost hysterical to me was that the first time I'd met him, I'd thought he was one of the most handsome men I'd ever seen, his powerful aura and utter dominance of everyone a huge turn-on. I'd even had a few delicious fantasies about him, ones I couldn't share with anyone lest they think I was a very sick woman. As I waited for the teleconference to begin, I allowed one of the visions to slide into my mind.

. . .

"Fuck you," I hissed just seconds before tossing the entire glass of wine in his face. He was a bastard, the kind of man you run away from instead of being lured into his darkness. I was certain other women had fallen for his lines of bullshit, but I wasn't like any other woman. I was strong, capable of shoving aside mongrels who were determined to best me. I stared at him defiantly, allowing a dark laugh to slide past my crimson-stained lips as I enjoyed watching him wipe the remnants of a luscious five hundred dollar bottle of wine from his gloriously chiseled face.

He said nothing, nor did he react in any other way. The asshole merely blinked several times until his vision was clear, taking a sip of his gin and tonic, the colorless liquid now stained from the deep, rich color of the cabernet. Seconds later, he lowered his tumbler to the coffee table, adjusting the ruined lapels on his expensive white tuxedo.

I continued laughing, savoring every moment of causing him discomfort.

With only two strides, he had me pinned to the wall, yanking my arms over my head and securing my wrists with a single hand. I should never have underestimated him, gloating on my small win. A coy grin crossed his face just seconds before he raked his fingers past the bodice of my dress, easily able to rip the front all the way down, exposing my naked breasts as well as the thin lace of my scarlet thong.

Undaunted, I kept a smug look on my face, refusing to give in to his tyranny. "As I said, Randolph. Fuck. You."

He tilted his head, his lavender eyes more luminescent than before. "That's a very good idea, my beautiful little pet. I think I'll do just that." Another laugh filtered into the room, the two bastards sharing ownership of Worth Dynamics gawking in the background, clapping their hands in encouragement as he unfastened his belt.

That's when I realized I wasn't getting away. My heart thumping, I struggled in his strong hold, my anxiety building as his fingers dug into the thin skin of my wrists. "Let me go, you bastard."

"You can call me anything you'd like, Scarlett. That won't change a thing. In fact," he murmured as he lowered his head, "that only makes me crave you more and I always get what I want."

I lowered my gaze, sucking in my breath when he released his cock. His thick, throbbing cock. A slight whimper threatened to give away how horrified I was, but I managed to purse my lips, holding my head high. The second I attempted to jam my knee into his groin, he threw his other hand around my throat, squeezing until breathing became difficult.

"I suggest you learn that you will obey me." His smile remaining, he added additional pressure then shifted his long, well-manicured fingers to my panties. With a single snap of his wrist, they were tossed aside. "We'll start with the fact I plan on fucking you as often as I desire."

After forcing one of my legs around his hips, he thrust the entire length of his shaft into my tight channel.

And a single moan escaped my lips.

I wrinkled my nose to keep from making a single sound, shifting in my chair as I felt my pussy juice trickling into my lace thong. Randolph Worth thought he was Prince Charming, God's gift to women. The man was nothing but a monstrous excuse for a man. I dragged my tongue across my lips, loathing how aroused I'd become from the ridiculous fantasy. The asshole would certainly never have a chance to touch me. If he dared to try, I would unleash a wrath like he'd never experienced.

I sat casually in my leather chair, wearing my signature power red suit as I waited for the bidding war to end. While I wasn't a fan of Zoom meetings, the man holding all the cards had insisted he present his decision with everyone on teleconference. I fingered my cup of coffee, keeping a smile on my face. The war zone had been narrowed down to three bidders, including Worth. All three rulers of Worth were present, crowded around the end of a beautiful mahogany conference table. Yeah, they thought they were kings. I couldn't wait to make them paupers.

What I enjoyed was the fact Randolph Worth was irritated as hell, his rich lavender eyes piercing the camera. I could almost swear he was contemplating all the nasty things he'd like to do to me.

He'd have a fat chance in hell. I could eat the bastard for breakfast.

While the man had always acted like I wasn't any kind of threat, he was learning just how wrong he'd been. I'd never been one to use unprincipled tactics before, but after losing the last bid to Worth Dynamics, I'd remembered something my father had told me years before and it had changed my way of doing business.

"When you know your true enemy, you will stop at nothing to get an advantage. Find out all the secrets he or she holds, the kind kept in dark closets and under lock and key. Once you do, you'll be the queen of your domain."

I'd never forgotten his words of wisdom again and he'd been right.

All three men who ruled Worth Dynamics held secrets. One was deliciously dark and deceptive. And in my mind disgusting as well. I'd learned everything I could about the three strapping men to use against them as necessary.

And as often as possible.

I hadn't always been this way. When I started the firm, I was determined to keep my head above murky waters, maintaining a heightened level of integrity. But thing changed over the years, the ugly insinuations that I'd stolen intellectual property almost costing me two contracts. All because the boys of Worth hadn't been able to handle the heat of having a woman as a tough competitor. So I'd learned to become more like them, including believing enough in myself that I'd scheduled a press conference for... I glanced at my watch, allowing a sly smile to cross my face. For exactly thirty minutes from now. I planned on announcing the glorious details of the contract with Dockett Industries.

Then I was planning on driving a stake right through the heart of Worth. They were such bad boys after all. They deserved to be knocked down a peg or two.

Or ten.

They belonged to an exclusive club, not the brick-and-mortar kind frequented after a long day at work, although it was my belief the members held regular, secret meetings on a bi-monthly basis. From what I could tell, the club was exclusive, highly secretive, and by invitation only.

That meant only the richest men could apply, deviant fantasies brought to life by one rich and powerful owner. Of course I hadn't been able to find out anything about him either. Hmmm...

If what little I'd learned was true, the club was also very kinky, although I'd found nothing on the internet regarding it myself. The private investigator I'd hired had only found limited details by checking Randolph's bank accounts and asking a few friends, or so he'd told me. It would seem Randolph had been careless in making a payment, but only once. At least I had a name of the organization.

The Clubhouse.

The name meant nothing, which was the point, but I'd kept my PI active, also drilling down on anything I could find. In truth, I wanted to bury the three men. Maybe I was taking their merciless behavior too personally. Then again, I'd had dealings with Randolph and his nasty father years before.

My PI had managed to follow a short trail with an abrupt end, unable to garner the special invitation himself. I planned on using the information at the right time if necessary, and I had no doubt it would be.

While enemies had attempted to thwart my success more than once, only the men of Worth Dynamics had the chutzpa to carry through with their implied threats.

"We will devour you in this industry."

"You'll never succeed in making it to the upper echelon."

"Be careful who you trust, Scarlett. You're a neophyte in an industry ruled by men."

Such arrogant pricks.

I'd heard more unsavory words and felt more intimidation from low level players, but Randolph had the means to carry through with his... promises.

I yawned, as if I didn't have a care in the world and settled back against my seat. Meanwhile, the third player was fidgety, sweating profusely. I almost felt sorry for the poor guy. If my reports were correct, the man had lost a significant portion of his business over the last year. If he failed to win this contract, his business would go under. What a shame. However, all was fair in war and business.

I took a sip of my bottle of water, calculating what winning the contract would mean to my increasing bank account. As expected, Mr. Dockett, the man awarding the bid, was late to the scheduled meeting. Of course, he'd done so on purpose just to see what the three bidders were made of.

While it was likely the decision had been made long before this gathering, that didn't mean bad behavior couldn't influence his announcement. While waiting, I took the time to study the other two owners of Worth.

Alexander Drummond had the sexiest dark eyes I'd ever seen. They were so black they almost glowed an iridescent blue depending on the light. He always seemed to wear a smirk on his face, as if business amused him. However, I'd learned early on his tactics were... questionable. I almost laughed at the thought. He was originally from Australia, his parents moving to the US when he turned twelve. He'd kept the accent, using it to his advantage with women. There was something hidden behind his obsidian eyes, as if he'd seen the worst of humanity.

A man not to be underestimated.

Trent Roark was formidable, although his fun-loving nature allowed him to get away with treating others badly. He had a boyish look about him with his sandy-colored hair and intense green eyes. It didn't hurt he had a hint of a cowboy twang from growing up in Texas. I'd also heard he had a dark, sadistic side that women couldn't stand. I had to admit the dichotomy intrigued me.

And of course, Randolph, son of the famous patriarch who'd changed the world of robotics for generations to come. He had something to prove, which made him extremely dangerous. He'd grown up with a silver spoon in his mouth, wanting for nothing even as a small child. His aristocratic features and chiseled jaw added to his don't-fuck-with-me persona. What I wouldn't give to 'fuck' with him my way.

And it had nothing to do with sex.

What a shame they were all so damn good looking, sexy in a deliciously divine way. I was aware they'd used their fabulous looks to their benefit on several occasions. However, I refused to succumb to the temptation even if they were scrumptious to look at.

If I lost the contract in question, I had other ways of establishing more of a reign in the industry. I snickered at the thought. I'd have the three men eating out of my hand by end of the year. Hell, I'd already been hailed as the woman to watch by several of the leading industry magazines, which I'd known had kept me from being on Worth's Christmas card list.

Exhaling, I glanced at my watch, curious how long the dog and pony show was going to take.

I wasn't a patient woman, but today I would wait as long as necessary in order to win the prize.

Then I'd celebrate my win with a tall glass of champagne and a luxurious bath. Maybe I'd even purchase a few trinkets; a nice piece of jewelry or a new car. Hmmm...

After five minutes, Mr. Dockett finally entered the room along with his sidekick attorney. After easing behind his desk, he took his time before lifting his head.

"Good afternoon. Thank you all for being present for my decision." He didn't bother acknowledging the players greeting him.

I remained silent. At this point, I had nothing else to say. I'd worked on the account for three months, preparations taking me long into every night. My employees hated me for being so diligent, but they'd revel in their upcoming paychecks if everything worked out the way I knew it would.

My instincts were never wrong.

"I'll cut to the chase. I'm certain all of you are very busy," Mr. Dockett continued. "I've taken into account all aspects of your companies, including your business ethics and determination to succeed. That made my decision much easier. And so..." he paused, finally staring into the camera, "I'm awarding the contract to Prestwood Automation. I believe Scarlett's company can best serve our needs. Thank you all for participating and Scarlett, I'll expect a call from you in two days. We need to finalize details prior to signing the contract."

I remained quiet, reveling in the moment, unable to take my eyes off Randolph's reaction. If I didn't know better, I'd say the pompous asshole was going to throw a temper tantrum.

Aww. Too bad.

"Thank you, Mr. Dockett, for your vote of confidence. You won't be disappointed." I clicked off before I was forced to watch the men crumble. Then I eased my arms behind my head, swiveling my chair.

Maybe it was time to break out the champagne for my entire staff. What the hell. I was only going to live once.

CHAPTER 3

A few minutes earlier...

Randolph

"I'm going to make this very easy for you, Michael," I stated with absolutely no emotion. The call had been an interruption, the man's insistence making my sweet assistant nervous, allowing her to ignore my command by entering the conference room without being invited. I would forgive her.

The asshole on the other end of the line was a different story.

I expected Michael to curse me, but he remained quiet for a few seconds, which pissed me off even more.

"No, Randolph. I'm going to make it easy for you. I'm taking my business elsewhere where it's appreciated. I think Prestwood Automation will suit my needs."

Rage tore through me but I kept my cool. "I'm only going to say this once to you."

"I don't care what you have to say, Randolph," Michael said before laughing.

"I think you will, and I suggest you listen very carefully. If you dare fuck with me or my company again, I will destroy you bit by bit in a way you will never see coming. Then I will feed you to the wolves."

I didn't have to turn my head to know my two partners were less than thrilled with the way I handled certain clients—former clients.

"Is that a threat, Randolph?"

"No, Michael. That's a promise." I ended the call, tossing the phone on the conference room table then taking a deep breath.

Alexander gave me a harsh look before motioning me to resume my place at the conference table. "Get over here so I can unmute."

Snorting, I took my time moving to and easing down on the leather chair, swiveling it back and forth. I returned my gaze to the screen. My, oh, my. Scarlett was positively beaming. My mouth watered from all the filthy thoughts racing through my mind. I would offer to take her under my wing. Then I would pounce like the predator I was. I couldn't wait to hear her call out my name as I fucked her long and hard.

"I'll cut to the chase. I'm certain all of you are very busy," Mr. Dockett stated, pulling me out of my vile fantasy.

As the fucker continued on, I found myself moving to edge of my seat. This was fucking insane. How could the little man give away our contract? How? "Turn it off," I said, barely keeping my voice low.

"Quiet," Trent whispered.

I took several raspy breaths, my mind shifting to thoughts of revenge. Not only would I fuck the gorgeous woman, I was going to break her. Goddamn it. Nothing like this happened to Worth

Dynamics. She would belong to me very soon. Every inch.

Watch out, Scarlett. I'm coming for you.

I could tell Trent was making nice to Mr. Dockett, obviously trying to stay in his good graces. I ignored the conversation, my anger shifting to rage, moving toward the window of the conference room and staring out at the Pittsburg skyline, the area now known as robotics row. My father had foretold the explosion of the industry years before the city was transformed into a mecca. He'd been the backbone, challenging the other Fortune 100 companies from the very beginning.

The man would roll over in his grave if he learned we'd lost the account.

I'd been far too arrogant in assuming we'd win the contract. When I slammed my hand against the glass, Alexander exhaled, the sound exaggerated.

"What the fuck was that?"

While I heard Alexander's question, I remained where I was.

"That was defeat with a capital D," Trent answered. "Did you see how Scarlett was gloating at the end?"

"This is… unexpected," Alexander muttered. "I need a damn drink."

My father had always been successful in squashing the hopes and dreams of fledgling companies, which is what I'd considered Scarlett's company until eighteen months ago. I'd been wrong and I was never wrong about anything.

"And what the hell was that conversation about with Wentworth?" Trent demanded.

"I was simply getting rid of unnecessary baggage," I finally answered.

Trent laughed. "At this rate, we won't have any clients. I think you should try and be nicer to a few of them."

"Let me guess, Michael has decided to work with Scarlett's company," Alexander said quietly.

I yanked off my jacket, tossing it across the back of one of the chairs. When I leaned over, I gave both of them a hard glare. "As I said. We don't need his brand of bullshit. We also don't need Dockett's bullshit."

Alexander exhaled before shaking his head. "Believe what you want, Randolph. While Wentworth was small potatoes, we put a lot into getting Dockett's account and we should have secured it. Something's off and you know it."

Off. That was an interesting word to use.

"That was exactly what the lovely Scarlett Prestwood wanted and expected to happen. If you ask me, Steven Dockett is enamored with her long legs and voluptuous figure." While Trent laughed again, he'd repeated the accusation more than once.

I shoved my hands into my pockets, hungering for revenge even though the bid war had been played fair and square.

Or so I'd been led to believe.

Given what Alexander had mentioned regarding our stock only minutes before, all bets were off.

"Wentworth she can have but Scarlett will make a fool of herself in the venture with Dockett. It's too large for her firm to handle," I said quietly, the twitch of my cock no longer surprising. I'd been attracted to the feisty redhead since the moment I'd met her, fighting to urge to ask her out on a date. Then I'd found out she had sharp teeth and claws. Then she'd become nothing but my enemy.

Our enemy.

"She's intelligent, sophisticated, and knows all aspects of the business," Alexander huffed as he pulled out his phone. "My guess is she'll succeed. That makes your concern regarding whether she purchased the stock more viable, although she never struck me as being that kind of businesswoman."

I rubbed my eyes, trying to control the still building fury. The stock would take a significant dip, especially since I'd alluded to the press about a huge announcement. Fuck. Fuck!

"Oh, shit. You have to see this," Alexander growled.

As I glanced over my shoulder, I could tell he was just as enraged as I was. He returned to the computer, his fingers flying on the keyboard. Seconds later, I heard the sound of Scarlett's voice.

"What is that?" Trent asked.

"That is a damn press conference. The woman knew she was going to win. What the hell?" Alexander snapped his head in my direction. "You need to hear this."

I moved closer, my jaw clenching. Just seeing her standing in front of a crowd of reporters only added gasoline to the raging fire. This had all been planned. What the hell did she do, buy someone off? I thought about two of our employees who'd recently quit without notice, going to work for Prestwood Automation. They'd been in a position to know trade secrets. Why the hell hadn't I thought of that before?

"You've been competing with Worth Dynamics for years, Ms. Prestwood. How does it feel to take a large chunk of the industry away from them?" the reporter asked as he shoved a microphone in her face.

She glanced straight into the camera, and I could swear she was able to see right through the screen, directing her answer at me alone. "I feel fantastic. I've worked very hard, able to keep my integrity in a sea of piranhas. Good people can win in the end."

"Are you suggesting the men who own Worth have no integrity?" another reporter asked.

"What do you think they're going to do given their loss?" Still another reporter stepped in, all bright-eyed and bushy-tailed. The fuckers thought this was their fifteen minutes of fame.

"What the hell is this about?" Trent hissed.

"This is all staged, boys," I answered, admiring her tenacity.

Sighing, she acted as if the question truly troubled her. What a consummate actress. I had to give her a lot of credit.

"I think Randolph, Alexander, and Trent have continued to build an amazing business. Sadly, they seem to have lost their way. As far as what they're going to do since being dealt such a blow. My guess is they'll retreat to one of their kink clubs to reenergize."

"What. The. Fuck?" Alexander snarled.

The feeding frenzy was just beginning, question flying from one of the press members then another. And all Scarlet did was smile to the cameras. She'd accomplished her goal without saying much of anything. People tended to shy away from anyone involved in a possible sex scandal. The woman was freaking brilliant.

"Turn it off," I said before taking a deep breath.

Alexander and Trent shared a look, but as the screen went dark, I tapped my fingers on the table, debating how to handle this. She'd just thrown a gauntlet, assuming she was powerful enough to take us on. The woman had another think coming.

"I'm surprised you haven't broken the laptop," Alexander said, half laughing.

I offered a sly smile. "She was grandstanding, but yes, she caught me off guard."

"Fuck the press conference. Just winning the contract alone will allow her to garner even more business," Trent added.

"Then there's the stock situation," Alexander added.

"If she gets control of even ten percent of our stock, we could have a nightmare on our hands." Trent lifted a single eyebrow.

My thoughts drifted to the fantasy, only this time I had even darker hungers in mind. If the woman had fucked with us in any way, she would pay the price. At minimum, what I planned was a hostile takeover. She'd just entered a big boy's game. Little did she know she wouldn't be able to handle the three of us. And that's exactly what she would be forced to do.

"Then we can't allow that to happen." I turned to face them, shifting my attention from one to the other. Suddenly, a huge smile crossed my face. "The contract isn't signed yet. Is it?"

"I'm not sure after her accusations that Mr. Dockett would consider working with us. He's a church-going man." Alexander shook his head.

"Trust me." Said the spider to the fly.

"Uh-oh. I can tell you have something in mind," Trent said as he lifted a single eyebrow.

"I do, although I would have to consider my thoughts brutal. Savage. Underhanded."

Alexander shook his head. "You're going to play dirty. It's funny how you work best when you embrace your beast, my friend. What do you have in mind?"

"Let's just say that it's time for a little power exchange and I know just how to begin the dance," I said, grinning as the thought turned into a plan.

"The dance?" Trent asked. "You're a sick man. Aren't you?"

"At this point, I'll entertain anything. She crossed the line." Alexander seemed insistent.

I walked toward the bar in the corner, sliding three crystal tumblers closer. After grabbing my favorite libation, I poured equal amounts in all the glasses, able to hear Alexander's deep baritone laugh. While I'd known both men since the early days of college, my dark-haired friend was nearly as cold-blooded as I was, sometimes even more so. Our antics in those days should have gotten us arrested.

Now we were savvy businessmen, our prominence in the industry and extreme wealth allowing us to enjoy everything our hearts desired.

Boats.

Fast cars.

And women, something we often participated in together. However, this time would be by far the sweetest. While indulging in our darkest fantasies, we'd also take down our number one enemy in the process.

What could be tastier?

As I brought all three drinks, handing two of them off, a smile slowly spread across my face from my vile ideas.

"Spill it, Randolph. At least I have other business to deal with today. Hopefully, they didn't catch the damn press conference." Trent gave me a harsh look before grabbing the drink from my hand.

"Fine," I said then sat on the edge of the conference table, crossing my legs. "Tomorrow night is the charity auction event."

"Fuck that," Alexander hissed. "I have no issues giving to charity, but I can't stand being forced to engage in small talk with political pinheads."

"No, I think you're going to enjoy what I have in mind." I swirled my drink, holding it up as a toast. "We're going to engage in a little wager with Ms. Prestwood. And if she's that curious about the dark kink we love so much, maybe it's time for her to get to know us better."

I could tell I had both their attention.

Trent pushed away from the table, rising to his feet. He looked smug as usual, but I could see his wheels turning. "Okay. Keep going."

As I explained what I had in mind, both my colleagues smiled.

Then they approached, allowing us to enjoy a toast.

"Here's to a fantastic game," Alexander growled.

"May the best... player win," Trent added.

I had no intentions of losing. By the end of tomorrow night, Scarlett Prestwood would embrace her three new owners.

Her brutal masters.

The Omni William Penn Hotel, a luxurious location in the heart of downtown Pittsburg, had been chosen as the host for the event. I'd spent several nights in the fine establishment while wining and dining prospects. Tonight was all about giving back.

As we walked into the ballroom, I was surprised the staff had managed to turn the stunning expansive room into a beautiful representation of Monte Carlo, complete with dozens of gambling tables. While no money changed hands, that didn't seem to alter the festive atmosphere in the least.

Several charities were being represented, every guest required to pay a hefty entrance fee.

Alexander moved in front of me, scanning the large crowd, a sly smile on his face. "Very nice."

"This should be a spectacular evening," Trent laughed as he flanked my side.

Within seconds, a waiter approached with a silver tray in his hand, offering what I expected was expensive champagne. While the two others accepted a glass, I waved him off. On a night like this, bourbon was required, the perfect accompaniment for a predatory game of poker.

"It would seem the entire city council is here," Alexander said casually.

"And celebrities," Trent added.

While both men were right, all eyes seemed to be on the three most powerful and eligible men in the city. We enjoyed our coveted position and had for years.

"Time for a drink," I told them, laughing softly as I headed toward one of the many bars spread throughout the room. I didn't have to wait long to place an order, but as I waited, I enjoyed the scenery as well as the half dozen women giving me a onceover. None of them interested me, just like every woman I'd had on my arm. They'd been little more than adornment for an event, a requirement to keep rumors from flying regarding my sexual appetite.

Little did anyone know how dark my needs had become.

After taking the glass, I headed for one of the tables, my breath actually stripped away from the sight of the most beautiful woman in the room by far.

Scarlett.

She was the kind of woman who could command a room just by walking inside. With her long neck and aristocratic features, glorious copper hair and glowing skin, she controlled men's fantasies by giving them a single look.

However, anyone who underestimated her business savvy soon learned a lesson. It was time to turn the tables.

I inched closer, allowing my gaze to fall from her face to the stunning, body-hugging dress she'd chosen for the event. Red in color of course, her signature hue. She didn't notice my approach, placing another bet on roulette.

She was fascinating to watch, the way her mouth twisted just before the ball dropped in the slot. As she started winning, all I could do was smile.

Scarlett always bet on red.

I brought the drink to my lips, dragging the tip of my tongue around the rim. She was up by almost two hundred thousand dollars. Good for her. Her performance had created quite the stir, at least three dozen people surrounding her.

But I maintained a bird's-eye view, enjoying the pleasant moment.

When she finally lifted her head, wrapping her long fingers around her glass of bubbly, I could tell she'd finally noticed my arrival. Amusement in her eyes, she lifted her glass, tipping it in my direction. The little vixen had no idea how fully aroused I'd become or that engaging with the devil would only get her burned.

But she would learn very soon.

"Last time," she said in her sexy voice. There wasn't a person watching who didn't lean over as the dealer spun the roulette wheel.

"Place your bets," he said about the din of the crowd.

Scarlett threw another look in my direction before sliding all her chips toward the large black and red numbers on the thick felt-covered table. After a few seconds, she moved from one number to the other. There wasn't a person surrounding her who didn't gasp given the risk she was taking.

I remained where I was, savoring every second of watching the little ball tumble from one slot to another. The loud roar as it dropped on the number she'd selected gave me another smile.

"She's good," Alexander said as he flanked my side.

"A risk taker," Trent chortled then lifted his glass in her direction in honor.

"Yes, she is," I whispered, licking the rim of my tumbler. I'd hungered for her for far too long, only my desires were entirely different than I'd felt with anyone else. She was special, someone to be cherished. That wasn't the kind of man I could be. I was sadistic and incapable of providing passion for anything longer than temporary. I'd molded myself after my father, his cold and calculating ways securing business deals while sadly pushing my mother aside.

I hadn't intended on becoming like my old man, but I'd been forced to realize I would never be the romantic. I smiled just watching her, my cock twitching until I knew I'd need release soon. She had no idea what she was about to face, including the consequences for her unscrupulous activities. I would not allow her to get away with attempting to destroy Worth.

"And she just won a little over a million dollars for her charity." Alexander shifted in my direction. "You're going to need to up the ante if you want to attract her attention."

"Oh, I plan on it, my friend. Just wait. She'll come to us." I was confident the lovely lady wouldn't simply walk away. She'd take the opportunity to gloat for two reasons. Her win the day before and her subsequent achievement on this glorious night.

True to form, after Scarlett enjoyed wallowing in the acclamation of her win, an assistant cleaning up her chips, she walked in our direction. Or I should say she was swaggering, sashaying her hips back and forth provocatively.

"Good evening, gentlemen," she purred in her sultry voice. "Is the game too hot for you? Are you worried you can't win?"

My cock ached, pushing hard against my trousers and filthy images took over my mind. "Quite the contrary. Roulette is a game for children."

She wrinkled her cute little nose then laughed. "And what game is man enough for the three big strapping hunks standing in front of me?"

Oh, the woman knew how to turn on the charm but there was no doubt she had venom in her bite.

I took a few seconds before answering, rubbing my jaw then turning my head in the direction of the poker tables. "Poker. Skill. Determination. Cunning. That's what it takes to win at such a glorious game." The adrenaline rush heightened as thoughts regarding my plans kept the air between us electrified.

After turning her head slowly, she took a deep breath. "An easy venture for novices. But I understand your attraction."

"Why don't we have a wager?" Alexander asked, following through with a portion of my nefarious plan.

"A wager?" she repeated, her face glistening from amusement but I sensed true curiosity.

"I think that's a marvelous idea," Trent added, inching closer to her.

Scarlett stood her ground, giving him a hard onceover. There was a crackle of electricity between the four of us, enough it could power the entire hotel. My mouth watered at all the delicious yet dark thoughts rummaging through my mind.

I glanced from one friend to the other, trying to keep my expression bland. "Actually, that's not a bad idea."

"Then what do you suggest?" she asked demurely, trying to act bored to death.

"How about we play for a million dollars to our two charities. If we win, you'll strike a check to the charity of our choice and vice versa."

Her laugh sparkled throughout the room. "You must be joking. I just won a million dollars in a few minutes for my beloved charity."

"Two million." Alexander tilted his head, his eyes piercing hers.

"Ummm... Still, not enough. I'm sorry, boys. If you want to play in the big leagues, then you're going to have to give up the goods." She started to turn away.

"Scarlett. I have an idea," I said in a husky voice, knowing the tone would draw her attention.

I was correct as always.

She lifted an eyebrow as she turned toward me, once again dragging her tongue across her ruby-stained lips. "I'm listening but make it quick."

Snorting, I closed the distance between us. "We'll make this easy for you. If you win, we'll provide five million dollars to that beloved charity you've mentioned."

"Hmmm... Well worth my while. And if I lose?"

I took a few seconds, allowing my heated gaze to fall all the way down her long leg peeking through the high slit in her fabulous dress. "If we win, then you're required to provide one million to our charity."

I could tell she realized there was more. She inched even closer until the scent of her perfume filtered into my system, forcing my balls to tighten and my pulse to skyrocket. "What else? I know there's a catch."

"A catch? You don't trust us, sweet Scarlett?"

At least I could tell my words bothered her.

"Not in the least, boys. However, I'm a betting woman so I'll repeat. What's the second part to the wager?"

"Simple," I breathed as I lowered my head. "If we win then you'll also be required to spend a solid week with us following every order, submitting to everything we command." I allowed the words to linger, taking several deep breaths.

"A week," she repeated. Was her brave façade fading?

"Yes. One. Full. Week. Do you think you have what it takes?" My partners and I were considered brutal men, although the people who'd spouted off the remark had no idea about the truth. We weren't just heartless. We were savages dressed in expensive attire. My needs knew no bounds and the woman standing in front of me had no real understanding of the fate she faced. That alone drove a hard ache into my system. I couldn't wait to peel away her layers, shoving aside her worthless attempt at becoming something she'd never wanted in the first place.

Scarlett Prestwood was submissive by nature, hiding behind a solid mask of steel. She'd pretended to be something she wasn't for so long it had become second nature to her.

Breaking her would be my greatest joy.

Women had a way of allowing men to glean their desires, but only for those who were astute, paying attention to every gesture a woman made. I could tell by the way she'd dragged her tongue across her lips for a third time, allowing her fingers to brush along the nape of her neck just how aroused she'd become. Her thirst to try what she considered forbidden was easy enough to read. I planned on using the information to my benefit.

She slowly returned her gaze toward the poker table. Her hand wasn't shaking nor was her breath skipping to any degree. She was calm and collected. However, I could tell she had more than a single doubt.

When she lifted her head, staring into my eyes, her smile screamed of her determination and confidence.

"I'll take that bet."

 *carlett*

Arrogant.

Unscrupulous.

Bastards.

I continued to repeat the words in my mind over and over again just to be able to keep the smile on my face. I abhorred the three men, everything about them. I'd spent hours studying their deceitful tactics, learning every weakness they had. While they might have studied me as well, they certainly didn't know about my roots, or what my father had done for a living.

He'd been a powerful poker player, winning millions of dollars on the circuit. He'd been considered one of the best, never allowing his opponents to catch a single glitch in his facial expressions, body language, or methodology.

And he'd taught me everything he knew.

I could remember standing just behind him, studying every move he made. Hours spent. I'd enjoyed the closeness we'd shared, which was rare at the time, my father spending half a month on the road. His winnings had provided my sister, mother, and me with a beautiful home and his children with fabulous educations. He'd even provided seed money for Prestwood Automation, determined to make certain I was well taken care of before his untimely death.

Death. Just thinking about the fact that he was gone gave me shivers.

He'd fallen into something that had changed everything.

A moment of sadness as well as reverence shifted into my mind. My dad would be proud of all I'd accomplished. I was dragged back into the moment by Randolph's intense stare. He was certain he would win, which continued to drive me to laughter.

I would enjoy taking all three men down a second time in two days. Yes, the press conference had gotten a bit out of hand. And yes, I'd crossed a line I'd promised myself I never would, but I couldn't lie that it felt so damn good. I could only imagine what people were saying about the three owners who enjoyed kinky clubs. I shuddered at the thought.

Whips.

Chains.

Cages.

How could people enjoy something so… sadistic?

"When would you like to indulge in this fantasy of yours?" I asked, enjoying another sip of the expensive champagne.

Randolph took a deep breath, his eyes never leaving mine. When he exhaled, his heated breath floating across my neck, I loathed the fact goosebumps appeared on both arms. Thankfully, the asshole didn't seem to be paying any attention.

"I suggest right now," he answered. "Why not?"

"Why, certainly. I do enjoy surprising my favorite dog shelter with checks, especially coming from someone of your… integrity."

His eyes flashed, allowing me to see his increasing anger. But damn if there wasn't something else in those lavender eyes of his.

Hunger.

It would be a cold day in hell before I'd ever consider succumbing to him or the other two brutes always by his side. I turned sharply, walking toward the set of poker tables. "We'd like a private game," I said to the dealer.

The lovely older woman gave me a smile then motioned toward one of the free tables. I took my seat, easing my glass away from the playing area. I had to admit that I couldn't wait to see how this unfolded.

Randolph took his time, but our appearance drew attention from a good portion of the guests. They surrounded the area as they'd done while I'd been at the roulette table, eager to see another battle between two powerful individuals.

While the dealer normally chose the game to be played, this time she asked what would be preferred.

"Lady's choice," Randolph said as he eased onto the seat, giving me a sly smile.

"Texas Hold 'Em," I answered, giving him a nod.

As the dealer explained the rules of the game, ones I knew very well, I kept my eyes locked on the man sitting at the opposite end of the table, his two partners flanking his sides as anticipated. It reminded me that the company was in Randolph's surname, his deceased father still considered an innovator in the world of robotics. Sadly, his son didn't seem to have the same talent for mechanics or engineering. That had given me a solid advantage. Randolph had come onto the scene a year after I'd delved into the market, but he'd had all the money and hype to back him where I'd been forced to start my company in the back room of an existing company with only two other employees working with me. Times had been tough, fighting the big boys of the industry taking almost everything out of me.

Meanwhile, he'd made his first million in six months. Yes, I was bitter as hell.

After the dealer laid down the blinds, I ran my fingers through the chips. It was going to be so much fun breaking the three men down again. I couldn't wait to revel in their expressions when I won.

"Seven card stud. Best out of three hands?" Randolph asked, already pulling the cards into his hands as they were dealt one by one.

"Sounds perfect."

My father had always told me that the worst thing a player could do was shift in their seat. It was a dead giveaway that the cards weren't in their favor. While I hated what I'd been dealt, there was opportunity depending on how fate as well as my skill played out.

And so we began.

As we played the first game, I studied the man intently. He'd kept the same smirk on his face as he'd had from the minute I'd laid eyes on him. "I'll raise." I tossed another hundred thousand dollars into the pile, enjoying the few gasps from the audience.

Randolph shook his head, tossing his chips into the pile. "Call."

Only a few minutes later, I won the round, which I could tell irritated the hell out of him. As we ventured into the second, our drinks had been refreshed, a larger crowd surrounding us. I found it interesting the group of people became very quiet every time I initiated a play.

When the bastard placed a full house onto the felt, trumping my hand, I inhaled, giving him the sweetest smile. So, he'd won a round. He wouldn't manage a second.

I was furious with myself for allowing the asshole to beat me. Now everything was riding on our last hand.

One I was determined to win.

All three men were unnerving, pushing me to the very edge of something I wasn't accustomed to. Fear. I couldn't lose this round. Not under any circumstances. The thought of spending a week in their presence, let alone doing their bidding, was revolting as hell. I took my time, realizing the dealer was waiting for my decision.

After yawning, a tactic I'd used a good portion of my life, I smiled as I stared down at my cards.

Even though the hand I'd been dealt was horrible.

Inhale.

Exhale.

I was able to gather a scent of various fragrances, all musky in nature. One was raw, the kind of earthy smell that tingled my senses. Another reminded me of a dense forest just after a spring rainstorm. And the third was all exotic spices. I found the combination draining, giving me a pulsing headache, something I didn't need. I had to concentrate, to anticipate the next few moves he made. Anything less was unacceptable.

"Ms. Prestwood?" the dealer asked, the woman's eyes imploring. I could easily tell she was cheering me on.

"I'll raise." I shifted my gaze toward the entire pile of chips I'd amassed, sliding them across the table. As anticipated, the crowd nearly went wild, some even moaning behind me. We'd caused quite a stir with our wager, which could bode well for increasing interest in my company. When I placed the cards on the table, I had no doubt what Randolph had in his hand was much worse than mine. I'd seen a single twitch of his upper lip.

That's all I'd needed to see.

He took a gulp of his drink, another dead giveaway.

Then he presented his cards.

I should have known a conniving bastard like Randolph Worth knew how to play the game, and not just the one involving cards. He'd played on my confidence, learning from my every move.

And in turn, I'd lost.

Humiliation spread through me like wildfire, fury wrapping around my throat and squeezing tight. For a few seconds I couldn't breathe, trying to make sense of how I could have dropped the ball. Even worse, there was no smugness to the man regarding his win over me. There was just the same calm and cool demeanor he'd tried to exhibit every time I'd been forced to run into him.

I made certain I kept my eyes pinned on his even as the crowd surrounded the table, every woman in close proximity vying for his as well as Alexander and Trent's attention. I remained mortified, even though I made certain and tipped the dealer before rising to a standing position. My stomach was in knots, my mind unable to process or accept the fact I'd lost.

As the three men were bombarded with congratulations as well as what I had to guess were offers from several women as they threw themselves at the assholes, I backed away, wanting some time to myself.

I'd spent sixteen hours a day building my company. I'd gone without food or sleep, had zero vacations and limited time spent with the family. I had no houseplants, certainly couldn't keep a pet alive, and my beautiful, spacious apartment was abysmal given the lack of furniture. I'd cared about nothing but growing my firm.

To be derailed in this manner wasn't acceptable.

I refused to abide by the terms of the wager. He'd played me and it was unacceptable.

They could sue me if they wanted, even if this was all supposed to be for the love of charitable organizations. I doubted the three men loved anything but themselves. I'd also never quit a damn thing in my life, not once. I'd fought my way through every tumultuous moment, refusing to back down or accept what didn't suit me.

But this was an arrangement I wouldn't accept.

There wasn't a human on the face of this earth that could force me into accepting the deal. As I turned away, I grabbed a glass of champagne from an oncoming waiter, gulping the entire contents down without pausing. Then I slammed the crystal stem onto a table as I passed by, heading out of the ballroom.

You're ridiculous, a coward.

It wasn't the first time I'd heard the words inside my head. Even with my successes, I'd felt like a failure more than once. However, I wasn't going to back down about spending time with them. If I did, I'd give them the upper hand in both my business and my personal life.

I scurried down the hallway, trying not to make eye contact with anyone, wanting nothing more than to get as far away from them as possible. Then I'd catch a cab.

Then what, hiding?

Hissing, I took long strides, ignoring the pain in my feet given the stilettos I'd chosen to wear. They were sexy alright, but not meant as getaway gear. As I rounded a corner, I shot a look over my shoulder, making certain I hadn't been followed. I managed to turn my head just seconds before I slammed into someone.

"Well, well. It would seem the sore loser is trying to back out on her wager," Alexander said gruffly as he crowded against me.

I took a purposeful step back, the single moan that had escaped my mouth irritating the hell out of me. The twinkle in his eyes was infuriating enough I was ready to slap him across the face. Then I did everything I could to regain my composure, glancing from Randolph to Trent. "I had a situation I needed to take care of."

"An emergency?" Trent asked.

"Yes."

"I find that difficult to believe, Scarlett. You've prided yourself that your company never has emergencies. Isn't that what you said in your recent interview?" Randolph was clearly amused. He stood against the wall, his arms folded, the sconce wall lighting highlighting his chiseled face and strong features.

"Things can happen, boys," I said as casually as possible.

"Yes. They can. But often they are contrived," Trent murmured under his breath.

"What's that supposed to mean?" I snarked.

Alexander moved closer, towering over me by several inches. "That means you're lying, which I find very difficult to believe since you also credit yourself for being a woman of virtue."

His superiority complex was just as strong as Randolph's.

"How dare you," I snarled.

Trent moved closer, crowding my space. "They were the rules of the game," he said almost in passing.

"Tell me, Scarlett. When one of your employees doesn't follow your rules, what do you do? Do you punish them? Do you fire or demote them?"

Randolph laughed. He was enjoying how uncomfortable all three of them were making me.

"Depends on the circumstances." I wasn't certain why I was playing *this* game. Then again, I'd never meant to lose. The thought remained like an infected knife. I couldn't help to think the bastard had managed to cheat somehow. This was a charity event. It was supposed to be in good fun. Then I'd allowed myself to get sucked into believing I was infallible. What a stupid mistake.

"These circumstances were clear, ones you accepted without hesitation. That means you broke the rules." Alexander's upper lip curled.

"Whatever." I tried to move away, only to have Alexander snap his hand around my wrist.

"Not so fast, sweetheart. You're coming with us."

Everything about his deep, throaty voice was enticing, but even with his stunning good looks and demanding demeanor, I wasn't falling into the kind of web I knew he spun around all the women he'd dated. The man was considered one of the most gorgeous creatures on the East Coast, sought after by debutants and celebrities. I found him reprehensible.

Given my four-inch heels, I was only a few inches shorter, which allowed me the advantage of being able to look him in the eyes with a slight tilt of my head. "I'm happy to write a check in the name of whatever charity you might give a damn about; however, I am *not* going with the three of you anywhere. I do hope you understand."

His laugh was just as husky as his usual tone of voice. He dared to lower his head until our lips were almost touching, taking the kind of deep breaths indicating he was drinking in my perfume. "You don't seem to understand the situation, which surprises me, Ms. Prestwood. You are a woman of integrity, always following through with terms of your contract no matter how difficult they may be. I find it fascinating that you accepted a deal, an implied contract, and now want to break those terms. I think I can speak for all three of us that your refusal to adhere to the contract you entered into freely is irresponsible and unacceptable."

The bastard was goading me, acting as if this was a normal business transaction. I smiled sweetly, even managing to brush my lips across his without reacting. The shock when a bolt of electricity surged into every cell and muscle left me breathless, my skin tingling. While I did everything in my power to pull away, Alexander used my faux pas to his advantage, pulling me against his massive chest.

I pressed one hand against him, able to feel his rapidly beating heart. It seemed to match mine, the erratic beats like small claps of thunder. My legs quivered, my mind trying to wrap around why I'd have this kind of reaction to a man I couldn't stand.

He dragged me onto the toes of my shoes, sliding his arm around me as he crushed his mouth over mine. His lips were soft, luscious in a way I couldn't fathom. No man was supposed to feel this good, the kiss like a long walk on a spring night. I was floored, stars floating in front of my eyes as the moment of intimacy quickly turned into a power exchange.

The man had the advantage, dragging me into his dark passion as his tongue swept into my mouth. He was dominating in all things, but this was a blatant disregard for what I wanted.

Or was it?

My body reacted in a treacherous manner, chills skating all the way down to my toes as my nipples hardened, slicing against the supple material of my dress. It had been a long time since any man caused this kind of reaction.

His subtle yet powerful growls filtered into my ears, filling my mind with dozens of filthy thoughts, the kind that would even make an avid reader of dark romance blush. I was thrown into a position I never thought would happen, but one that awakened all my deepest hungers.

Then something snapped in my mind, the woman who'd fought to gain a top position on a rung typically held by men kicked in. Using both hands, I shoved hard against him, able to break free.

Then I slapped him across the face.

"You are truly an interesting piece of work, Mr. Drummond. Is this how you handle all the women who come into your life? And is that why your reputation as a snake follows you no matter where you go?" I felt smug, enjoying the way his eyes flashed in anger. He actually thought he could ensure my complete surrender by kissing me? The man was stupid as well as disgusting.

The man didn't look stunned in the least. In fact, the asshole was amused.

And he wasted no time snapping his hand around my wrist again, dragging me several feet down the corridor, opening first one door then another until he found an empty room.

"What are you doing?" I demanded.

"Handling business," he huffed.

He pulled me inside, flicking on the overhead light. The small ballroom was in utter disarray, but he grabbed one of the chairs as his asshole partners slipped inside the room, grins on their faces.

When he sat down on the chair, yanking me across his lap, I was so stunned I couldn't react.

Until the bastard brought his hand down from one side of my bottom to the other.

Indignation rushed through my system, my mind still one big blur. As the fog started to lift, the fact he was spanking me like a bad little girl was so repugnant I sputtered out an array of nasty words.

"Asshole. Fucker. Son of a bitch. Bastard. Piece of shit."

"Such nasty words for a professional. Tsk. Tsk."

I shot my head in Trent's direction, wanting nothing more than to launch my body at him. I would have had Alexander not pinned the bottom half of my torso with one of his massive legs. I was going nowhere.

"Trent is right. Perhaps we should wash your mouth out with soap," Alexander suggested, continuing to issue one hard strike after another.

Nothing could have prepared me for what he was doing. I continued to struggle, hissing when he dared to yank on my gorgeous dress, managing to pull it up and over my already aching bottom. The fact I'd worn a thong forced a blast of heat to erupt across my cheeks.

"Bad girls need to be spanked fully naked, but I'll spare you the humiliation," he growled.

Was he kidding me? I wanted to scream but was terrified I'd call unwanted attention. I bit my lower lip as he resumed the spanking, each strike harder than the one before. I realized I was counting off the number of brutal smacks.

One.

Two.

Eight.

Ten.

Oh, my God. What was wrong with me?

Another guttural sound floated from the bastard's mouth as he dared to caress my aching bottom.

"You're doing very well," he said. "Only twenty more."

Twenty? My throat was tight, nearly suffocating me.

He smacked me several more times, two on the top of my thighs. Then he had the audacity to slide his fingers between my legs.

"I can tell how excited you are, Scarlett. I think you've hungered to have dominant men in your life."

"You're out of your mind," I hissed, my body shivering when he brushed the tips of his fingers across my lace-covered pussy, the scent of my desire floating into the air, betraying my conviction.

He chuckled darkly then started again, the sound of his palm smacking against my naked skin repulsive.

Only a few seconds later, I finally came to my senses, flailing my arms as several people walked by the partially open door. God. There was nothing more embarrassing than the thought of someone seeing me in a compromising position. Nothing. "Please, just stop," I finally said.

No, I begged. I was whining, for God's sake.

"I don't think so," Alexander answered, his smugness increasing. One day I would use his gorgeous face for dart practice. Maybe tossing knives.

I wiggled again, searching the area around me for a weapon of any kind. There was nothing within reach. "I hate you! I'll get you for this." I couldn't believe I'd actually issued the words. What was I, ten?

When Alexander leaned over, his body shifted. He was hard as a rock. Shit. "Little pet," he half whispered. "I'd like to see you try." He cracked his hand down so hard I jumped, the pain biting.

Shifting, the realization his cock was rock hard was even more disgusting than what they were doing.

"I suggest you remain in position, or this is going to be much worse." Alexander growled after making the statement. He freaking growled. Was he some Neanderthal?

I gulped for air as the spanking continued, two people stopping close enough I could listen in on their conversation. My God. This was horrifying.

"One day you will learn to be a good girl."

Alexander chuckled darkly, his words filtering into my mind. A good girl. They had no idea what I was made of. I bit back another cry, refusing to give them one damn minute of satisfaction.

And still he smacked me on one side then the other. I loathed the fact I was tingling all over, my mind a blur as the pain mixed with pleasure. That confused the hell out of me.

After Alexander delivered several more in rapid succession, Trent cleared his throat. "I think we should continue this another time."

Continue? Over my dead body.

"Sad but true." Just as quickly as I'd been yanked over his lap, I was returned to my feet. The experience had created a wave of stars, the rush of adrenaline forcing my heart to pump wildly.

When he let me go, I caught the concentrated look on Randolph's face. The bastards had planned this all along. I'd fallen into their trap. I was such an idiot.

I backed away, giving all three of them my signature smile. Never let them see you sweat. Then I turned, prepared to flee when I noticed a group of photographers standing about fifty yards from the door. Shit. This was the last thing I needed. While experts would say bad press was better than nothing, I disagreed and had learned the hard way that there were far too many people eager to see my fall from grace. Several would do anything to make that happen.

I'd been threatened by enough anonymous assholes to know that to be the truth. While I wasn't going to panic, I also had no intention of talking to them at this point. I'd already said what I'd needed for them to hear at the press conference.

Suddenly, Randolph took over the situation.

"Why, lovely Scarlett. You wouldn't be thinking about backing out on the wager. Now, would you?" Randolph preened for the cameras, his upper lip curling.

All I could do was exhale and try not to launch into him. I turned ever so slowly, cocking my head as I wrapped my arms around his neck. When I dug my nails into his skin, I made certain only his two buddies would be able to see my tight hold. "Randolph. You should know me better by now. I play to win, and our game is far from being over." This time, I became the aggressor, yanking on his head until he was forced to lower down. Then I whispered ever so sweetly so only he could hear, "Don't fuck with me, Randolph. You have far too much to lose. I know all your dirty little secrets and I intend on using them."

When I pressed my lips against his, I could tell his breathing was labored. I'd caught him off guard just a touch. He had no idea what or how I knew anything about him. I had to admit, I was enjoying the hell out of the moment.

As well as the taste of the man.

Damn it. That wasn't supposed to happen.

When he pulled away, he placed his hands against my sides, his eyes even more piercing than before. "Darling, I suggest you learn very quickly that you will honor the wager, or you won't like what happens."

"Are you threatening me, Randolph?"

He lowered his head, nuzzling against my neck. "I'm making you a promise, beautiful, sexy Scarlett. We are men you don't fuck with. If you learn to obey, you're going to enjoy a fabulous week of nothing but pleasure. But if you don't, your punishments will be ones you remember for a long time."

"You don't scare me," I managed, although my throat was tightening.

"You should be very afraid."

I bristled, not by his words but by his tone. It was dark, ominous, and ultra-exciting, leaving my mind spinning and my panties soaked.

"You will arrive at our offices tomorrow by eleven. If you don't, we will hunt you down. And bring a bag full of your most intimate clothing. We will be traveling. After that, you will belong to us." He brushed his lips across the base of my ear before pulling away, his smile reeking of danger. "But first things first."

"Meaning what?"

Alexander moved closer, enjoying the curious look on my face. "You're coming with us."

Randolph kept the smirk on his face as he raked his eyes all the way down to my toes. "From what I could tell at the press conference yesterday, you're eager to experience the joy of embracing the darkness inside all of us, the hunger that eats at our very souls."

"What are you talking about?" His eyes were far too mesmerizing, his scent staining my skin.

"You know exactly what I'm talking about, sweet and beautiful Scarlett. Pain and pleasure, ecstasy and agony, all because you're able to let go. I'm going to grant you that wish."

My mouth suddenly went dry, my heart racing. What the hell were they talking about? "You're insane. I don't want that."

"Yes, you do. As the saying goes, Scarlett. Be careful what you wish for."

When he and Trent flanked my sides, wrapping their massive hands around my arms, I resisted reacting in any way, but I continued planning my revenge.

Where the hell did the bastards think they were taking me? I shuddered at the thought.

While nothing usually bothered me, not a thunder-storm or a scary movie, I was shaken more than I cared to admit.

What in the hell had I allowed myself to get in the middle of?

 *carlett*

"Where are you taking me?" I demanded for the fifth time. They'd shoved me into a huge black SUV, locking the doors. Even the windows were tinted so no one could see inside. Who did they think they were, true celebrities? Muscle men?

Maybe the cartel.

I almost laughed, although I remained jittery as hell. All I could think about was how stupid I'd been at the press conference. I hadn't just been playing with fire. I'd caused an inferno. At this point, I wasn't certain I could handle the three of them together.

Together. They're going to fuck you.

My inner voice just wouldn't shut the hell up.

"We're going to club that happens to be a favorite of ours," Alexander answered.

Oh, God. Oh, dear God. They were taking me to some horrible BDSM club. I could only imagine what they were planning. "A club?" I managed, more uncomfortable than ever. This I hadn't planned.

"Absolutely. You are all dressed up, a beautiful creation. It would be a shame to waste such a gorgeous dress when the night is still young. Don't you agree with me, our beautiful pet?" Randolph growled.

I wanted to scratch Randolph's eyes out. He'd insisted on being the one to sit next to me in the backseat, no doubt making certain I didn't jump out at a stoplight. That wasn't a bad idea, but I knew I couldn't get away with it.

"I'm not your pet, asshole," I retorted.

"Such bad language again," Trent said from the front passenger seat. "I do think washing her mouth out with soap will be in her best interest."

"That's not going to happen," I snarled in return, trying to pay attention to where we were going as

Alexander turned off the main roads. I thought I knew the city like the back of my hand, but as the bright lights of downtown Pittsburg changed, so did the scenery, the skyscrapers becoming smaller buildings and brownstones. I was being taken to the industrial area of town. A moment of fear trickled into my system, thoughts about what little I knew about the Clubhouse rushing into the back of my mind.

Randolph growled the moment he wrapped his hand around the back of my neck, dragging me closer to his heated body. I slammed my hands against his chest, loathing the way his eyes flashed as the fluorescent lights of the street filtered in through the windows. The illumination was startling, the longing in his eyes intense. The man was like a live wire, the electricity shooting between us fueling the desire that I'd felt for far too long.

I needed to continue hating the man, refusing to succumb to whatever previous lurid thoughts I might have experienced. I'd keep telling myself he was the enemy.

"I suggest you learn to be nicer to us or it's going to be a very long week," he said oh-so quietly, allowing his hot breath to slide across my cheek. Then he rolled a single finger along my hairline and down my face, moving ever so slowly to my neck. "Do you understand me?"

"You don't scare me, Randolph."

He laughed then pressed his lips against my forehead. "I don't want to scare you, Scarlett. I simply want to make certain you understand the rules for the upcoming week."

I continued shoving my hands against him until I was able to push myself away by a few inches. "What rules?"

"You obey everything we say. It's that simple." When he let go of me, I almost slapped his face but thought better of it. One night I could endure. A week? My stomach churned at the thought. The last thing I wanted to do was spend additional time with them.

Well, maybe that wasn't entirely true.

He pulled me into his lap, forcing me to wrap my arm around his shoulders.

My God. The man was amusing himself, the bastard. If he thought for one second that I was going to do everything he or the other two animals demanded, he was dead wrong. "What I understand is that you are Neanderthals who act like women are possessions."

"In this case and for a solid week, you are our possession, perhaps for even longer," Alexander answered.

I gawked at the rearview mirror, trying to stomach what I'd just heard. "Longer. Oh, no. There isn't a chance in hell I'll spend more time with you."

Trent turned his head, studying me intently. I didn't need to see his eyes clearly to know they were ripe with the same kind of desire I'd seen in Randolph.

"Where are you taking me?" I choked out again. My nerves were now kicking in to the point butterflies were swarming in my stomach. I also couldn't feel my legs any longer.

"As I told you, a club, one that will entice your senses and begin to open your mind," Randolph said far too casually as he brushed his fingers up and down my back. This was far too intimate, more so than I'd anticipated, although quite frankly, I hadn't really planned out what I would do if I lost.

The bet had seemed ridiculous, an easy win for me. Another shiver skated down my spine. I'd always been the one in control, refusing to surrender to any man. I'd also never done anything kinky in my life, aside from using the occasional vibrator.

Swallowing hard, I tried to concentrate on staring outside even though Randolph's touch tormented me in the most delicious of ways. The spanking had been painful enough but the moment I shifted on his lap, I sucked in my breath, several curse words remaining in the front of my mind.

Randolph was rock hard, his cock throbbing. A part of me was far too excited, breaking through my defenses. Even his damn cologne was driving me crazy, giving me an entirely different kind of chills.

I dragged my tongue across my lips, cognizant that Alexander was watching me closely in the rearview mirror. I'd never had a single man look at me as if he wanted to devour me, let alone three. The entire evening was a huge blur in my mind. I'd gone from enjoying expensive champagne, relishing a huge win to being won in a poker game.

You did it to yourself. You have no one to blame.

My inner voice was far too active, always reminding me when I'd done something stupid. However, I would use the time to get the upper hand on all three men, finding a way to break through their defenses. They couldn't hide behind their glorious masks of steel but for so long.

As Alexander began to make several turns, eventually slowing down, I felt my entire body tense. When he drove into a dimly lit but very large parking lot, I was shocked to see the number of cars, expensive vehicles.

Mercedes.

Porsches.

Lexus.

Ferraris.

Jesus. Where the hell was I?

After Alexander parked, Randolph kept a firm grip, wrapping his arm around me. "I want you to listen to me. You are going to obey our rules. You will stay by our side at all times. Is that clear?"

"Where are we?" I asked again, now uncertain I wanted to know the answer.

"Club Velvet," Trent answered.

As soon as he said the words, I recognized the name. This was only the darkest, kinkiest club in town. Of course they'd belong to what was considered a men's club, where every fantasy came true.

Or maybe this was really a meeting of the members of the Clubhouse.

Alexander pulled me out of the vehicle, keeping his hand firmly wrapped around my fingers. After the other two approached, I was tugged down a long alley, a single light positioned above a steel door. Randolph knocked once then took a step back, cocking his head in my direction.

"Are you prepared to indulge in your fantasies, Scarlett?" he asked, his upper lip curling.

"I don't know."

"Tell me, what are they? Don't be shy."

Swallowing, the rush of heat sliding from my neck across my jaw was a small indication of how uncomfortable I felt with his question. I'd never told my best girlfriend anything so intimate. Why the hell should I tell him anything personal? "I'm not shy. I just don't have any. I don't have time for them."

All three men laughed, sending tingles dancing down the backs of my legs. Fortunately, the door was opened, a huge burly man giving all four of us a onceover.

"Welcome, Mr. Worth, Mr. Drummond, and Mr. Roark. I see you've brought a guest."

The eloquence at the bouncer's greeting surprised me. Did he remember the names of every member? That was impossible.

"Yes, Jameson. I'm certain there will be no issues with the club's owner."

Jameson gave him a respectful nod. "Of course not. Please come in. The show is about to start." He held the door open, allowing us to pass. The show? I couldn't imagine what that could mean.

There were no additional checks, no requirement for payment like the clubs I was used to going into. I was no fool and certainly had read enough books to know what to expect from a kink club; however, walking inside one brought a series of strangling sensations around my neck.

My apprehension was short lived, the long corridor opening to a typical-looking club, including two main bars and a beautiful stage complete with crimson velvet drapes. For some reason I thought I'd see women in chains and cages, but the atmosphere was sophisticated, black tie in appearance.

Randolph led the way, heading toward one of the few empty tables. I'd also expected to see mostly men in the audience, their submissives kept behind closed doors, but I was wrong again. There were dozens of beautiful-looking couples, all dressed in elegant attire.

Alexander pulled out a chair, giving me a commanding look when I hesitated. They were serious about my requirement to obey. After I lowered onto the plush cushion seat, he brushed his hand along my neckline, moving slowly until he wrapped it around the back of my neck in a possessive hold. He squeezed once before leaning over and whispering in my ear.

"It's alright to be frightened, Scarlett, but we won't allow anything to happen to you."

My breath caught in my throat from the way he issued the words. As if the man was reading my mind. There was no reason for me to be fearful, but my mouth was dry, my throat threatening to close. I was so used to being in power that this was far too uncomfortable.

Within seconds, we were offered a drink. I found it interesting that Randolph ordered for me, selecting what I knew was an expensive glass of cabernet. The man knew what I enjoyed drinking? He'd snooped into my life.

Just like I'd snooped into theirs.

Touché.

"I can tell you're surprised," Randolph said as he studied me.

"This isn't what I thought it would be."

He chuckled. "Couples enjoy the shows as you can see. This is just date night."

Who the hell was he kidding?

Before the drinks arrived, the subtle warm glow of the sconces adorning the walls were replaced with pinpricks of twinkling blue lights showering down from the dark ceiling. Almost immediately, the stage was illuminated with a darker shade of blue, the colorations beautiful. I was pulled into the moment, leaning forward in my seat as the curtains slowly drew aside, exposing a steel St. Andrew's cross. I held my breath as two masked men walked onto the stage, both holding a lovely blonde in a gorgeous, gilded robe.

As they led her toward the cross, I was surprised that almost no one in the audience was paying close attention. They continued with their conversations and celebrations, as if the show they were about to see was typical of a night out on the town. I heard myself whimper when the robe was ripped away, revealing her naked body.

Alexander crowded closer. I was able to see him out of the corner of my eye as he studied me, watching how I reacted to the unfolding show.

When her wrists and ankles were shackled by thick straps, I started to shiver.

"What do you see, Scarlett?" he asked, his husky voice like a jolt of current skittering throughout my body.

"I don't know," I half whispered, uncertain whether he'd heard me. I didn't like the feeling of being out of control. They were going to force me to do this, to accept their brutal discipline.

"Yes, you do. Open up your mind." In another possessive move, he placed his hand on my thigh. I wasn't certain whether it was meant to comfort me, but the touch was sensual enough that my heart fluttered.

"Pain."

"Nothing has happened yet."

"But it will," I retorted. "They will hurt her."

"That's not what this is about, Scarlett. While pain is often necessary in order to provide guidance, the joy of letting go, placing yourself in someone else's hands is the beginning of true ecstasy. One day, you will be able to let go."

Who the hell was he kidding? There was no way I would trust any of them this way. Never.

He kept his hand in the same place as the two masked men began to flog her. When the wine arrived, I took an immediate sip, refusing to allow them to know I was out of sorts. They would likely use it against me.

I wanted to look away, to pretend I was in a typical club, but I continued to be drawn back to the stage, the combination of sensuality and brutality breath-taking. With every crack of the flogger, I shifted in my seat, finally realizing I was far too aroused, my nipples aching and the scent of my pussy's reaction floating into my nostrils. I was mortified, the warm flush returning to my face.

This wasn't expected nor was it something I wanted, yet there was no denying my attraction to the merci-less event. Why had they brought me here, to gloat about what they were planning? To prepare me for a week required to submit to moments of utter pain? They wouldn't give me a solid answer. This was nothing more than a tease, all three men trying to see just how thick my bravado truly was. They would soon learn. Nothing would be able to break me.

Especially not their attempt at requiring full surrender.

I had no way of knowing how long the show lasted, but when it was over, I continued to stare at the stage, trying to process what I'd just seen. I felt an odd sense of loss, a haunting sadness that made no sense to me.

"Finish your drink, Scarlett. There is much more to see." Trent's words filtered into my ears, but I couldn't bring the glass to my lips, my stomach in knots. I lifted my head, studying his face. He was pensive, but I sensed his continued arousal as well, his eyes now half closed as he stared at me. There was no doubt in my mind these three men were going to use me.

Spank me.

Taste me.

Fuck me.

Alexander pushed the wineglass toward me, his dark presence overpowering. I managed to take a few sips, the delicious taste soothing at least one of my senses.

Trent took me by the hand, leading me away from the table and toward one of several corridors, the others following. When he stopped at one of the closed doors toward the end, he didn't bother knocking. That's the moment when I knew they'd planned the poker game, gambling that Randolph wouldn't lose. And I'll fallen for it. God, what the hell was wrong with me?

Arrogance.

I'd allowed a moment of overconfidence to shadow my decision-making capabilities. Shame on me.

Even though I'd anticipated where they were taking me, seeing an empty X cross in the middle of the private room, the apparatus made of a dark, rich wood, kept me quivering. While there were couches located on the outer perimeters, pillows adorning the plush rug, the center of attention was the cross. Even though Trent pushed me further into the room, I found it difficult to move, my legs stiff. What better way to break down an enemy than to drag out their dark fantasies, pulling them into a world of darkness. Maybe they knew I wanted to expose their membership in the Clubhouse. This would certainly be a perfect blackmail to keep me from acting on my plan.

"Why am I here?" I whispered the question.

All three men surrounded me, the combination of their colognes having the same effect as before. The allure of their exotic aftershaves titillated my senses, tugging at my innermost desires. I held my breath, refusing to become intoxicated by this simple act.

"You are here to begin your training," Randolph said casually. He reached out, gently rubbing his knuckles across my cheek. I flinched, pulling my head away. Laughing, he gave the other two a look then closed the distance. "Don't fight me, Scarlett. You know you want this. You've craved this your entire life."

"You don't know me at all and you're not going to."

"You will allow your guard to fall. That is a promise to you. Only when you do can you truly enjoy the sublime spaces we'll take you," Alexander added.

"All three of you have been reading too many erotic books," I shot back.

Randolph chuckled but his commanding tone returned. "Go closer to the cross. I want you to feel the power of the apparatus."

I rolled my eyes, wanting nothing more than to refuse his command, but I'd make a firm commitment to tolerate at least one night. I would honor the pledge to myself. I held my head high as I walked toward the cross. The closer I came, the more scattered my breath became. By the time I was standing directly in front of it, my heart was racing. I didn't need further direction to lift my hand, but my fingers were tingling as I brushed the tips across the surface.

The wood was surprisingly cool to the touch, softer than I would have imagined. The draw from before continued, pulling me into visions of what I'd just witnessed. I found myself stroking the wood with a gentle touch, admiring the workmanship. The creation was a masterpiece of craftsmanship, every detail beautiful in design.

I sensed Randolph's presence behind me, yet he remained quiet, just watching my reaction. It seemed so important to them to capture the experience. I'd never felt like such a specimen in a jar. The situation was strange but alluring in an unusual way. I continued to tingle all over, my breasts aching more than before.

"Remove your clothes," Alexander said from behind me.

While I opened my mouth to retort, I bit my lower lip instead. I turned my head, once again studying Trent's expression. He seemed mesmerized, the wry smile on his face indicating how much fun he was having at my expense.

"Remember the terms of the wager," Randolph said casually.

I turned my head in his direction, exhaling as he removed his jacket and bowtie, tossing both on one of the couches. Then he unbuttoned his cuffs, taking his time to roll up his sleeves, his hard cold stare never leaving me.

"I remember," I said between clenched teeth.

"I don't think you want us ripping that beautiful dress, or do you?" Alexander asked.

I tried to control my temper, moving away from them and toward the same couch, running my fingers over Randolph's jacket before removing my heels. Then I turned around to face them. I wasn't ashamed of undressing in front of them. Fuck them. They wouldn't get the best of me no matter how hard they tried.

As I slowly lowered one slender strap then another, I allowed a sly smile to cross my face. Just seeing the way their eyes slanted, lust filling all three pairs was delicious indeed. If this was just a game to them, I would come out the winner.

I took my sweet time, turning slightly but twisting my neck so I could watch their reactions as I slowly tugged on the dress, shimmying my hips until the material had fallen to my thighs. When I allowed gravity to take it to the floor, I heard one of them issue an exaggerated breath.

"Turn around," Alexander ordered.

Now my nerves kicked in. They were going to ogle me, defile me in whatever way they wanted. Rules of the wager. Penance for the loser. I did as I was told, trying to keep from tearing up the moment I turned around.

I'd had my share of men look at me as if there was no other woman for them in the world, but the way the three of them were looking at me left me aching inside. Their expressions of lust and need created another wave of electricity dancing through every pore and muscle.

Randolph came forward, lowering his gaze then moving behind me. I followed with my head, trying to control my breathing.

"Magnificent," he breathed. "Remove your thong."

I closed my eyes finally. The little slip of fabric had allowed me to maintain some sense of modesty. Now it was being taken away from me. I slid my quivering fingers under the thin elastic, dragging my tongue across my lips, trying not to focus on their face. When I stepped out of them, I wanted to fold one arm across my breasts, placing my other hand in front of my bare pussy, but I fought my natural reaction again. No weakness. They could never see any vulnerability within me.

"Go to the cross," Trent instructed.

Another tremor of fear drilled holes into my skin, but I walked stiffly toward the cross. They were really going to do this. Damn them.

"Place your hands over your head and open your legs, spread them wide for me." Alexander's tone was huskier than ever before, gravelly and sensual.

I obeyed, making promises to myself of all the ugly things I was going to do to them. The thought of them shackling me was horrifying, but I would endure the humiliation as well as the pain. As fingers brushed down my spine, I closed my eyes, preparing myself to be shackled for an extended period of time.

"You are truly beautiful, but you need to understand that you're no longer in control." Randolph's voice skipped along my skin like a smooth slice of velvet. He fisted my hair, twisting my long locks then lowering his head, pressing his lips against my cheek. His whisper only added to the horrible dichotomy of terror and excitement. "This is your first real lesson in a power exchange. If what I suspect is true about you, you'll never want to return."

I couldn't think of the right thing to say, nor did I want to give them any satisfaction that I cared.

"I suggest we use a flogger," Alexander growled.

"Perfect," Trent added.

"Keep your body in position, little pet," Randolph commanded, his hold on my hair remaining in place.

I counted the footsteps that Trent made as he walked to one of the three cabinets in the room. Then I held my breath, trying to shove my mind into another reality. By the time he returned, my pulse was rapid, my heart thudding against my chest.

"There is nothing like the feel of leather against your naked skin," Trent murmured. Seconds later, he dragged the implement down the length of my spine, swirling it from one butt cheek to the other. "What you will experience are the most incredible height-ened sensations, but only if you give in to your dark desires."

"You need to trust us," Alexander added. "You won't be given anything you can't tolerate."

Every muscle in my body tensed. How was I going to be able to endure their oppressive actions? When he slid the flogger between my legs, I flinched involuntarily, fisting my hands and rising onto my toes. "Are you going to chain me to this ugly cross?"

"You and I both know the cross is beautiful, Scarlett. Do you need to be tethered?" Randolph's question was just another jab at my heightened level of usual control.

But finding the answer was difficult.

"I... No. No, I do not." My emphatic tone likely gave all three of them total amusement.

"When someone agrees to submit, there is no need to shackle them," Alexander said half under his breath.

Swallowing hard, lights flashed in front of my eyes as I thought about what he'd said. Maybe he was right, except I hadn't agreed, at least not by choice.

Trent continued his exploration of my body, sliding the thin leather ends down up one leg and up the other. I heard the snap of his wrist before I felt the initial jolt, but I was so tense I pushed away from the cross.

One of them pressed their hand against the small of my back. Gently. Almost lovingly. As if they wanted to reinforce what I was doing was my decision. At least the pain wasn't significant, although every inch of my body tingled.

When two more were delivered in rapid succession, I moaned once, the mild hint of anguish from before blossoming into something else entirely. The discomfort I could tolerate. Their control was more questionable.

I kept my eyes closed, fighting the tears that threatened to give away just how anxious I was. I'd handled tragedies in my life. This was nothing in comparison. I wasn't certain who had control of the implement, but another series of hard smacks were given, including two across the tops of my thighs. Then I felt hot breath skating from one shoulder to the other.

"Your skin is even more luscious," Randolph murmured. I could tell it was his hand sliding down one side of my body, a single finger rolling back and forth from one leg to the other before the bastard had the nerve to tease me. He swirled the tip around my clit several times, forcing a series of unwanted deep breaths from my lips.

I was more aroused than ever before, the full weight of my body resting against the cross. When he thrust his finger deep inside my pussy, my body stiffened but I arched my back, hungering to have his fingers drive me to an orgasm.

What is wrong with you? What are you doing?

Over the course of the next several minutes, the sensual combination of pain and pleasure ripped away at my armor, allowing my vulnerable side to show. I couldn't stop my body's reaction, the wafting scent of my feminine wiles. I was driven close to a climax then it was yanked away from me, leaving me panting, wet and hot all over.

"What do you want, Scarlett?" Alexander asked as he cupped my mound, using all four fingers to taunt me even more.

"Nothing," I lied, unable to bring myself to admitting how much I was enjoying the experience.

The hard crack of the strap was jolting, forcing a slight scream from my mouth.

"Let's try that again," he growled. "You will tell me the truth, or you won't be allowed to come. What. Do. You. Want?"

I dragged my tongue across my parched lips, still panting from the exertion of trying to keep from reacting. But there was no way around answering. There was also no reason not to tell them the truth. My mind remained a blur, my nipples aching. When I was given another hard smack, the single strike more brutal than any of the others, I slapped my palms against the cross, words flowing from my mouth.

"I want to come. Please."

"That's very good, Scarlett. Keep your legs wide open for us. You're going to be granted your wish." Randolph's tone was even more dominating than before. He yanked on my hair, forcing my head to an awkward angle as he pushed his hand between my legs, rubbing up and down several times.

I realized I was bucking against him, enjoying the increasing friction. Within seconds, everything around me faded away as I became lost in the extreme pleasure. Something snapped within me, and I let go just as I'd been told, succumbing to the wanton need I'd felt for so long. As an orgasm swept through me like the strongest tidal wave, I opened my eyes wide, my entire body shaking violently.

He refused to stop, thrusting several fingers deep inside, flexing them open even as my muscles clamped tightly around them. Nothing had ever felt so good.

"Oh. Oh!" My scream rushed up toward the ceiling, my body sagging against the wood. I wasn't certain how I remained standing as one climax morphed into a second. When Randolph removed his hand seconds later, I whimpered, almost ready to beg him not to stop.

His growl was guttural, filtering into my ears, his hold on my hair constricting. "You did very well for your first lesson, our little pet. Now, open your mouth."

I did so, hating the fact I didn't hesitate to follow his orders. When he slipped his cum-soaked fingers inside my mouth, pushing them deep inside, I thought I would gag.

"Suck on them," he demanded.

While I did as he commanded, I tried to pull my rational mind together. It was no use. I was overwhelmed by stunning vibrations, the continuing electricity all four of us shared.

After he seemed satisfied, removing them a full two minutes later, he patted my aching bottom then turned me around to face him. Even though my eyes were hazy, barely able to focus, I was able to see his were dilated, his entire face filled with lust.

"Do you know what's going to happen now?" he asked, lifting a single eyebrow.

"No." Although the little voice inside my head told me exactly what they had planned.

"Now, we fuck you. After that, you will never be with another man again."

CHAPTER 6

rent

Ours for the taking.

Those were the words I'd heard out of Randolph's mouth more than once, along with his determination to break her, molding her into exactly what we wanted. All three of us found the same type of woman attractive, although those we'd shared together had never meant anything to us. We'd been called callous, unfeeling, and heartless.

Maybe that was the truth.

We'd made a pact in college, one that had remained with us all these years later. Business would always come first, women nothing more than pleasure for a single night, maybe a weekend. I'd been the one to think differently over the years, longing for something more permanent. While we had discussed sharing someone on that kind of basis more than a couple of times, the subject hadn't been brought up recently.

We were three of the most eligible bachelors, men to be admired as well as feared. We'd worked tirelessly, often seven days a week to make Worth Dynamics into a powerhouse. The fact Scarlett's much smaller company had managed to snag some of our intended clients was troubling, but for Randolph, it was as if a portion of his soul had been ripped away.

That was if he still had one.

We weren't good men. No one would ever accuse of us of being kind or sympathetic. Even the monies we'd given to various charities had been seen as empty attempts at making ourselves humans. Up until now, we hadn't cared. But everything had changed, at least in my mind.

Yes, I wanted nothing more than to shove my cock deep inside her wet pussy, filling her with my seed. Yes, I enjoyed watching her body writhe from the subtle yet effective pain she'd been given. And without a doubt, I'd turned into a money hungry beast just like the other two. But that hadn't brought me happiness, only satisfaction. And now that wasn't enough.

Scarlett had mocked us to the point I'd handled several awkward conversations regarding her claims in the press, including two from current clients. It would seem being involved in the world of BDSM was both riveting as well as off-putting. She'd managed to drive morality questions into several people. I should be furious with her, unwavering about what Randolph had in mind, but I found it difficult to engage in anything else but fulfilling my carnal desires.

Time would tell if she'd managed to damage our reputations as well as future possibilities. Could she had purchased several shares of our stock? Yes, but I had my doubts.

My cock was throbbing as I backed away, keeping my gaze firmly locked on Scarlett's naked body. I was impressed she'd managed to hold her own, her rebellious nature the same as she'd used during every competitive bid. I admired her strength and resolve, but tonight I wanted nothing but pleasure, just like my partners. I would let go of my chivalrous ways, if only for a single night.

After all, she had accepted the wager.

After tossing my jacket onto one of the sofas and losing the confining black tie, I walked closer to the cross. My hand still tingled from using the tawse, the adrenaline flow keeping my blood pumping. Randolph grinned as he watched my reaction, backing away and moving toward the small bar in the corner of the room.

I shifted my attention to Alexander, chuckling as I noticed his expression. The man was going to ravage her like the beast he truly was.

"Scarlett," I growled, drawing her attention.

She turned her head ever so slowly, the hellion refusing to back down.

"When we address you, you will answer."

A smirk crossed her face before she gave in. "Why, yes, sir. What can I do for you?"

"Come to me. Crawl."

While I expected her to balk, refusing to follow the egregious order, she surprised me as almost every-thing about her did, slowly dropping to her knees. When she was on all fours, she tossed her head up high, her eyes shining from the fire burning deep within her. I had no doubt she was planning her revenge, which made the evening that much more enjoyable.

At least she obeyed, crawling toward me, pursing her lips provocatively. She was pulling out all the stops to keep us on our toes, disarming us with our carnal needs. The sensual beauty had no idea that there was no way she could do that.

None.

I unbuttoned a portion of my shirt, my cuffs included, my cock now pushing hard against the tight confines of my trousers. The woman was irresistible, dragging the savage from deep inside me to the surface. My desires had always been dark, my exploration of my sadistic side more enjoyable than I would have thought. While tonight was tame in comparison, Randolph was right that she needed to learn her place.

When she was beneath my legs, the vixen slid the tip of her tongue all the way around her mouth, baiting me as I'd seen her do in various meetings. My balls tightened as the thought of what I wanted to do to her rushed into the back of my mind.

The second she rubbed her face against my leg, I shot a look toward Randolph, shaking my head. He was enjoying watching the little show, leaning against the bar and swirling his drink.

Alexander continued undressing, waiting in the background to see what I was going to do. If I had my choice, I'd strap her to one of the swinging chains, fucking her over and over again, but tonight was different.

"Undress me, Scarlett."

Her heated look remained, her eyes turning cold as steel. She had no way of knowing how much she enticed me, pushing my boundaries. There was no reason to believe we could actually engage in a more formal, permanent relationship, but time would tell.

I took a deep breath, lifting my head and enjoying the moment as she tugged off my shoes, tossing them aside then running her fingers along the insides of my legs. As she began to unfasten my belt, the heat of her body being so close was like gasoline ripping through every muscle.

I'd been considered the most patient of the three of us, as well as the most reasonable. Tonight, my hunger had already risen off the charts. I yanked off my shirt, not bothering to unbutton it. Her murmurs were a sweet reward, even if they were contrived.

When she slowly slid the material past my hips, I peered down at her. Her nipples were hard as perfect pebbles, the scent of her pussy driving me crazy. After she pulled them to the floor, easing one leg out and yanking the unwanted material away then the other leg, I issued another command.

"Suck me until I tell you that you can stop."

Purring, she kept up her little act, pressing kisses from one side of my leg to the other. Just the touch of her fingers was enough to push my heartrate higher. I could barely contain my raging hunger as she blew across the tip of my cock. Damn, my balls were aching, the pain biting.

I allowed her to play a little longer, darting her tongue across my sensitive slit then around my cockhead several times. My entire body stiffened, the need only increasing. It had been a long time since I'd been with a woman, even longer since we'd shared one. Maybe Randolph had provided a good idea after all.

She finally slid one hand between my legs, tickling my balls before wrapping her hand around them. The second she squeezed, the pressure was almost too much to bear.

"Fuck. Don't tease me too long, Scarlett."

"Or what?" she purred.

"Or you will suffer the consequences."

"It might be worth the risk."

When she engulfed the tip, using her strong jaw muscles to suck fervently, I rolled onto the balls of my feet. The sound of Randolph's quiet chuckles almost pissed me off, but I knew she'd have a field day with him, taunting him relentlessly.

She continued rolling my testicles between her fingers, daring to give me a mischievous look. I couldn't believe she continued to think she held some kind of control. That would make breaking her even more delicious.

"I said. Suck me." I pushed down on her head, forcing her to take several more inches. Then I tangled my fingers in her long hair, adoring the way her soft locks felt in my fingers.

After that, I took full control, forcing her to take all of me. When the tip hit the back of her throat, a smile slid across my face. Her mouth was so damn hot.

Alexander approached a few seconds later, his sly look one I'd seen dozens of times. He waited as I pumped her head up and down, staying behind her without touching. I was surprised at his level of control. The man usually had none.

The sensations were far too electric, driving me close to an orgasm. When Alexander fisted her hair, I took a deep breath, allowing him to take over. My breathing remained ragged, beads of sweat forming along my hairline. I wanted nothing more than to fill her throat with my seed, requiring her to swallow every drop. That would come, but not tonight. My hunger was far too intense.

"You're going to suck me as well, sweet Scarlett. Now, open that gorgeous mouth of yours," Alexander instructed, wasting no time shoving his cock inside.

Watching the way he was with her almost pissed me off. I'd never had that feeling before, but as I stood behind her, it was difficult not to rip her from his arms. I purposely turned my head in Randolph's direction, realizing that he'd finally undressed and was standing only a few feet away. He remained unblinking, staring down at her with an expression I couldn't read.

Randolph was an unforgiving man, refusing to accept anyone's weakness, including his own. He'd been tough on himself, pushing so hard I'd often wondered how young he'd be when he died of a heart attack. However, his animosity for Scarlett was more intense than I'd ever seen in him.

When he finally gave me a hard look as well as a nod, I chuckled under my breath. It was past time to fulfill our promise.

As well as satiate our needs.

Alexander seemed to sense what we were thinking, lifting her off the floor and into his arms. While she didn't fight him, her breathing remained ragged.

"It's time, little pet. Soon, you will belong to us." His husky statement set the tone as he eased her onto the rug.

I lowered to my knees, watching as Randolph dropped down as well, only he immediately lay down, folding his arms behind his head.

Alexander whispered something in her ear and while she cinched her eyes shut, she obeyed his orders seconds later, moving stiffly toward Randolph.

The electricity crackling in the air was even more significant, the current adding to the combustible aura surrounding us. We could burst into flames easily. I snickered at the thought. I wasn't a philosophical guy, although I did fashion myself to be more of a romantic than the other two.

Randolph growled as he pulled her arms, tugging her toward him, forcing her to straddle his hips. When he cupped her breasts, another wave of desire burst into my system.

There was no reason to talk, no need for discussion. Randolph pinched her nipples, his eyes flashing as his predator rushed to the surface. Then he slid his hands down her arms, shifting his fingers to her hips.

I moved behind them, dragging the rough pad of my finger down her spine. Almost instantly, goosebumps floated across her skin, the single whimper she issued one I could tell she loathed doing. There was no doubt she felt attracted to all of us, but refused to give in.

Just yet.

But she would.

As Randolph lifted her hips, pushing the tip of his cock just inside her pussy, I pulled her arms away, sliding my hands under them, coddling her breasts. He yanked her down, issuing a series of guttural sounds as he filled her completely.

"Ride me, Scarlett. Ride me hard," he instructed.

I lowered my head, nipping the nape of her neck as I pinched and twisted her nipples. Every sound she made, every slight moan echoed in my ears, adding to the combustible heat building between us.

Scarlett remained silent, even trying to control her breathing as she bucked against him, her knees firmly planted against his thighs.

"You do enjoy pain. Don't you, Scarlett?" I murmured then licked the base of her earlobe.

"Never."

"You're a terrible liar." I blew across the back of her neck before sliding my fingers into my mouth. She cocked her head to the side, narrowing her eyes. I allowed her to watch as I made certain my fingers were nice and wet.

Then her eyes opened wide when I eased them into the cleft of her bottom.

"What are you doing?" she asked, although her tone was just as demanding as before.

"Getting you ready." I could tell Alexander was growing impatient, pacing the floor as he stroked his cock.

I loved the way she squirmed, her body shifting back and forth. Soon, I wouldn't be able to hold back, taking her like a true barbarian. I slid a single finger inside her dark hole, marveling at the explosive heat and how tight she was.

She whimpered, her chest rising and falling. I continued pinching her nipple, enjoying the way she shivered in my arms. Then I added a second and finally a third finger, driving them long and hard into her sweet asshole. She threw back her head, her body shaking as I pumped savagely, but I could tell by the sheen on her face that she was enjoying the combination of pleasure and pain.

Randolph let off another series of growls, drawing her attention to him. As he bucked his hips, plunging into her, the strain on his face indicated he wasn't going to last for long.

I continued finger fucking her tight hole, whispering all the dirty things we were going to do to her.

"We're going to taste you before fucking you in every hole. Then we're going to mark every inch of your gorgeous body. Would you like that? Would you enjoy allowing everyone to see who you belong to?"

Her answer was a slight laugh, but that only fueled the fire even more.

I finally added a fourth finger, flexing them open as her muscles strained to accept the thick invasion. She was so damn tight I could tell she wasn't used to the joys of anal sex. She would soon learn. As I thrust hard and fast, Randolph dug his fingers into her skin, tossing his head back and forth, the sounds he made more like an animal than a man.

She did everything she could to hold back, refusing once again to succumb to her own pleasure. Her shoulders tightened and she smacked her hands on his chest, breathless sounds sliding up from her tight throat.

Randolph couldn't hold on any longer, bucking hard against her. As his face contorted, I knew he was close to coming.

As his body began to shake, I pulled away, moving onto one of the couches. The way she turned her head, staring at me was telling. She wouldn't give in without a strong fight. My cock remained fully extended, the veins on both sides pulsing. When she rolled her tongue around her lips in another provocative move, I gave her a single nod. If she wanted to continue playing the game, then so be it.

The little woman should be very careful what she asked for. I stroked my cock in a lazy manner as Alexander pulled her onto her feet, turning her swiftly and crushing his mouth over hers. I tipped my head back, visions of her voluptuous body remaining.

I was jarred seconds later by the feel of her delicate fingers rubbing up and down my chest, the weight of her body as she crawled onto my lap sizzling. While the poker game had taken a different turn, there was something in her eyes that pierced my very soul.

Perhaps she sensed it given her features softened, her gaze falling as she slid her fingers down my chest, fingering my cock before wrapping her hand around the base of my shaft. As she rose off my legs, she rubbed the tip up and down her pussy before slowly pushing it past her swollen folds.

There was no need to guide her, or to push her in any way. I enjoyed watching her, giving her a moment of control. We were like oil and water, but the connection we shared was stronger than I'd ever felt with another woman.

Scarlett threw back her head, staring up at the ceiling as she gripped my arms, clinging to me as she lowered her body. Nothing could have prepared me for the way her muscles clenched around my cock, pulling me in even deeper.

"Fuck," I whispered, my heart thumping hard against my chest. She was so damn tight, pushing another wave of electricity into my extremities.

"Mmm…" she murmured, slowly lowering her head. There was a hazy look in her eyes, her mouth twisting before she gave me a sly smile. Then she started riding me harder than she'd done with Randolph, her breasts jiggling just enough my mouth watered.

I wrapped my hand around her neck, forcing her into a deep arch, allowing me to lower my head and savor licking one nipple then the other. When I bit down on one, she issued a ragged cry. The taste of her skin was so sweet, almost as much as I knew kissing her would be.

"Don't forget about me, sweetheart," Alexander huffed as he knelt beside her.

I rubbed my lips across her chest to her other nipple, sucking and nipping before pulling back. Alexander's grin was laced with evil, the glint in his eyes just like what I'd seen in Randolph's. I pulled her closer, cupping her chin and capturing her mouth.

She squirmed in my hold, pushing her hands against my chest. When she tensed as Alexander pushed the tip of his cock inside her dark hole, I thrust my tongue inside her mouth. I was right. The taste of her was like warm honey, her scent exotic and intoxicating. When he was finally fully seated inside, we moved to a well-known rhythm we'd used many times before.

While my needs were usually much darker, the only way I could gain satisfaction, the time spent with her would go down as special.

Even if I didn't know exactly what the hell that meant.

She raked her nails down my chest, shoving hard against me and forcing the moment of intimacy to end. A strange look had appeared in her eyes as she rocked her body forward and backward, following our orchestrated dance almost perfectly. She was doing everything in her power to bring us to an orgasm. She wanted this over with.

I remained unblinking, my jaw tightening as I realized just how manipulative she could be. The fear she'd shown before was nothing more than an act. I had to admit she was a damn good actress, more so than I'd originally thought. Exhaling, I dug my fingers into her hips, forcing her to ride my cock like a wild stallion. The thought of breaking her was now firmly planted in the darkest reaches of my mind.

Her smile continued to grow as we fucked her long and hard, until neither Alexander nor I could take it any longer. Another jolt of fire and heat swept through me as my balls swelled, the ache increasing. Within seconds, I threw my head back and roared, the sound of Alexander's cry of relief matching the timbre of my own.

My body continued to shake after erupting deep inside of her, my muscles tight as drums. Panting, I locked eyes with her one last time, growling when she lowered down, nipping my earlobe before whispering into my ear.

Her words? They were enough to push me into moving into round two of the game.

"Don't think I'll ever fall for any of you. You couldn't handle me if you tried."

Scarlett

"No, Marjorie. I won't accept those terms. I've told you as well as Michael this before. Why is he suddenly changing his mind?" I rubbed my forehead, pacing the floor of my office as I talked to my attorney. I'd been working on another deal, while smaller also one that would keep our name in the forefront of people's minds. When Wentworth had gone to Worth, I'd almost lost my confidence. The fact Michael had reached out again meant Randolph had managed to piss him off. Or maybe he'd seen my press conference. Either way, I knew the three men who'd wrangled me into a filthy wager remained angry. I should agree to Wentworth's terms without question, but I couldn't afford to fuck up either account.

My illicit wager just might cost me everything.

Including my heart.

I bit my tongue to keep from moaning. Why was I thinking about this as anything other than what it was, their attempt to force me to surrender. I knew it wouldn't end with a single week spent with them. They'd require more.

Including with regards to my company.

"I suggest you think about this. We're only talking about an earlier timeframe," Marjorie insisted. "Michael Wentworth has a big mouth and a lot of friends."

Hissing, I glared out the window at the bright sun. Since I hadn't slept a wink, I winced from the glare. There wasn't enough coffee in the world to help. To say I was grumpy was an understatement.

You fucked them. You allowed them to spank you. And fuck you. You are insane.

The inner voice also continued to nag me. While her nasty words were all true, I didn't need to be reminded by my conscience. I couldn't seem to get their scents off my even though the shower had been red-hot. The three assholes hadn't just stained my skin. They'd gotten under it.

"I have other business that's pressing. And…" I hesitated, swallowing hard as I glanced at my watch. "I have to go out of town for an unexpected meeting for a week. You're going to need to push them off at least until I get back."

"This isn't like you at all, Scarlett. I'll do what I can do but I hope you're prepared to lose both contracts."

Over my dead body. "Talk to Dockett and Wentworth for me. They like you. Tell them whatever you want about why I'm out of town. I will try and talk to Mr. Dockett myself. He needs more hand holding than Michael does. Plus, the profits are larger. And I'll call you when I can. I promise."

"Does this sudden departure have anything to do with the charity event? I heard they were in attendance," she said, only her tone of voice had changed, becoming more admonishing. "Are you hiding from the Worth boys?"

Boys wasn't a term I'd ever use. Groaning, I could barely get my mind off the three men. The three disturbingly sexy men. "No, it does not," I said, trying to sound sincere.

Her exhale told me enough. She didn't approve of my tactics.

"Be careful around Mr. Worth, Scarlett. He's just like his father. He'll stop at nothing to get what he wants. You should already know that."

"Stop worrying. I can handle Randolph."

"I'm serious. The three men together are formidable as hell. Whatever you're doing, you're definitely playing with fire."

"Don't you mean they're dangerous?" I chided as I glanced at my watch.

Marjorie exhaled loudly enough I could hear the sound clearly. "I'm serious. Sampson Worth was known to have some very... interesting associates."

This was news. What kind of associates was she talking about?

"Meaning what?"

"Meaning the kind you don't want to cross."

"What have you heard?"

She sighed. "Just that he was in over his head with debt. If rumors are true, he sought help to dig himself out."

Hmmm... That was interesting. "With whom?"

"That I don't know."

I was surprised she was listening to rumors, but I made a note to keep it in the back of my mind. I looked at my watch again. Eleven o'clock was too close for comfort. "He's dead, Marjorie."

"But his son is very much alive. Randolph has made no bones about crushing the competition. I've warned you about his tactics before."

I certainly couldn't worry about whatever associates Sampson liked to play with. Maybe I should push forward with exposing the three men in another way altogether. So far, my plan was at least drawing questions. I'd had three emails from several firms I thought were unattainable. And all after I'd exposed a penchant for kink.

Stay brutal. Stay focused. You need to crush them. Huh. I hadn't thought of my attorney's dog-to-the-bone kind of mentality. "Have you ever heard of an elite men's club called the Clubhouse?"

"Please do not tell me you're getting involved with something kinky!" she chided. "I don't know what you were doing with that press conference, but whatever it was, you have eyebrows raised, questions being asked."

"I don't participate in anything kinky. You know me better than that. However, I don't mind highlighting all the filthy things those men do. It's just business. So… What I do want to do is discover everything I can about this secretive society. I think all three men are members. I would love to expose their proclivities." I hated lying to her, but I remained embarrassed about my behavior the night before.

"What in the hell has gotten into you, Scarlett? You always told me that you wanted to keep your integrity no matter the circumstances. Who cares what they do in their private time?"

"The public has their own views on what's moral and what isn't, Marjorie. So I made the most out my success. So what? That's what they would do without question. Find out what you can, no matter what it takes."

"You might be opening a lion's den. Men like that don't take being investigated lying down. They also don't like having their proclivities exposed. They will lash out."

"So be it. Bring it on."

I heard the hesitation in her voice as well as the angst. She'd been very much like a second mother to me, nurturing while providing tough love when needed. I valued her guidance and her ability to keep me from heading onto a steep ledge, but this was something I had to do.

"Don't lose yourself in this, Scarlett, and I'm not talking about your business acumen. You've suffered enough through the years, trying to get over your father's murder. This is your time to shine, not wallow in the kind of muddy waters you're planning on sliding into."

"I get it, Marjorie. I really do."

"Just be careful where you're headed doesn't turn into quicksand."

"Yes, ma'am." I ended the conversation, tossing my phone onto my desk then leaning over. I allowed my thoughts to shift to my father. He hadn't been the most upstanding citizen in the world, but he was my father and I'd loved him with all my heart. His murder had nearly destroyed me. Even worse, his killer had never been found. What did the cops care? He was a card shark. A man who lost as much money gambling as he won playing poker. I shook off the ugliness, trying to concentrate on what I was planning.

Had I really agreed to spend a week with the assholes? That wasn't like me. I'd had far too much champagne, which had obviously led to my bad decision. Bad? Hell, it was horrible.

And exciting.

And delicious.

And...

Then the incident in the club. I certainly couldn't admit to anyone, especially myself that I'd enjoyed the evening with them. What I couldn't figure out is why they hadn't shackled me to the cross. A mystery I wasn't going to find an answer for. Maybe I didn't want to. Maybe it was a tactic the three men used in seducing women. I rubbed my forehead, the headache I'd developed after leaving their… company like tiny sharp knives sticking into my brain. Maybe I could take those knives and shove them into all three men.

I shoved the thoughts aside as I heard a knock on the door. "Come in."

As my assistant walked in the door, she pointed to her watch. "You asked me to remind you about the appointment you have."

"Yes, I did. Thank you."

"No problem, Ms. Prestwood. Is there anything else?"

I glanced at Ashley, the young girl the best assistant I'd ever had. She was also a tiger when it came to research, making certain I knew what rival companies were doing. If I didn't watch out, the girl would take over in five years. At least that thought gave me a smile. "Ashley, let me ask you something. Do you know anything about the men of Worth Dynamics?"

When her face turned bright red and she dragged her tongue across her lips, that told me enough. The girl was enamored with them, just like almost everyone else in the city, maybe the damn country.

"I know they're the hottest bachelors in town. I know they aren't very nice to the women they date. I know they belong to a secret club."

My ear perked up like crazy. I moved around my desk, noticing just how uncomfortable she seemed after telling me. "Secret club?"

"I'm sorry. I shouldn't have said anything." She looked everywhere but into my eyes.

"It's okay, Ashley. We're just talking. How do you know about the club?"

The girl seemed nervous as hell. "I really can't say. I promised."

"You promised? What does that mean?"

"My roommate. She dated Trent for maybe two weeks. Things were... weird."

"Define weird."

She glanced over her shoulder. I'd never seen her acting so jittery. That wasn't like her at all. "You promise you won't say anything?"

"I have no one to tell. I'm just trying to get an angle on how to handle them if they threaten me in any way."

"Be careful around them, Ms. Prestwood. They are dangerous and pushy, the kind of men who won't take no for an answer."

"Now you have me intrigued." I folded my arms, walking closer. "You know I can handle men like that."

"Normal men. I don't think they have a normal bone in their bodies. I know that sounds rude."

"No, not at all. What do you know?"

Ashley held the file in her hands so close to her chest and with such force her knuckles were white. What the hell was bothering her so much?

"Madisen, that's my roommate, wouldn't tell me much but she said Trent took her to some club one night, but not a real club. It was being held in some mansion. I don't know where, but it was in the city. Anyway, there were girls there, but not like dates."

"Prostitutes?"

"No. That's the crazy thing. Some were doctors, lawyers, teachers," Ashley continued. "But she got the feeling that they were there for a... nefarious reason. Fulfilling fantasies."

Nefarious. That was a very good word to use at this point. "Why did Madisen stop seeing Trent?"

"Honestly? She wouldn't tell me exactly, but I knew she was offput by his dominating tactics."

"Interesting," I said half under my breath. "Well, I appreciate you telling me that." I continued wavering between ignoring the three self-imposed powerful men and fulfilling the ridiculous obligations. I'd always been the kind of woman who charged into any situation. The proclamation from Randolph alone should have been enough to create self-doubt, but instead I was more intrigued than ever. Besides, perhaps I could delve more into the Clubhouse, discovering what was really going on.

Maybe if I exposed them for their sadistic needs, I could finally shove the three men aside as a competitor.

"I'm heading out for a business trip," I told her in passing.

"I don't have anything on the schedule."

"No, this was unexpected. I should return in a week. You can call me if anything comes up." I glanced at my watch for the fourth time that morning. Eleven would roll around far too soon.

"What about Mr. Dockett? Aren't you supposed to finalize the contract tomorrow?" Ashley asked.

I could tell the girl was still nervous about what she'd told me. What in God's name had her roommate gone through that was so bad she couldn't mention it? Maybe the boys had forced the girl to sign a nondisclosure agreement. I was growing more curious by the minute.

"I assure you that I'll be handling business while I'm gone. Marjorie is working on the final contract now."

She nodded then moved toward the door. "Just be careful, Ms. Prestwood. Madisen isn't the same after spending time with Trent."

"Duly noted, Ashley. Stop worrying. I can take care of myself."

She nodded then walked out the door, still quivering as if she'd told me her deepest, darkest secret.

As I grabbed my briefcase, closing then shoving my laptop inside, all I could think about were Randolph's words.

And his promise.

Somehow, I had the feeling I would soon learn all about their well-kept secret.

Only I wondered if I would return the same woman as when I'd left.

Or if I'd considered myself owned.

I laughed as I headed toward the door. The bastards had another think coming if they thought I'd surrender to them on any level.

Hell would freeze over first.

Last night had proven that they were piranhas. I would have to show them I was the bigger predator.

"Ms. Prestwood, your car is waiting. I'll handle all your calls." Her smile was positively mischievous.

"Thank you, Ashley. I'll see you in a week."

By the time I moved through the all glass doors into the dim lighting of the day, I felt far better than I had the night before. Armed with new information, what I was planning should be considered treacherous, but at this point, I no longer cared. I eased into the back of the Cadillac, still donning my sunglasses even though it was a gray day. While the driver tossed my bags into the trunk, I took a moment to gaze out the window, marveling at how far I'd come.

Life truly was glorious, and three men were never going to derail it.

The drive was without incident, my phone remaining quiet. That was the first time in so long I couldn't remember. When the driver pulled into the destination, I took a deep breath, a sly smile remaining on my face. I couldn't wait to delve into their psyches, to find out what made them tick.

Then I would destroy them.

The wind had kicked up, my hair a mess as I walked across the tarmac and onto the waiting charter flight. Once inside, I removed my shades, taking a seat in one of the luxurious leather seats. Within seconds, I was offered a glass of champagne, just as I'd required. The second the exterior door was closed, I took a deep breath.

"Ms. Prestwood," the pilot said as he headed in my direction. "Your flight is on schedule. We'll break free from the oncoming storm within minutes. The rest of the trip should prove to be relaxing."

"Thank you, Bart. I appreciate how quickly you managed to arrange the flight."

"Not a problem, Ms. Prestwood," he said. "Happy to do so."

As I sipped my champagne, I glanced out the window. This week should prove to be exciting.

But not for the reason the three men of Worth Dynamics intended. I was taking the upper hand.

And I would never let it go.

CHAPTER 7

lexander

Women.

Sometimes I felt as if they were the bane of my existence. While I adored them—the way they laughed, the twinkling of their eyes, and definitely the sultry way they acted when realizing they'd attracted a man's attention—up until now, I'd found no use for keeping one longer than what was absolutely necessary.

In order to fulfill my carnal needs.

However, there was something enticingly different about Scarlett. She wasn't just a typical female who enjoyed being wined and dined, finally seduced by a man. The formidable woman preferred, no, demanded to be in charge. I found that intriguing as well as infuriating. Her behavior the night before had been... spectacular. I laughed at the thought as I flexed my fingers, still able to feel the sensations from spanking her delicious bottom. Just seeing her standing against the cross had been entirely too incredible. I'd wanted to see her in shackles, but last night wouldn't have been the right time.

While Randolph had enjoyed every moment of seducing her at the club, he'd acted cold and aloof after driving her back to the hotel. Then he'd been furious, fuming since she'd walked away with her head held high and her morals intact.

I'd also seen no guilt for attempting to destroy our reputation.

Yes, I was pissed, but I also admired her spunk. Her challenging all three of us at the same time had filled me with the kind of carnal hunger that knew no bounds. Just thinking about her kept me fully aroused. Did she deserve punishment? In the worst way. Spanking her had been enough of a taste that I wanted more. As far as retaliation? I had mixed feelings about what ramifications it could bring.

While I knew what Randolph wanted from her body, it was easy to tell he had other plans in mind as well, including forcefully taking over her company. While I'd participated in, even encouraged his titan-like decisions, something about the entire situation bothered me and had since the night before.

I was certain Randolph would tell me I'd allowed Scarlett to crawl inside, breaking down my defenses. Yes, she was beautiful, the draw to her more than I'd felt for any other woman; my reaction was complex even if I couldn't put my finger on what I was thinking.

It wasn't just the wager with Scarlett. I felt like another game was being played and the four of us were nothing more than puppets. I couldn't get the thought out of my mind given recent incidents within the company. There was no logical explana-tion for my reasoning, just a gut feeling.

I stood at the window of my office, peering out over the city. The day was dark and gray, which matched my mood perfectly. Up to this point, I'd had no desire to engage in my partner's unseemly wager.

However, seeing, tasting, and fucking her the evening before had kept me awake all night, my hunger far from being satisfied. I'd been considered the bachelor of choice throughout the city for almost two years, not that the title meant anything to me. I was the kind of man who reveled in dollars, not in accolades. I was rich, just like Trent and Randolph. I could have anything or anyone I wanted. That's why being a member of two selective clubs had been perfect for my personality. I'd enjoyed encouraging the darker side of my need, indulging in vile fantasies on several occasions, some darker than others. Last night had been tame in comparison.

Had I had more than a single thought about what I would like to do to the feisty redhead? Absolutely.

But somehow, I'd known Scarlett had been off limits, until the unseemly wager. My cock ached at the thought. Last night had changed everything, including my line of thinking. She thought she'd maintained the upper hand after her win with the self-righteous Steven Dockett. Soon, she would learn otherwise.

And I would enjoy spending quality time with her, exploring every detail of her luscious body. I also had a feeling Randolph was correct in his assumptions. While I'd been unable to find any additional information on the purchaser, I was slowly making headway. It was only a matter of time before the owner of what appeared to be a shell company was exposed.

"You're in deep thought this morning," Trent said from behind me.

I cocked my head, realizing he'd made himself home in one of my leather chairs as he always had, the same smile he always wore on his face. There were times I wondered about his work ethics, but he'd always seem to come through, no matter the circumstances.

"Just business," I answered, although it was far from the truth.

"Uh-huh. The one thing you aren't is a good liar."

I chuckled, turning to face him. "And what do you think I have on my mind?"

"I would say the very sexy Scarlett Prestwood." He inhaled, holding his breath and closing his eyes as if remembering her subtle yet provocative perfume.

"Yes, she is quite the woman."

"She's a barracuda."

"In her mind, my friend. In her mind."

"She was very clear last night was just another portion of the game and one she still believes she's going to win."

I lifted a single eyebrow. "What did she say?"

"That we couldn't handle her."

Interesting words given she'd come close to succumbing fully.

"We will take her down, but I don't think she's going to respond to typical business tactics no matter how ruthless they might be."

The smirk on his face widened. "What do you have in mind?"

"Let's just say I think she needs to fully understand who she's dealing with. Maybe Club Velvet wasn't a strong enough reminder."

"Wait a minute. You're thinking about taking her to the Clubhouse?"

"Why not?" I asked, my balls tightening from the filthy thoughts I'd had for hours. "A dark fantasy would be delicious."

Shrugging, Trent looked away for a few seconds, his eyes glassy.

"Do you have something else in mind?" I asked, curious as to what he was thinking.

"Do you remember how many times we talked about sharing a woman?"

"Yes, and we have. Several of them. That's what happened last night and will again. What are you getting at?"

He exhaled before turning to face me. "I'm tired of the circuit as well as the events involving the Clubhouse. Don't get me wrong, I've enjoyed participating but we've been involved for three years. It's time for a change."

"Is this about money?" Not only was the yearly fee closing in on five hundred thousand dollars for each of us, but every fantasy also had a steep price as well.

Trent snorted. "You know better."

I couldn't help but laugh. "You want to settle down. You're buying into the 'we own her' bullshit."

"Maybe. Is that such a bad thing?"

Sadly, I didn't get a chance to answer him, Randolph exploding into the room as he usually did. At least there was excitement on his face for the first time in almost two months. Still, I thought about Trent's comments and his question. No, it wouldn't be such a bad thing, but I wasn't certain the three of us could handle sharing a woman on a permanent basis. Although... Scarlett was certainly the kind of creature who could keep us on our toes.

"It's almost eleven," Randolph said as if we were preparing for acceptance of a million-dollar contract.

"Yes. I will be curious if she's on time," Trent said, his eyes flashing.

"She will be. She wouldn't risk disobeying." Randolph's statement meant he was so damn sure of himself, just like always. Granted, Scarlett had remained quiet after our visit to the club. She certainly had a mind of her own, refusing to be pushed. And she'd been pissed at herself for losing the poker game.

"And what if she ignores her end of the deal?" There was something challenging about Trent's question. Almost instantly, Randolph bristled. The man didn't like being challenged on any level by anyone.

"Trust me. She won't." Randolph headed toward the bar, preparing three drinks.

"A little early, isn't it?" I asked.

"We're officially on vacation as of today," Randolph answered. "Why not celebrate a delicious win?"

His idea of a 'win' was different than mine; however, taking a few days off was enticing. I couldn't remember when any of the three of us had spent time away from the office and the various business deals. Maybe sun, sand, and surf would inspire our creational efforts, something that had been amiss lately.

As he swaggered toward us, his expression one of utter confidence, all I could think about was that Scarlett would remain disobedient on purpose, pushing our buttons. Her punishments could be harsh and often. I had to admit my cock twitched all over again just thinking about it. What a pleasure it would be to see her reddened bottom and the sheen of perspiration on her glorious skin.

"Gentlemen, I think this adventure is going to be our best." After handing off the glasses, Randolph raised his.

"Here's to one of the most beautiful creatures on the face of this earth surrendering," Trent toasted.

"I second that," Randolph growled.

While I enjoyed the moment, my instinct told me our venture wasn't going to be that easy.

Fifteen minutes later and I knew I'd been right.

Scarlett was a no-show.

"What. The. Fuck?" Randolph hissed.

"I'd say Scarlett has more backbone than we believed." Trent's amusement clearly angered Randolph.

"Maybe last night was too much for her," I muttered, thinking about what Trent had told me.

"She handled it just fine," Trent offered. "In fact, she's upping the wager."

I finished my drink, remaining calm. When Randolph tossed his glass against the wall, the thin tumbler shattering into dozens of pieces, all I could do was sigh. He'd been on edge for far too long, his increasing anger levels and sadistic needs finally a concern that could no longer be ignored. "Then we need to raise the stakes. Perhaps we should consider other options."

The tension in the room increased. While Randolph remained quiet, Trent lifted a single eyebrow as he glanced in my direction.

"I don't want to use other options, at least not for the time being," Randolph said a full minute later. "Although I agree about upping the amount of the wager and I'm not talking about money."

"Then what do you suggest?" I did my best to keep fury from my voice. That wouldn't do any good at this point. Granted, there were times I hated being the voice of reason, today included.

When Randolph finally shifted to face us, the smile on his face was unexpected. "It's simple. We hunt her down. Then we make certain she realizes that she now belongs to us. After that, we're going to insist she become a part of the Worth enterprise."

This time I shot Trent a look, curious as to his reaction.

He rolled his eyes first then polished off his drink. "What the hell? Scarlett accepted the terms of the deal. She should be made to honor them. If that also exposes her less than ethical business tactics, even better for Worth Dynamics. However, taking over her company is harsh."

"Not really. We'll make certain she's compensated. If she's a good little girl, then maybe we'll offer her a job." Randolph exhaled, narrowing his eyes then heading in my direction. "And what do you think, partner of mine?"

"Does it matter? You've already made up your mind." I closed the distance until we were only inches apart, my six-foot five-inch frame giving me a slight advantage at this moment. I usually jumped at the chance of taking over a smaller company. This time, it bothered me.

Randolph always thought himself to be the alpha in charge, needing reminders that all three of us were savage in nature. Now he acted as if his word was final. Everything about his plan bothered me, especially given my gut feeling.

"Yes, it does." His answer was just as conceited as I'd expected. "All three of us need to be on board with this."

I had to think it over. It was entirely possible that Scarlett was behind the threats. If that was the case, we should be able to find that out, but only if she felt squeezed. Still, what we were considering was risky as hell.

"We have to play it carefully," Trent added. "I don't want her destroyed. I won't accept that."

"Only her company," Randolph laughed, but I could see so many emotions in his eyes. This was very personal for him.

"Fine. Then I have no problem hunting her down, requiring her to follow our rules. However, there is one amendment to the rules of the game that will not be altered." I was surprised at my pattern of thinking, but it felt right.

In fact, a portion of my mind was almost delirious with thoughts of the future.

"Alright. What's the exception?" Randolph lifted his head, his eyes burning into mine.

"This time we play for keeps."

Todos Santos, Baja California Sur

Scarlett

While city life had its purpose, including being required for the business I was in, I loathed everything about the smog and traffic, noise and crowds. I'd always preferred a quiet beach setting, a location where I could kick back and relax after a hard day of work. I'd always told myself that I would purchase a little house somewhere tropical, the perfect getaway. Sadly, business had always interfered.

I was thrilled I'd made the decision to come to Todos Santos, a pristine location where the desert met the sea. The water was turquoise, the beaches almost empty, and the quaint town set back in another time.

The house was right off the beach on a high knoll, the views from every room spectacular. All I'd had to do was made a single phone call and I'd secured the location for my use.

Women often refused to maintain contact with men they'd formerly dated, but I'd found several advantages of remaining friendly. This was one of them. Roger had even made certain someone stocked the refrigerator and bar before my arrival. There was nothing quite like sipping a margarita while the sun began to drift below the horizon. I'd been here little more than a day and I was already more relaxed than I'd been for months, maybe years. Perhaps tonight I'd take a late-night snorkel.

I sat back in the lounge chair, soaking up the last of the rays of sun, marveling in just being there. While I'd worked on the flight, finding out as much as I could about Randolph, Alexander, and Trent, I'd been forced to realize they'd worked hard to maintain a heightened level of privacy. What little I'd found had been press releases and opportunity photos.

But thoughts regarding the Clubhouse weren't far from my mind. What kink were the three men into? When should I use what limited information I'd gathered? So far, Marjorie hadn't found anything my private investigator hadn't. But she was tenacious. It was obvious the three macho men had held back at Club Velvet. Maybe they thought they'd lure me into their dark web.

I'd been tempted to talk to Ashley's roommate but resisted given my assistant's odd reaction. A smile crossed my face. I'd also thought about what Marjorie's phone call, going ahead and giving her the authorization to finalize the contract with the changes the client had wanted. In doing so, I'd stripped another opportunity away from Worth, even if it meant I had to scramble for a few weeks. The boys had no idea how much I was crowding in on their territory.

I was truly an evil woman, more so than my father would ever have believed.

However, my mind remained troubled. Marjorie had also told me someone had been making several inquiries regarding the company without divulging the reason why. That didn't sit well with me, but at this point, there was nothing I could do about it. At least Marjorie had finally shut them down.

My thoughts drifted to the incident at Club Velvet. I still couldn't get it off my mind or the sight of their naked bodies. My God, the three men were built.

Bad girl. Very bad girl.

I licked salt from the rim, the light breeze tickling my skin. After taking a few more sips, I left my drink on the table, moving inside and grabbing my snorkel gear. The shimmer of sun should still allow me to enjoy visions of the beautiful marine life and corals less than fifty yards from the villa.

When my feet touched the sand, a series of shivers skated down my spine. Maybe it was time to purchase the house I'd been fantasizing about for years. I dropped my towel and eased into the water, taking a few seconds to glance back at the outline of the massive house. One week wasn't long enough.

There was nothing more spectacular than a swim near twilight with the sun illuminating so many of the vibrant colors of tropical fish and sea life. While I hadn't gone scuba diving in years, my favorite recreational activity, this was a fabulous second.

I managed to get lost in the moment, savoring the peaceful time alone.

By the time I returned to the beach, stars were brightly decorating the sky, the breeze now creating a chill coursing down to my toes. After wrapping myself in the towel, I headed back to the villa.

Tonight I'd make pasta to go along with the fresh seafood, pairing it with a delicious pinot noir.

As I jogged up the stairs, I realized just how dark it was around the house. While there was no one within a mile of the villa, any oncoming vehicles easy to see from the upstairs windows, I stopped on the landing. Why? There was no reason. Then why was my skin tingling all over? Swallowing, I slid the panel on the living room door, heading inside.

Then my skin began to crawl.

"Hello, Scarlett. You really thought you could get away that easily?"

Oh, dear God. There was no way the assholes had found me.

As Randolph began to laugh, I allowed my eyes to become accustomed to the darkness, thankful the bright moon was slipping in through the windows. It was easy to see three silhouettes lurking in the shadows. How the hell did the bastards find me? I'd taken great steps to ensure that didn't happen. I wasn't going to give them the satisfaction of asking.

I hated the way their colognes mixed, the scent a combustible combination of exotic spices and musky odors, all infused with their heightened level of testosterone. My God. I loathed Randolph's smugness.

"Well, well. It would seem you broke into my house. How daring of you." I moved toward one of the table lamps, switching it on and glaring at them. They were relaxed, enjoying their slight revelry, all three positioned on the leather furniture. They'd even taken the opportunity to prepare themselves a drink. Who the hell did they think they were?

"Let's be frank with one another, Scarlett. I think we owe each other that," Alexander piped in. "You don't own this house. In fact, this is one of several properties owned by a former flame of yours. Isn't that correct?"

All I could do was laugh, even though my heart was already skipping several beats. "No, but I don't need to. I have several good friends who share anything I ask for." There was something very carnal about the way they were looking at me, allowing their primal nature to show. While I knew Roger owned several weapons, I had no idea where he'd stored them inside the house. The best I could do was race into the kitchen, grabbing one of the butcher knives.

I chastised my thoughts, although I had to get the fuckers out of here. Then what? The little nagging voice in the back of my mind told me they would never just walk away.

Not until they got exactly what they wanted.

I hated how relaxed they seemed, their casual attire unexpected yet forcing some crazy wanton desires close to the surface.

"I can only imagine what you were required to do for such special attention," Randolph snickered.

"How dare you. I find it interesting you'd challenge my integrity when the three of you broke in."

Randolph was on his feet, heading in my direction. While I didn't want to back away, giving him any indication that I was nervous as hell, that's exactly what I did.

"Let's check some facts. Again. You accepted the wager, playing the game of poker fair and square. You lost. Then you attempted to flee moments after. We showed you leniency. We wanted to introduce you to our lifestyle, allowing you to understand what to expect. What did you do? You ran. You disrespected us. That won't happen again. This is going to be rule number one, Scarlett. You will respect us at all times."

A laugh slipped easily from my mouth. "Not a chance." I could tell the man was serious.

He smiled, as if my words were nothing but a joke. "Rule number two, you will do everything we tell you to do, no matter the request."

I stared at him incredulously.

"Rule number three. You will hand over your cell phone. There will be no endeavors to seek help of any kind. If you attempt to do so, you will be punished."

Hatred tore through me unlike anything I'd ever felt before. "Is there a rule number four?"

"Why, yes, there is. You will be coming with us to another destination. Any attempt at escaping will not only be met with harsh punishment, but it will also mean you're going to be confined."

Confined? The fucker had another think coming.

"You don't own me," I managed.

"That's where you're wrong. We do for one. Solid. Week." Randolph laughed again, the sound sending more than just chills down my spine. He meant every word. "Given you ran, the time officially starts now."

When the other two barbarians flanked my sides, I realized my legs were trembling.

"I think it's time that Scarlett realizes that disobeying us isn't in her best interest." Trent's voice was deeper than normal, grittier while still managing to slide across my skin sinfully. While he appeared to be the most unassuming of the three, I sensed a darker vibe than normal.

"And I think it's time you realize that I'm not in the mood to play games," I countered.

"The problem is that you don't have any choice in the matter." Alexander's words skittered over me like a tumultuous wave, his hot breath skipping along my shoulder. Before I had a chance to say anything in return, he'd grabbed my towel, yanking and tossing it then advancing. Even in the dim light, I could see just how aroused he'd become.

All three of them were hungry, prepared to take what they wanted.

Not a fucking chance. Not now. Not ever.

"I suggest the three of you get out of here right now or I'll call the authorities." I did my best to maintain an authoritative voice, shifting my angry gaze from one to the other.

All the bastards did was smile, as if I was enjoying this.

Encouraging them.

Hungry for them.

"That's not going to happen. You will honor the terms of the wager." Randolph brushed the tip of single finger down the side of my cheek. His actions brought a hiss from my mouth but a fevered response from my body, my skimpy swimsuit unable to hide my fully aroused nipples.

"I think we should start with a round of discipline," Trent half whispered. Was he trying to be subtle or just pretending he wasn't an asshole?

"If you touch me, I will kill you." While I issued the words through clenched teeth, trying to sound authoritative, I was forced to realize I was in a horrible position. No one but the pilot and Roger knew of my destination. The pilot had been told to leave me alone until my return date and Roger was jetting off to parts unknown.

I was all alone with three hulking brutes.

I should have known they'd do everything in their power to hunt me down.

Alexander laughed then grabbed my wrists, yanking them over my head with one hand. I immediately kicked out, struggling to get away from him but he was far too strong, able to keep me in place easily.

"Tsk. Tsk. Bad little girls shouldn't anger their captors." The man was obviously enjoying my discomfort.

"I think what she needs is a hard spanking to fully understand the error of her ways." Trent glowered in front of me, raking his fingers down from my neck past my cleavage to my stomach.

"Agreed," Randolph growled, the sound reverberating in my ears.

Words stuck in my throat, my mind reeling from what they were suggesting. No man had ever dared to lay a finger on me in some crazy attempt to punish me. I should have known from what they'd done the night before how much they enjoyed treating me like a child.

I continued wiggling, jerking on my arms until Trent produced a pocketknife. Suddenly, this didn't seem like a game any longer. Anxiety coursed through me, tensing every muscle. I held my tongue, trying to control my breathing as Trent continued smiling, expertly maneuvering the knife, the sharp blade easily cutting through the thin fabric of my one piece. Within seconds, he'd removed it, lowering his gaze as the slick of material fell away.

I'd never felt so exposed in my life, including what I endured at the club. Heat built along my neck and jaw, creating a dull ache in my teeth from how hard I was clenching. As it exploded across my face, I bit back a cry. This was really happening.

Randolph eased behind me and while I jerked my head as far over my shoulder as possible, I couldn't tell what he was doing. When he wrapped his hand around my hair, twisting then pulling my long strands aside, I shivered from the jolt of current shifting down my spine. I was supposed to be disgusted, not turned on by what he was doing.

He slid my hair over my shoulder then raked his nail all the way down my spine to the crack of my ass. "Yes, a very brutal spanking is what you need. They always do a woman some good. Last night was just a taste of what you can expect."

"What are you, fucking Neanderthals?" I spouted off, hating the erratic sound of my voice.

Randolph fisted the back of my head at the scalp, yanking by several inches. Then he was able to look down at me, his eyes narrowing. "As I told you, respect. If you don't learn that right away, things will be even more difficult for you."

"My God. You are the most arrogant man I've ever met." I was still seething, trying to both use and curtail the burning rage churning deep within. The last thing I would ever do was respect any of them.

"I'll take that as a compliment. However, you are getting punished for running from us and for ignoring your obligations." Randolph's smile was almost sinister, his words rumbling in my mind.

Had they found out about my other game? I couldn't be certain and until I was, I'd have to pretend I was simply refusing to honor the win from the charity event.

When Randolph slipped his hand around the back of my neck, his fingers digging into my skin in a possessive hold, I made a promise to myself that I would take the man down first. Then I'd circle around for the others, eliminating every ounce of power they believed they still had.

"Make no mistake, Scarlett," he hissed, the sound sending a wave of electricity shooting through every cell and vein. "We are going to devour you, enjoying every moment of exposing every one of your vulner-abilities, savoring every ounce of flesh. You're going to experience anguish like you've never known, ecstasy that will drive you into a whole new world. Then after the week is finished, you will belong to us. Permanently."

Chills continued to form, layer after layer until it was almost impossible to see clearly, let alone think in a rational manner. They had me right where they wanted me, acting as if their ownership was a God-given right. All the nasty thoughts about what I wanted to do faded away.

But only for now.

Soon I would regroup.

Then they would suffer.

I watched almost in horror as Alexander cleared the massive wooden coffee table. When he returned, a damn look of utter dominance on his face, he took several deep breaths as he gazed down the length of me.

"Get on the table on all fours," he instructed.

"Not a chance. You're going to have to make me." While I knew my statement was ridiculous, a part of me wanted to see just how far they'd go.

I didn't have to wait long.

Trent tossed me over his shoulder, taking long strides in the direction of the table. When he put me down, he gave me a stern look. "Do not move. If you do, your punishment will increase tenfold. Do you understand?"

"Who the hell do you think you are?" I demanded.

"One of your masters."

A laugh erupted from my throat before I could stop it, but for some reason, I stayed right where I was. There were three of them and one of me. I didn't like the odds. They were obviously irritated, but I couldn't be certain they wouldn't do something much worse than just spanking me.

Like a bad little girl.

The thought was revolting, churning in my stomach. I tried to control my breathing as the three men conversed in privacy, making certain I didn't hear what they were talking about.

When I finally noticed Randolph unbuckling his belt, I was lightheaded, no longer able to feel my fingers or toes. This had to be a nightmare I couldn't wake from. There was no other answer. I closed my eyes, trying to keep my resolve as well as my anger. The last thing I needed to do was show any kind of weakness.

Eventually, they would learn to be very afraid of me.

When I felt their presence, was able to gather their scents, I became woozy. They were even more gorgeous in their casual attire, but I couldn't allow myself to think that way. They were the enemy and nothing else. Period.

But you hunger for them.

No, the thought was disgusting. I could never want anything or anyone like the three men.

Then why is your skin tingling, your heart thudding?

Fuck this. I closed my eyes, prepared to shut down the world around me in order to block out what was happening. The fools would never get the advantage. Never.

"I think our lovely prisoner deserves thirty lashes. What do you think, gentlemen?" Randolph asked. The frivolity in his tone was as repulsive as his dominating one.

"I think thirty-six would be more in line," Alexander stated, laughing softly after doing so.

"Perfect. A dozen each. However, if she gets out of line we start again." Trent was more controlling than I'd ever heard him. The entire situation was surreal.

"Thirty-six it is. Why don't you start, Trent?" Randolph suggested.

Trent exhaled. "I would be happy to."

I could swear he was taking his time on purpose, making the anticipation even more sickening. When I felt his fingers brushing down my spine, I reacted instantly, kicking out, my foot able to connect with a portion of his body.

There was silence for at least a minute. Then Trent moved closer. "I'll chalk that up to being nervous, Scarlett, but if you act out again, we're going to double your round of punishment. Do you understand?"

"Yes," I hissed between clenched teeth.

The hard smack he issued with his hand hadn't been anticipated. I yelped, immediately sucking the sound back in. I refused to show them any sign of weakness.

"Respect. Isn't that what Randolph told you?" Trent growled, the sound sending a dozen vibrations dancing from my shoulders to my toes.

The bastard actually thought I'd use the word 'sir.' They weren't just arrogant. They were absolute assholes. However, if I didn't play the game, there wasn't a snowball's chance in hell I'd get away from them. "Fine. Yes. Sir."

"Not good enough."

What? What the hell was he getting at? Then it dawned on me. The fuckers wanted me to call them my masters. I was sickened to the point my throat was almost closed and my jaw clenched until my teeth hurt.

Play along. Just play along.

"Yes, Master."

"Much better. There is a good chance you can be taught your place."

Trent had never acted this way, but I'd pegged him as a wolf in expensive sheep's clothing. I should realize that nothing was as it seemed with them. I wrapped my fingers around the edge of the coffee table, bracing for impact. At least I didn't have to wait long. He delivered a volley of four in rapid succession, every slap of the strap hitting me directly in the center of my buttocks.

While the pain was instant, it was tolerable, although I gritted my teeth to keep from making any sound. I was surprised the force shoved me forward, enough so if I didn't keep a strong hold then I'd be launched off the furniture.

"Excellent. Randolph, turn on another light for me. Will you? I want to see the warm blush as it builds on her beautiful skin." Trent exhaled, the sound like a deep rumble of a powerful engine.

"Brilliant idea," Randolph muttered and within seconds, light flooded the room.

I winced, blinking several times, hating myself for the fact a few tears had formed. This was more humiliating than anything I'd ever been through in my life.

Trent took a few seconds to rub one side of my bottom then the other before starting again. I counted six this time, although I could be wrong. The pain had already started to build, my legs quivering. Panting, I tried to look forward, but seeing Alexander lounging on one of the leather chairs, watching me intently was almost too much to deal with. Yet I persevered, glaring at him with all the hatred I could manage. When I shifted my gaze, studying the Australian, I had a feeling he was doing nothing more than biding his time.

Alexander's eyes were so dark and intense, yet the way he was sitting was casual; one leg crossed over the other, his elbow on the arm so he could rub the tip of his finger back and forth across his succulent lips. He knew exactly how attractive he was. He was imagining what he was going to do to me when it was his turn.

Trent took another deep breath, still caressing my skin. I realized I was wiggling, shifting my hips back and forth.

"You are truly delightful," he whispered in his husky, throaty voice. "But so naughty."

"Yes, she is," Randolph mused. "But we'll take care of that. When we're finished, she'll be very docile, begging us for punishment any time she disobeys us."

Yep. The man had gone psycho.

"Last two," Trent whispered, and gave them. There was no doubt he wanted to continue.

"Alexander. You're up next," Randolph directed.

"Are you two his lackeys?" I couldn't resist asking. While I knew I would suffer the consequences, it was worth it to see the changing expression on Alexander's face as he rose to his feet. Yes, there was some discord in the hierarchy of their relationship. At some point, I would use that to my advantage.

Alexander said nothing as he took the belt from Trent's hand, but before he began, he widened my legs until my knees were near the edges of the table. When he moved in front of me, I jerked my head until I was able to look into his eyes.

His expression wasn't just about possession or desire to punish me. There was something else, darker and more obsessive. Then he slapped the belt, the end hitting my bottom as well as slicing against my pussy lips.

I jerked up, unable to keep from gasping. "Bastard!"

"That's going to cost you, little pet. I'm making the executive decision to add four more strikes. Would you care to continue?"

It was suddenly as if every bit of humanity had left him. He repeated the same action four times and every brutal strike brought tears to my eyes.

"That's enough," Randolph snarled. "Not until she's ready."

Ready? For what?

I took several deep breaths, concentrating on staring down at the table. I heard Alexander cursing under his breath, but he didn't fight Randolph, talking two long strides until he was behind me. When he started spanking me in earnest, I noticed Trent walking toward the triple glass doors. The man was suddenly unreadable, but his body language told me many things.

He was uncomfortable with the situation.

He wasn't happy with Randolph.

And... he wanted something else entirely.

He would be my first candidate to work my magic on. I'd break him down so fast, he wouldn't know what hit him.

Then I'd shift to Alexander.

My thoughts regarding revenge eased the pain, even though Alexander's strikes were harder than Trent's had been, making certain he covered the backs of my thighs. I squirmed but managed to keep from issuing another sound.

When the dark-souled man was finished, he tossed the belt onto the floor, immediately yanking his glass into his hand and heading toward the bar.

Randolph chuckled behind me then dragged his fingers across my neck and down my spine to the crack of my ass. "Are you beginning to understand your circumstances?"

That I'm going to destroy you?

That if I could, I would stick a knife in your heart?

That all three of you are small men, and likely your cocks are minuscule?

"Yes. Master." At least the ugly thoughts gave me a smile.

"Excellent. We're already getting somewhere," Randolph murmured, continuing to finger the cleft between my buttocks. When he slowly slipped the tip to my tender pussy lips, I tensed. Until the night before, I hadn't been touched by a man in a very long time.

"You're already wet, glistening for us. I think you enjoy being punished."

Just the way his voice swept across my skin was mind boggling, my body's reaction an even worse betrayal. I gritted my teeth to keep from saying anything as he pushed a single finger past my swollen folds.

Teasing me.

Reminding me of my place.

Telling me in no uncertain terms that I belonged to them.

God, I hated this. All of it.

He chuckled in his usual dark, demanding way before starting his version of discipline. Just the cracking sound of his wrist as he snapped the belt pushed a wave of heat into me, but the whooshing noise the strap made going through the air kept me on edge. I wasn't certain I could endure any more.

"Count them off for me, little pet," he commanded.

Was he kidding me? I wasn't even certain how many he'd issued, my mind almost numb that from realization alone.

"Twelve more. That should help you."

"Yes. Master."

He snapped the belt twice, waiting until I obeyed.

"One and two, Master." I envisioned gutting him.

Crack!

Four more in rapid succession.

"Three, four, five, and six, Master." I imagined slicing his throat with a dull blade.

Randolph took his time, doling out only one.

"Seven, Master." I could see him writhing in pain, begging me for forgiveness.

He smacked me twice more, leaving the last three. He liked hearing me call him my master. Fucker.

"Eight and nine, Master." I was so going to love forcing him to call me Mistress.

When he took his damn sweet time kneading my bruised and aching bottom, humming while doing so, I allowed the evil portion of my mind to imagine several hard blows to his gorgeous face.

"So beautiful and talented. So disobedient. It will be a sheer joy when we finally break you. And Scarlett? That is going to happen."

When he delivered the last three strikes, they caused the most anguish, every nerve ending on fire. Electricity shared between the four of us was also shooting off inside like bottle rockets. I was breathless, a series of stars floating in front of my eyes. I could barely think let alone talk, but I managed to give the bastard what he wanted.

For now.

"Ten. Eleven. Twelve! Master." Yes, the man would suffer more at my hands than he had in his worst nightmare.

And I would enjoy every minute of it.

"Now, you're going to stand in the corner, little pet. That is until we're ready for you. After that? We're going to begin another lesson, one you won't forget. Would you like to know what's in store for you?"

Jesus. The asshole was gloating more than he had when winning a contract. "Yes. Master."

"We're going to fuck you long and hard until you beg us for more. And Scarlett? There will be no second chances. You belong to us, body and soul."

CHAPTER 8

rent

Anger.

I'd felt it several times over the last few years since coming to Worth Dynamics. I'd never questioned why since I was making more money than I ever dreamed of. But now, I was questioning everything, including why the hell I'd followed along with this scheme of Randolph's. I couldn't escape the feeling all three of us would crash and burn. Hissing, I closed my eyes, allowing several visions of Scarlett's naked body to filter into my mind.

Randolph was right about one thing. She'd gotten in over her head in attempting to sabotage us. Although she'd gotten very good at making us uncomfortable. Snickering, I shifted my weight, relieving some pressure on my aching cock.

I didn't bother retrieving my drink, although I wanted to consume an entire bottle of alcohol at this point.

Instead, I walked out onto the deck, leaning over the edge of the railing and allowing the sound of the surf to provide relief. Maybe comfort. I wanted Scarlett more than any woman I'd ever met in my life. Yes, I was dominating, even sadistic with my needs, but she was far too precious to try to destroy.

As I raked my hand through my hair, enjoying the night breeze, I sensed Alexander's presence and bristled. I didn't need a goddamn pep talk. He'd signed on board as if destroying both her resolve and her company meant nothing. I'd agreed to give her a fair price for her company, but maybe I'd been stupid enough to believe that's what he meant. Randolph obviously had no plans for keeping her on as an employee. As far as the three of us owning her? That would happen if hell froze over ten times. Jesus. We'd been so arrogant in our thinking.

When he placed a glass in front of me, I rolled my eyes but accepted the offer. Still, I remained quiet. At this point I had nothing to say. My cock ached, my balls so tight I was in pain, but I was having difficulty accepting any part of this.

"Are you going to tell me what the hell is going on with you?" he asked after a full minute had passed.

"What do you want me to say?"

"The fucking truth. You've been hot and cold the entire time with this."

"The question is, why aren't you? You're happy with the way this is turning out?" My tone was as demanding as it had ever been. Maybe I needed to do that more, asserting my authority for once. I'd thought of little else but Scarlett since indulging in her flesh, and her words had cut through me, as much as I hated to admit it. I liked the girl. Hell, I wanted to be closer. That wasn't like me.

Alexander laughed as he leaned over the railing, staring into the sky. He'd always been the dreamer, the one with high hopes of becoming the richest man in the world. Me? I'd wanted to make a good living and find a happy home. I almost laughed at my simple needs. A lovely wife, maybe three kids and two dogs. A modest home with a large yard.

Okay, a boat would be nice, not the yacht I partially owned with the other two. I would even love a damn garden of all the stupid things.

I didn't see that in my future. Not now. Not ever.

After this, Scarlett would spend the rest of her life trying to destroy us, no matter what Randolph thought he could do. Hostile takeover, my ass. She was far too intelligent to allow anyone to walk all over her.

"I'm excited, Trent. I'm enjoying the moment. Keep in mind that Scarlett is no shrinking violet nor is she an innocent bystander in all of this. Is it such a big deal that I want her begging for more?"

I shook my head. "Not if you're a monster."

"Oh, come on. What the hell is that supposed to mean?"

"It means we hunted her down like an animal, flying thousands of miles in order to do so. It means we just spanked her like some bad girl in need of constant discipline. And it means we're going to fuck her not once, but as often as we desire."

"I don't see the issue. We've disciplined women before. We've fucked them before. She enjoyed what happened at Club Velvet. You know it as well as I do."

"That's the problem, Alexander. Neither you nor Randolph see the risks or the potential problems in the future. You treat her like... like a damn object, for Christ's sake."

Alexander exhaled, but I could hear clear discord in the sound. "Are you forgetting that she has plans on sabotaging our company? Do you not see that she's using her feminine wiles to try and disguise her ruthless tactics? They worked on Steven Dockett like a charm. They certainly allowed her an audience with several reporters."

"What I see is that we don't have a clue who purchased that stock. We are assuming. Yes, we need to find out, but there are other ways of doing it. As far as the prank she pulled? Please don't try and tell me Randolph wouldn't have done the same." I shook my head several times before continuing. "Do you know how many anonymous threats I've gotten over the last year? Phone calls. Emails. Hell, a damn letter arrived in my mailbox one day in cutout block letters. If you really think Scarlett has spent all that time trying to scare us, then you're out of your mind."

He turned toward me, cocking his head. "You never mentioned these threats."

"Are you trying to tell me that you haven't received one or two?"

"In passing, maybe, but not in such egregious ways. You shouldn't have kept that a secret."

"What secret?" I barked. "Randolph told me the day I signed the contracts becoming an owner to expect my share of threats. So I have. It's no big deal. The purchase of the stock might be something else, but until you can provide a name of the purchaser, I refuse to buy Scarlett has anything to do with it."

"Shit. You're in love with her."

Huffing, I paced the deck, trying to figure out why I felt so strongly about her. "No, I don't know her."

"Damn it, Trent," Alexander said after a few seconds.

I could tell he was holding back. "What the hell is really bothering you?" He hesitated and Alexander had never had any problem telling me what was on his mind.

"I don't like what's going on. My gut tells me Randolph isn't sharing something important with us. Whatever the case, it's obvious the threats are escalating. That makes the situation a very big deal."

He glanced toward the door, and I twisted my head to see what he was looking at. Randolph was sitting in one of the chairs, staring at Scarlett as if she was a prized deer hanging on the wall. My heart raced at the thought.

"Okay, fine. Maybe I should have taken them more seriously, but until you mentioned the issue with the stock, I hadn't noticed anything else strange within the company." In the bright light of the full moon, I could see just how hard his jaw was clenched. "Wait a minute. You really do think Randolph is keeping secrets." Not that I would put it past him in the least. Randolph was hardheaded as fuck, his upbringing keeping the damn silver spoon in his mouth.

He took a swig then a gulp of his drink, swirling the rest of the liquid in his glass before polishing it off. I'd never seen the man nervous in all the years I'd known him. He'd been the cool as a cucumber guy, laughing when anything remotely bad happened. He was also the tough man, even getting into fistfights when we'd been in college. This was unexpected as hell.

"Talk to me, Alexander," I insisted.

"There are a few discrepancies that have been bothering me. Things that aren't adding up."

"What are you talking about?"

He glanced over his shoulder. "I'm the CFO, for Christ's sake. It's my job to analyze our profitability in comparison to other years. A few of the original accounts took a huge jump just before Randolph took over from his father. I wanted to follow up on the details. They are... sketchy at best."

"Bad record keeping?"

His sighs were labored. "That's what I thought, but two years of records were doctored. I don't have any doubt about it. Numbers don't lie. Either Worth Dynamics was given a boost in contract terms by a hefty amount, or the books had been doctored. And that doesn't make any sense."

"Does Randolph know what you've found?" I tried to think through what he was saying. Maybe Sampson had used the inflated numbers as collateral for a loan.

After shaking his head, he finally looked me in the eyes once again. "No, and I'm not ready to tell him anything. I'm also not ready to accuse him of keeping things from us."

"That's why you have no issue treating Scarlett as an object."

"If there are some purposeful discrepancies, they might be criminal in nature."

I shook my head, glaring at him. "That's a huge stretch. No wonder you aren't ready to repeat it. You want to keep her with us, so she doesn't have a chance of finding anything."

"Exactly. Don't get me wrong, I adore the woman, probably more than I should. The thought of enjoying her on a more permanent basis keeps my cock hard. But I don't believe that fantasies can be anything but just that."

I thought about what he was saying. Did Randolph know and had he kept us in the dark? "Why do I have the feeling you've buying into Randolph's thoughts, wanting her company destroyed?"

"At minimum I think it would be best if Prestwood Automation was under our corporate veil but coaxing her to become a part of our company isn't going to happen. You're romancing the idea that she would ever work for us. You know better. She would never take orders, just like she's acting now."

"Do you blame her?" The tension between us was palpable.

"Why don't I make a suggestion? Let's just enjoy the next couple of days. We deserve that," he said more in passing.

Deserve. The word seemed out of character even for him. At this point, I'd bought in, agreeing to this ridiculous game.

"Sure," I managed.

"Don't take too long out here brooding. You know how Randolph gets." When he headed toward the door, I snarled under my breath. Yeah, I knew exactly how Randolph got.

The fucker usually 'got' everything he wanted. Well, I doubted it was going to happen this time. After we were finished with her, I had no doubt in my mind that she'd not only find a way to destroy us, but she'd also manage to have us arrested.

When he continued to hesitate, I had a feeling he was more burdened by the knowledge he was holding secret than he wanted to display.

"Do you have an idea of who might be behind this?" I asked.

Alexander sighed, the sound ragged. "Look. I knew more about Randolph's father than you did. Randolph still worships that man, even though he was unscrupulous as hell. He also had some friends who could be considered criminals. I don't know if it means anything given what little I know, but I'm going to try and find out if that has anything to do with the threats being made."

Alexander had been closer to Randolph over the years. What little I knew about Sampson seemed to corroborate what he was telling me. I'd never liked the man, especially the way he'd treated his family. However, the man was dead. What the hell did he have to do with someone making threats?

"Just be careful, my friend. Harboring secrets isn't the best thing for the company."

He shook his head, laughing in his deep baritone. "Point taken, Trent, but the last thing we need to do is make the wrong assumption."

"Like we're doing with Scarlett?"

"You were the one who told me you wanted to settle down." He lifted a single eyebrow, staring at me intently.

I wasn't certain what or if I wanted to say anything at this point. He looked over his shoulder. Although I was unable to read his expression, I could feel his remaining tension. He was also hungry, perhaps even more so than I'd become. Still, the game we were playing was risky as hell.

The reason?

We could actually lose our hearts in the process.

After he went inside, I realized my grip on the railing was tight, my entire body aching from desire.

Oh, what the hell. My life was nothing but making money anyway. I laughed softly, taking a swig of my drink as I took another look at the rolling ocean.

Yet as I walked inside, I had a bad feeling the threats would only continue. What if we had another enemy to contend with?

* * *

Scarlett

They were going to fuck me long and hard?

Hadn't they already done that?

I couldn't seem to stop shivering at the thought. Yes, I'd actually fantasized about sharing a bed with the three of them for a single night, but that had been after drinking far too much wine. Too much had happened between the four of us, including the night after the charity event.

And you enjoyed every moment. Stop lying to yourself.

Exhaling, I realized my little voice was right.

I remained lightheaded, but my nipples were still hard, small pebbles that were aching as much as my bottom, heat continuing to build.

Even my mouth was dry, unable to process what had occurred in the last thirty minutes.

I'd been sent to the corner like a bad child who'd thrown a temper tantrum. While the rational side of me continued to remind the irrational side that I was still playing a game and one I'd been stupid enough to agree to, I wasn't certain how long I could handle pretending I was submitting.

I was well aware Randolph was hovering over me as if he owned me, but I also knew Trent and Alexander were having some kind of discussion outside. I'd love to be a fly on the wall. The three men were similar but oh-so different. I wanted nothing more than to get inside their minds, finding out exactly what made them tick.

While Randolph was hungry for power, he was driven by a very personal reason. I was determined to find out what, using the details along with everything else I'd learned against him.

"Come here," Randolph suddenly beckoned.

I closed my eyes, fisting my hands and digging my nails into my palms in a crazy effort to keep from spewing something nasty.

"I said. Come here. Don't make me tell you again."

If he was this way with all the women he dated, no wonder he remained single. I turned stiffly, glaring at him with all the venom I could muster. My feet felt heavy as I attempted to walk in his direction, but I managed to keep from swaying in front of him. When I was only five feet away, I lifted my head in continuing defiance. "I'm here."

He lifted his eyebrows, giving me another one of his filthy yet controlling looks.

"Master," I added, biting my lower lip to keep from screaming. That wouldn't do me any good.

"On your knees. Crawl to me." He pointed to the floor then settled back in the plush leather, widening his legs.

My God, the audacity of the man was increasing by the minute. Forcing me to crawl to one of them seemed to be their signature move. Was that supposed to make a woman feel inferior? It would take a hell of a lot more than that. Nasty things slipped into my mind.

I took a deep breath as I slowly dropped to my knees and onto all fours, crawling toward him at a snail's pace. He was fucking amused at my hesitance, his eyes glistening as he studied me intently. However, he allowed me to take my time until I was less than a foot away.

"Come closer. I don't bite, at least not at this point," he growled.

If he only knew the ugly, murderous thoughts I'd had earlier. Still, I had no way of ignoring him, so I inched closer, the scent of his cologne floating around me, the fragrance far too intoxicating. He reached down ever so slowly, placing his hand on top of my head and stroking.

"That's a good little pet. You can follow orders."

How many times was he going to say that shit to me? What did he want, for me to purr for him?

"Purr for me, sweet kitten. I want to know how much you want me."

I'll be damned. I continued to tamp down all the nasty things I should do and say, issuing several purrs that sounded more like a cat dying in some freaking alley.

"Softer, more seductive," he ordered.

I did as I was told, trying to keep my composure. He continued stroking my hair, tangling his fingers in my long strands as his breathing became more erratic. I even dared to rub my face against the inside of his leg.

"Now, you're going to suck me."

Fine. If the man wanted me to suck him, I was going to do it my way. I lifted my head and slowly slid my fingers along his calves, moving ever so slowly over his knees. His eyes had become little more than slits, his chest heaving. By the time I reached his inner thighs, his cock was throbbing hard against his trousers. My mouth and throat had gone from bone dry to very wet. There was no denying my attraction to him or the burning desire that continued to build.

So much of me wanted to lash out, but as another jolt of electricity shot through me, my entire body ached to be touched.

And tasted.

And fucked.

What was happening to me?

The desire for them hadn't left since the time I'd been forced against the cross.

He pressed my face against his bulge for a few seconds then moved his arm away, reaching for his drink. This was the epitome of a power exchange. I fell into a routine, trying to remember that the endgame would be spectacular. As I slowly unfastened his pants, tugging the zipper, he let out a series of growls.

When I peeled back the edges, I realized he wasn't wearing any underwear. A commando man. How very true to the kind of person he was.

He raised his hips, allowing me to slide the unwanted material away, exposing his cock. I was shocked at the size as well as the thickness, excitement coursing through me. The veins on both sides were full of blood, pulsing even more when I rubbed the tip of my index finger around his cockhead. His masculine scent was almost overpowering, pulling the bad girl version of me to the surface.

I was forced to admit I wanted to taste him, to lick up every drop of his sweet cum. My mind became a blur as I fingered the side, slowly drawing a straight line to his swollen balls. I wrapped my hand around them, marveling how they felt in my fingers.

"That's it," he breathed, his eyelids remaining half closed even as he tried to take a sip of his drink, almost spilling it in the process.

I realized I was in full control, able to do anything I wanted. The thought was riveting, keeping me on edge. I remained on my knees, squeezing his balls with enough pressure he threw his head back and moaned. When I darted my tongue across his sensitive slit, his entire body began to shake.

There was something so filthy about what I was doing, and I did enjoy his every reaction. When I engulfed the tip, using my strong jaw muscles to suck, he lifted his hips off the chair.

"Your mouth is freaking hot," he managed, although his words were little more than a garbled whisper.

I continued sucking, sliding my tongue back and forth for several seconds. Then I rolled my tongue down the underside until I was able to dart the tip around first one testicle then the other.

Randolph shifted in his seat, taking several deep breaths then fisting my hair. "I don't think it's wise to tease me, little pet."

I hated being called their pet but at the same time, the single word was thrilling in some sick, twisted way. With another loud purr, I took a portion of his sac into my mouth, swirling my tongue as I sucked gently. His entire body began to shake, every sound he made guttural.

Within seconds, I was enjoying myself, finally licking up the length of his shaft then returning his cockhead to my mouth. The taste of him was intense, sweet yet tangy, my mind whirling from what I was doing. I wrapped my hand around the base, twisting it back and forth until I created wave after wave of friction.

He jerked up from the chair, fighting to return his glass to the table. I'd never seen such a look of bliss on his face. His eyes remained closed as I took another inch into my mouth, my jaws struggling to accept the wide girth. Within seconds, he took over full control, pushing my head until I was forced to take every single inch, the tip hitting the back of my throat.

I struggled to breathe, trying to keep from gagging.

"That's a good girl. You're doing so well," he whispered, panting hard after saying the words.

When I was able to relax, he loosened his hold, allowing me to start sucking in earnest. Within seconds, I'd developed the perfect rhythm, moving up and down. As the taste of his pre-cum slid into my mouth, my legs started quivering. I realized I was enjoying this, more so than I'd intended.

Randolph threw out a series of husky growls, his fingers never leaving my head. Less than a minute later, I could tell he was close to coming.

That's when he pushed me away with enough force that I was dumped on my aching bottom. He stared at me with lazy eyes, dragging his tongue across his lips.

"I have to fuck you first."

He didn't get the chance, Alexander moving into the room, making savage sounds of his own.

"I see the party started without us," he said, half laughing.

"You took your sweet time," Randolph answered, struggling to get to his feet. As he peered down at me, I could almost read his mind, his brutal desires as they swam to the surface. "Don't move."

I watched as the two men undressed, Trent joining in only seconds later. Even though their suits had always been well tailored, they'd never been able to accentuate just how damn good looking they truly were. All three were muscular with chiseled arms and legs, barrel chests and narrow hips. It was hard to believe such ruthless creatures could have such exquisite features. All three cocks were creations of beauty, thick and hard and... Whew. I allowed myself to become mesmerized for a few delicious seconds before turning away.

This wasn't some ultimate fantasy. There would be no decent ending. This wasn't just about the poker game. Hunting me down was all about winning the war between our companies, including not allowing me to sign the recent contract. While I'd had a single phone conversation with Mr. Dockett, trying to explain I had a family emergency, he hadn't been too keen on allowing me leeway. For now, I'd calmed him down. That would only last for so long. I prayed Marjorie could work her magic on the man.

Only a few seconds later, Alexander pulled me to my feet, taking his time to draw a zigzagging line down the side of my face. Then he cupped my jaw, pulling me onto my toes. I pressed my hands against his chest and almost immediately my fingers were seared from the explosive heat between us.

He noticed our intense chemistry as well, his dark eyes flashing as he lowered his head. "I can't wait to thrust my cock inside that sweet pussy of yours." As he captured my mouth, my body tensed. I realized I was digging my nails into his skin, pushing hard against him, but there was no getting out of his clutches.

While I didn't expect to enjoy the moment of passion, as before, I was wrong. He tasted of bourbon and cinnamon, a delicious combination. When he put his arm around me, cupping my bottom and drawing me even closer, I moaned into the kiss.

I knew without needing to look that Randolph was watching us intently. There was so much heat, jolt after jolt of current, that my heart hammered against my chest. I shouldn't enjoy his touch.

But I did.

I shouldn't want to feel his thick cock.

But I couldn't hold back, crawling my fingers down his stomach, wrapping them around his shaft.

His body shuddered from my touch, the kiss becoming more aggressive as his tongue dominated mine. When he finally pulled away, his grip on my jaw remained. He nipped on my lower lip then under my chin, licking back and forth.

I clung to him, my resolve starting to crumble. The man was sexy as hell, pushing all the right buttons.

"So luscious," he breathed. This time, his accent washed over me like a warm blanket, heightening my yearning.

As I opened my eyes, all I could focus on was Trent and the way he was looking at me, devouring me with his eyes. When he started to walk closer, I couldn't keep from issuing several strangled whimpers.

As he moved behind me, brushing his fingers over my shoulders before running them down my back, I knew I would have dropped to the floor if Alexander's massive hands weren't holding me. There was so much passion brewing between us, leaving me breathless and in awe at the way my body tingled from head to toe.

Trent murmured dirty things, telling me in no uncertain terms what he wanted to do to me. As he rubbed his fingers up and down the crack of my ass, I didn't tense as I'd done before. In fact, I arched my back as much as Alexander's hold would allow. There wasn't an inch of my skin not covered in goosebumps.

"I'm going to fuck you in your ass, our sweet pet, not once but several times. Would you like that?" Trent asked, whispering into my ear then nipping my earlobe.

I found myself nodding several times, the simple pleasure keeping butterflies swarming in my stomach. We'd sparred so many times over the past two years that it had become second nature to me. I'd always been able to ignore my feelings around them. I couldn't any longer.

Alexander shifted back and forth, grinding his cock against my stomach. I was far too lightheaded to think clearly, enjoying the warmth of their two heated bodies, a slight buzz echoing in my ears.

Trent turned me around to face him, using both hands to cup my face. He was gentler in his actions as he rubbed both his thumbs across my skin, staring into my eyes with such blatant hunger my legs began to quiver all over again.

"I want you," he managed then crushed his mouth over mine.

For a few seconds, everything else was blurred out, the heated moment between us something special. The man was a fantastic kisser, taking his time to explore the dark recesses of my mouth. I rubbed my hands along his arms, marveling just how muscular he was. Then I eased them over his shoulders, daring to tangle my fingers in his shaggy hair.

He seemed to enjoy my actions, pulling me even closer. I couldn't resist, wrapping one leg around his hip. The scent of my desire wafted between us like a beacon of sin. There was no doubt he could tell just how wet I remained, the hunger pushing me toward a sharp precipice. Everything about his hold was different than that of the others. While still possessive, it was also reeking with passion.

When he broke the kiss, he took the time to drag his tongue around my lips then across the seam of my mouth, his nostrils flaring as a smile crossed his face. There was no doubt he was famished, ready to devour every inch of me.

"Soon I'll be inside of you," he muttered. "And I can't wait to taste you."

Shuddering, I turned my head, able to tell Randolph was growing impatient.

He advanced like the predator I knew him to be, taking my hand and pulling me away from them. As he tugged me toward the open kitchen, I held my breath. What the hell did the man think he was going to do?

With a primal growl, Randolph lifted me onto the kitchen island, pushing me down and spreading my legs within seconds. As he leaned over, his hot breath cascading across my stomach, I pressed my hand over my mouth to keep from making any sounds. The second he swirled his tongue around my clit, I failed as I'd done before, my whimper floating toward the ceiling.

Every sound he made was like a beast in the wild hunting for its prey. He held me wide open, licking up and down the length of my pussy, but the bastard was teasing me, pulling away every few seconds.

He wanted me to know that he was the one in full control.

I lolled my head when he finally drove his tongue into my tight channel, flicking it feverishly as he grunted several times. He truly was a savage, but as he brought me closer and closer to an orgasm, I didn't care who he was, only the joyous pleasure he was bringing me.

The bliss he was *allowing* me.

I was being manipulated but I didn't care. Seconds later, I was vaguely aware that both Trent and Alexander were leaning over from opposite directions. When I felt their hot mouths over my nipples, I fell into a peaceful moment of bliss, mewing as they sucked and nipped my hardened buds. The orgasm continued to build, pushing me past the point of no return.

Randolph seemed to sense my condition, thrusting several fingers deep inside. His actions were perfectly orchestrated, driving me closer and closer.

Gasping, I tossed my head back and forth as Trent pinched my nipple, twisting it roughly. I was nothing but a ragdoll, succumbing to whatever they wanted to do. Everything was a beautiful blur as the climax finally roared into my system.

"Oh. Oh… My…"

"That's it, little pet. Come for me," Randolph growled, his actions becoming rougher.

I couldn't hold back, the eruption sparking embers into a raging fire. I was quickly overwhelmed, a single orgasm morphing into an incredible wave, leaving me wet and tingling, my skin extra sensitive.

Every moan I issued was scattered, every breath I took labored, my heart racing until my pulse skipped in my throat. And still they continued, Randolph feasting on me as if he was a starved man.

Stars floated in my periphery of vision, allowing me to fall further into a moment of sheer ecstasy, enough so it took me a few seconds to realize both

Trent and Alexander had moved away once again. When I opened my eyes, everything was hazy, my body warm.

Randolph leaned over, planting his hands on either side of me. "I take you first."

The four words were said with such authority I realized I was holding my breath.

He dragged me to the edge of the counter, rolling onto the balls of his feet as he placed the tip of his cock against my pussy lips. His expression was one of almost desperate need, as if he was riddled with pain. When he gripped my hips, he wasted no time in thrusting the entire length of his cock inside.

I slapped my hands against the counter, shaking all over as my muscles tried to accommodate him, stretching then clamping down. "Oh, yes. I..." I bit my lower lip, stunned by the connection we shared. He was so powerful in his actions, pulling out then driving into me again and again, as if he couldn't breathe without fucking me like a wild animal.

My mind a huge blur, I found it even more difficult to think clearly, my pulse continuing to increase. As he became even more brutal, yanking me into a sitting position, forcing me to wrap my legs around his hips, I allowed myself to become lost in his eyes.

Everything about him was mesmerizing, but so much was hidden behind his golden irises, dirty little secrets I would find a way to uncover. I slapped one hand on the counter, pushing the other one against his chest as we stared at each other. This was some kind of line being drawn in the sand, forcing me to withdraw my rebellious nature.

Fat chance in hell.

I purred, raking my nails down his chest, able to create lines on his skin. I hoped at least one of them would start to bleed. He laughed softly then lowered his head.

His whispered words were said with no emotion, as if this was nothing more than a business transaction.

"Don't fight us, Scarlett. You won't like what happens if you do."

If the man thought he was going to scare me off, he had another think coming. I arched my back, bucking hard against him. He had no idea what kind of woman I was, the steel I'd been made from. I couldn't wait until he was the one begging.

But there would be no salvation. Not for him or for the other two. This was nothing but a dance, a prelude to much more.

When a sly smile curled on the corner of his mouth, I closed my eyes, tilting my head back until I was able to study the ornate carved wooden ceiling. Then I allowed another orgasm to rush into me. This time, when I opened my mouth there was no sound. None at all. Even my breathing was calmer.

Randolph wrapped his hand around my head, forcing me to look him in the eyes. His smile remained and just before he captured my mouth, he issued another warning.

"Breaking you won't be enough. Then I'm going to savor every moment of ruling you for the rest of your life."

 lexander

Throes of passion.

I'd heard the line coming out of every movie and book about sinful love affairs, although I couldn't stand those that included anything but hard fucking. Still, the sight of Scarlett's naked body alone was enough to keep my hunger on edge, my desires bursting through the steel armor I'd placed around my emotions and longing for a relationship years before. Scarlet had managed to rip a hole through every layer. Yet I couldn't stop thinking about Trent's ideas regarding the future, still finding it difficult to believe he was ready to settle down.

Then again, none of us were getting any younger. Even I was sick of walking into a cold, barren condo, no matter how many toys and expensive items of furniture I'd purchased for the expansive space. I had the best of everything in my life, but I hadn't been truly happy for one hell of a long time.

Maybe money could buy happiness for some people, but after a while, even raking in the bucks did nothing more than pad my bank account even more. Trent had been right. The fantasies both shared at the Clubhouse as well as those I'd experienced on my own had been enjoyable, but they lacked substance. The simple truth was no woman had sparked such desire in me.

Well, with the exception of one. I'd almost destroyed her life given my arrogance and lack of emotion. That was one aspect of my life I regretted more than anything else. Sadly, it felt like we were doing the same thing to Scarlett, keeping her a prisoner of a wicked wager while determining whether we wanted to wreck her world entirely.

I eased my hand to my cock, wrapping it around the base. Watching Randolph fucking her irritated me. That had never happened before. We'd shared several women over the years, the first one of our professors in college. That had been a truly dicey experience, one that could have gotten us expelled, but we'd enjoyed living dangerously. Nothing had changed since then. The need to take risks had followed us.

After graduating from college, we'd even joked about sharing a woman on a permanent basis. We'd had out last discussion as soon as we'd made our first billion, considering ideas and possibilities over a bottle of tequila on some tropical beach I couldn't remember the name of. No decisions had been made. Since then, there hadn't been a single woman who'd enticed us enough to open the discussion again.

Until now.

Still, I couldn't shake the concerns brewing in the back of my mind. Someone was attempting to shake us down. My gut also told me it had to do with whatever decisions Sampson Worth had made years before. If Scarlett was behind the attempt, the week spent together could fuel her efforts. However, if this had something to do with Randolph's father then all bets were off, and if that was the case, then Scarlett was in danger of losing business by just being around us.

And maybe more.

Her lingering perfume had already stained my skin and the way her breath had skipped across my face left me aching inside. As soon as Randolph eased her to the floor, I swept around the corner of the island, taking her into my arms, forcing her to straddle me as I got onto the barstool.

Scarlett cooed on purpose, giving me a pouty look. I knew she was only playing the part, trying to take back as much control as possible. The little game we were playing was enjoyable.

For now.

I held her aloft, toying with her. She peered down at me, keeping the same mischievous smile on her face I'd seen earlier. I knew I wasn't going to be able to stand doing this for long, my needs increasing by the second.

"What's wrong?" she asked. "You don't think you can handle me?"

Chuckling, I gazed down from her neck to her voluptuous breasts, refusing to allow her to reach my cock. "Randolph is right. You should be careful what you say to us. You're no longer in control, something very important for you to remember."

I adored the way she narrowed her eyes, every gesture she made sexy as hell. I'd had enough, my patience ripped away. When I pulled her down slowly, the way her muscles expanded, the explosive heat was even more powerful than disciplining her.

"Ride me, Scarlet."

She dragged her tongue across her lips, her seductive action meant to break down my defenses. That wasn't going to happen.

Her soft mews became ragged pants as she gripped my shoulders, pressing her knees against me as her pussy muscles clenched and released several times. A rumble erupted from deep within me, the sound penetrating the air. I pulled her all the way up until the tip was just inside before yanking her down again.

Every sound she made fueled a fire that already threatened to consume me. I was losing the battle of control, my balls already aching for release. Yet I was determined to make this last, to enjoy every moment.

Scarlett continued to cling to me, bucking hard as she dug her fingers into my shoulders. I nodded toward Trent, realizing he was waiting more patiently than I'd been able to do. As he approached, she tensed, sensing what was about to happen.

"Relax, little pet. We'll take good care of you," I growled, sliding my hand around her throat and pulling her down until our lips brushed together.

She palmed my chest, a series of short whimpers escaping her mouth as her eyes darted back and forth. For the first time, I saw a hint of weakness in those big green eyes of hers, as if she didn't know what to expect.

Trent seemed to sense her anxiety, caressing her arm for several seconds.

"Open your mouth, Scarlett," he directed.

While she did as she was told, she kept her gaze locked on my face, her lower lip quivering. When he shoved several of his fingers inside, she instinctively closed her mouth, sucking on them with pretended eagerness. The vision was delightful, filthy in an entirely different kind of way. My cock continued to pulse deep inside, my heart thudding against my chest.

"That's it. Suck them like the good little girl you can be," he murmured, giving me a wry smile.

She finally closed her eyes, but she remained tense, the sound of her strong jaws sucking on his fingers driving me crazy.

As he slowly removed them, she let out another whimper.

"Relax. I'm not going to hurt you," Trent whispered then licked down the back of her neck before easing his fingers along the crack of her ass.

I pulled her up by several inches, allowing him to slide the tip against her asshole.

Hissing, she looked over her shoulder. When he pushed the tip further inside, she threw her head back with a series of ragged whimpers.

"Jesus. That's..." she started, panting several times.

"Breathe for me, kitten. Just breathe. It's going to feel so good," he whispered, pressing kisses from one side of her neck to the other.

"You breathe," she snarked, her face twisting as Trent pushed his cock in even deeper.

When her body started to shake, I tilted her face, once again capturing her mouth. I couldn't seem to get enough of the taste of her, immediately plunging my tongue inside. As she'd done before, her fingers dug into me, moaning when Trent was fully seated inside.

He pressed his body against her, holding his stance for several seconds. When he finally started riding her, I eased away, lifting her up and down.

Within seconds, the look of discomfort on her face changed, her eyelids now half closed as she pursed her lovely mouth. Together, we formed a perfect orchestration, moving together seamlessly. I kept my hands on her hips, pulling her up and down as she rocked against me. The building heat was more combustible than before, every moan she issued filtering into my ears.

There was nothing like the feel of being deep inside her, maybe fulfilling some kind of dark fantasy. I couldn't help but smile as her moans increased, knowing that soon she should have another mind-blowing orgasm.

Our combined sounds were nothing but those of animals mating, our ragged breathing heating up the space around us. I continued to be shocked at the level of electricity surging through all three of us, and the way our bodies molded together was utter perfection.

"Mmm..." she whispered, tossing her head back and forth. When her body began to stiffen, I bucked against her, thrusting hard and fast.

Within seconds, she was pushed over the edge, tipping back her head with a scattered scream.

"That's it, little pet. That's it," Trent huffed as he rose onto the balls of his feet, plunging even harder.

My body began to shake violently, forcing me to realize that I couldn't hold back much longer.

When Trent flashed his eyes, I knew he was close as well. As we pounded into her, she lolled her head to the side, every whimper keeping me fully aroused.

"Yes. Yes. Yes!" I yelled as cum rushed to the surface, releasing deep inside of her, filling her with my seed. Trent's roar was within seconds, his deep rumble echoing in the gorgeous room.

As her body slumped against me, I knew that no matter what Randolph believed, she would always belong to us.

Even if it meant destroying our company.

Randolph

The ocean had always given me some sense of peace ever since I was a boy. While my parents had rarely gone on trips together, the few times had always been to a tropical location. That had allowed me a sense of freedom, as if the huge waves could sweep me away into another time and another place. Tonight was no exception.

I stood with a drink in my hand, savoring the experience in my mind. Just touching Scarlett had awakened something I'd thought long dead. However, the various thoughts as well as the continued electricity confused the hell out of me. Just two days ago, I'd wanted nothing more than to take the woman down, breaking her in every way possible. Even though I'd known the other two wanted more before hunting her down and I'd gone along with it, that had never been on my mind.

Until now.

I exhaled and lifted my glass, toasting to the woman who always managed to get under my skin. She had a way about her, refusing to take no for an answer no matter the circumstances. Maybe I was just as attracted to her powerful ways and formidable demeanor as I was to her gorgeous body.

Either way, it was a dangerous combination, one I hadn't expected would bother me so much. Maybe there was a part of me left that could enjoy a normal relationship. As if I had any clue what that was. I'd never seen any affection between my parents. I'd been the only child, not a single family member ever attending a family outing. My mother had told me that it was because of how nasty my father had been over the years, alienating both sides of the family.

Still, I'd worshipped him during my early years, joyful any time he came home from a business trip. Sadly, he'd never seemed to have any real time for me, preferring to work seven days a week. However, he'd certainly built a name and a reputation for himself, as well as an empire. Was that what I ultimately wanted? I was no longer certain.

What continued to trouble me was the fact Alexander suspected more than he was telling me. Then again, I wasn't stupid by any means. I was just like my father. The same attitude. The same instincts. The same arrogance. That had been fuel for many who'd attempted to derail Worth over the years, including the kind of men who rarely took no for an answer. Maybe my friend was feeding off vibes I'd given off since the threats had begun. I'd changed, becoming colder, completely uncaring about anything or anyone else.

Like father. Like son.

I would never forget staying up late one night, seeing my father when he'd arrived home late, which was usually the case. He'd staggered into the front door, stumbling as if he was drunk. I'd remained in the shadows, terrified to approach him. He didn't like to be bothered when he'd had a few too many. Only I'd sensed something else was wrong and followed him to the hallway outside his office. What I'd overheard had been confusing for a kid of only ten or eleven. He'd made a few phone calls, telling someone he'd finished his assignment. His voice and body had been shaking the entire time.

I'd stood in the background, terrified to move. I'd never heard such angst in my father's voice before. He was pleading with whoever was on the other end of the phone to let the nightmare end, whatever the hell that had meant. My father had never begged for anything in his life. Quite the opposite. He'd been the one to force men of great power and stature to kowtow to him. I'd seen blood, although at the time I'd thought it was nothing more than a prank.

However, now I understood that he'd been doing what he could to provide extra protection for his family, including hiring twenty-four-hour security. For a full year I was followed everywhere I went.

To school.

The playground.

Especially when I went somewhere with my mother.

I'd heard my parents arguing about the reason why, what she'd called his break with reality. That had been a significant source of bad blood between them that had eventually led to their separation. But that had taken years.

It was several years later when I'd learned a portion of the reason for my father's concern.

He'd been threatened. Not in the way I'd become accustomed to; some two-bit asshole sending a threatening note or making a deranged phone call. No, my father had been beaten for something he'd either done or not done, whatever enemy he'd made keeping him on a short leash. At least that's the way it had seemed. While I'd never had the courage to ask my father what had happened, the incident had changed him forever. He'd fallen into a deep depression that even his work hadn't been able to pull him out of.

He'd died taking the secret to his grave, my mother refusing to talk about what she knew. I wondered if he'd bothered telling her the truth. Now I wished I'd pushed him more than the little I had.

Ever since the night he'd come home bloody, a shadow had fallen over the family, whatever dirty little deception he'd played lurking in the darkness like a monster waiting for the right time to strike once again. Sighing, I loathed the fact he'd succumbed to the kind of hungers that had ultimately destroyed him.

I'd asked him twice if he was keeping something from his family and he'd shot me down both times. The last time had remained with me for months, although I hadn't bothered to think about his violent reaction in years.

"What in the hell are you hiding from us, Dad?" I stood in my father's office. Confronting him was never a good idea, but this time it was necessary. I'd overheard two phone calls, both reminding me that my father had a secret part of his life that he'd refused to talk about with anyone.

"You barge into my office with a question like that?" He laughed until he saw just how serious I was. "What are you getting at, Randolph?"

"I was there the night you came home all those years ago. You were covered in blood and not all of it was yours. What are you mixed up in?"

He rushed toward me, wrapping his hand around my throat and shoving me against the wall. I was too shocked to react at first, throwing my hands up beside me. He'd been stern, even cold to me over the years, but he'd never laid a hand on me.

"Don't you ever ask me about that again! Do you hear me? Do you?" All the color drained from his face, beads of sweat instantly forming, trickling down his cheeks. At that moment, I could see utter terror in his eyes.

"Yes. Okay, Dad. I won't." I knew better than to challenge him any further.

After a few seconds, he seemed to realize what he was doing, slowly pulling his hand away and wiping his palm on his trousers roughly. Then he staggered backward a few steps, dropping his head into his hands.

I remained quiet, my heart racing.

He tipped his head over his shoulder a few seconds later. "Look, son. I've done some bad things in my life. At first, I was able to convince myself that I was doing so to protect you and your mother. After a while, I couldn't lie to myself any longer." He lifted his fist into the air, the strangled sound he emitted unlike anything I'd ever heard. "You need to promise me something."

"Anything, Dad."

"You'll take care of your mother if anything happens to me. I did my best, but she's not going to be able to take *living on her own without help."*

"What are you trying to tell me?"

He seemed to regroup, but I could tell he was shaking. When he turned around, he had a smile on his face.

A fake smile.

"I'm fine, son. Nothing is going to happen. I'm just getting older. Which is why," he said as he walked closer, as if the incident hadn't just occurred, "we need to continue getting you ready to take over the company."

"I'm still in college."

"You'll be graduating soon. Then you'll be ready."

A cold shiver raced through me. He'd died only two months after that, leaving his shares of the company in my name, willing me almost all his personal possessions and a hefty sum of money as well. At least my mother well taken care of. I'd been angry with him for months. Hell, years. Maybe I still hadn't forgiven him after all this time.

What no one knew is that I'd snooped in my father's office after he'd finally gone to bed the night after he'd been beaten. What I'd learned had changed my opinion of him. A crude promissory note, even

231

though no amount had been listed. He owed someone money. Fucking money. I hadn't thought about the bullshit in years, although what little I'd found hadn't shared the entire picture of what he'd fallen into. Now I had a feeling I couldn't keep it locked away for long. Someone was seeking additional revenge, planning on destroying my father's legacy once and for all. What debt hadn't my father paid? What loyalty had he betrayed? More important, why had he allowed himself to get mixed up in something out of his control?

He'd enjoyed a blessed life, his company thriving. Then he'd allowed his greed or maybe his proclivities to get in the way of what he'd managed to achieve. Nothing made any sense. I'd searched through his records later in life, again after the first threat had been issued months before. The warning had made no sense, none at all, which is why I'd shoved it aside initially.

But I would never forget the ugly words written in block letters on a fine piece of linen paper.

Like father, like son. Your sins need to be repented.

"Goddamn it, Pops. What the hell was wrong with you?" I closed my eyes, remembering the ugly night like it happened yesterday. Fuck. Fuck! I refused to lose this company.

I hung my head, trying to catch my breath and rationalize what little I knew.

While I had no reason to believe the same people had any intention of attempting a move against Worth now, my instinct continued to rear its ugly head. I didn't like what I was thinking.

That Scarlett was involved. That she'd been used as a plant, hoping she'd be able to expose my weakness or play the game long and hard enough I wouldn't notice until it was too late.

As I wrapped my hand around the railing, I didn't realize just how tight my grip was until my fingers started to ache. I ripped it away, flexing then fisting my hand. No one was going to threaten me and live.

After seething for a full minute, I chuckled, staring out at the ocean as if it could provide all the answers. As I swirled my drink, I sensed someone behind me. I turned my neck, exhaling after seeing Alexander. "You're up late, my friend."

"I was tasked with securing Scarlett for the night. Remember?" he said, half laughing. "She's a fighter."

"Yes," I whispered then took a sip of my drink. "She is."

"Interesting. You are very distant around her. If I didn't know better, I'd think you despised the woman."

"How could I despise something so beautiful?"

"Yes, she is that and more."

"And if I didn't know better, I'd say you like this girl far too much."

Alexander joined me at the railing, taking a deep breath of the ocean breeze. "What's wrong with that? We made a deal, the three of us. She's ours for the long haul."

"We shall see."

"What are you afraid of, Randolph, actually falling for the woman?"

"I'm not afraid of anything." I heard the indignation in my voice and sighed. I hadn't intended on being so forceful.

"Uh-huh. The stock purchases are bothering you."

"And that isn't bothering you?"

"Yes, but your behavior is what's really getting to me."

"My behavior?" I challenged.

He exhaled as he stared up at the sky. "I know you better than you know yourself. Something is off and has been since you lost your father. Maybe it started before that."

"What are you getting at?"

"That we have a serious issue to deal with but you're putting all the blame on Scarlett, which is ridiculous," Alexander answered with no emotion in his tone.

"Then I suggest you share what you know and are purposely keeping from me." I turned my head in his direction. He didn't seem fazed in the least.

"Alright. If that's how you want to play it. What I know is that Trent received several threats, although he didn't tell me the details. What I also know is that someone has been sniffing around the company asking questions. My assistant received a call almost a month ago she finally mentioned to me last week, one that was very disturbing."

"What the hell? Why didn't you tell me this before?"

Alexander nodded. "Because I wasn't concerned until the stock purchases. This entity was asking about when we were in the office. Maggie assumed the caller was hopeful to drop in and find us. She knew better than to provide any information. Then the call got weird. Her word. The man on the other end of the phone started asking more personal questions about our work ethics and whether she was happy working for me, what we did in our private time. Maggie hung up after that, thinking it was just some asshole."

"Interesting. Why didn't Trent say anything?"

"Because he was told from the start to expect our enemies to stoop to something that low. But I can tell they bothered him."

Sighing, I returned my attention to the shore. A small part of me had the feeling we were being watched, which was impossible. Still, I couldn't shake the feeling. "Let's hope they're nothing more than a prank." Was it possible the past was rearing its ugly head?

"Yeah, let's hope. You're serious about going to Cancun?"

"A perfect location," I said, my thoughts turning vile.

"It's also where one of the owners of the Clubhouse lives. That's not a coincidence, is it? What are you going to do, shove her into some dark fantasy that will force her total surrender to us?"

I polished off the rest of my drink. "Nothing that happens in life is a coincidence, my friend, but I do own a villa there as well. We'll have home court advantage. As far as allowing her to participate in a fantasy, the thought has crossed my mind. Maybe if she understood the power of an auction."

"An auction? My God. This really is a game to you, isn't it? You're going to scare her by acting as if some unknown man is going to purchase her?"

"It's just a fantasy."

Alexander inched closer. "You and I both know some of the members take it very seriously. Some of them are dangerous men who won't like being toyed with. He or they will want to take her and that just isn't going to happen. I suggest you rethink this."

Maybe he was right, but I had another reason for talking to the owner of what had often been referred to as a society, not just a kink club. However, that was something I would keep to myself for now.

When I turned to walk inside, I stopped short. "A storm is brewing, Alexander. I can feel it in my bones. We all need to be prepared for the outcome. And you're right that what I'm doing is risky."

"A storm. Why do I have the feeling you're keeping something from Trent and me? You know what's interesting? You never talk much about your father, other than in terms of business, but something happened that terrified you years ago. Why do I have a feeling whatever the reason, it's part of what's going on? And why do I think your father wasn't always on the up and up with regards to business tactics?"

"What are you getting at?" What the hell did he think he'd found?

Alexander gave me a hard look. "Was your father in financial trouble at some point?"

"That's not something he would discuss with me."

"Then how about his personal life?"

Jesus Christ. I felt like I was being interrogated.

"There's not much to tell you," I insisted. "Other than he's dead. Besides, what happened in the past is my burden to bear, not yours. I value your friendship more than you know but leave it alone."

"Don't do that shit, Randolph. I remember the terse phone calls you had from him at college. I know how much he pushed you to excel. When he died, that changed you. You closed up, refusing to care about anyone, but you were damn determined to work yourself to death. Why?"

I took a deep breath, holding it for an extended period of time before exhaling. "It doesn't matter any longer."

"I'd say it does if that's the reason we're under duress."

He knew I hated being challenged on any level.

"Just find out the person behind the company purchasing the stock." After hearing the nastiness in my tone, I shook my head. "I'm sorry, Alex. I'm not trying to take this out on you, but this is something I need to handle alone."

"I'll keep that in mind," he said curtly. "But you won't destroy Scarlett in the process. She's not playing games with us any longer."

"You do care about her."

"I don't know her, but I intend on making that happen," he said, this time his voice full of emotion.

"Good for you." I had no idea what else to say to him. *Sins of the father...* I couldn't get it out of my mind. Maybe he'd sold his soul to the devil for his prosperity, and I was to pay the price.

"Look, buddy. I know we've been working long hours, but something's been eating you for a lot longer than the contract miss with Dockett. I *am* your friend, or at least I thought I was. You can talk to me about anything."

Alexander and I had been like brothers, at least from what I knew about siblings. I knew I could trust him with anything, including my life. Maybe I didn't want to admit my family wasn't as special as I continued insisting we'd always been. Maybe I was fooling myself for believing there had been any decent qualities.

If what I knew was correct, my father had done everything in order to get what he wanted.

Including the possibility of resorting to murder.

"I know that, Alex. Do you know why I brought you and Trent on as partners?"

"Honestly, I have no freaking clue. You certainly didn't need to. You sold huge portions of stock for seventy cents on the dollar, which really wasn't good business for you."

I laughed for a few seconds, prepared to give him an honest answer. "I calculated the risks. I knew that bringing the two of you on would expand our empire, making all three of us a hell of a lot more money than I could do by myself. Both you and Trent are much better engineers than I could ever be. My father forced me into the program. I wanted to stay on the business side. He refused, threatening to yank my tuition. Robotics isn't my strength, even though I love the industry. Obtaining contracts is. I can't allow Worth to slide on any level. That's unacceptable. If that means Scarlett is knocked down a peg or two, then so be it. Business is business."

The ugly tension between us was happening more often. Tonight it was thick as molasses.

"Well, the offer stands, if you can tolerate providing the truth for once."

I swiveled, taking two long strides in his direction. Without thinking, I threw a hard punch, the force shoving him against the side of the building. "I just told you the truth."

Snarling, he slapped his hand against his jaw, his entire body bristling as he lunged toward me, his fist in the air.

"Go ahead. Take a jab at me. I know that's something you've been wanting to do for a hell of a long time!" I taunted, sliding my sleeves past my elbows. "Don't think I don't know about your dirty little secrets."

"What the fuck are you talking about?"

"That girl. The fantasy you forced her to participate in. I know exactly what happened to her." As soon as

I issued the words, I regretted them. What in the hell was wrong with me? This was my friend, one of the few people I trusted.

He took a deep breath, holding his stance for several seconds before lowering his arm. "While I didn't force her to do anything, I should have known better than to involve her. I think about that moment every day. Every. Single. Day." His voice was haunted as fuck.

What the hell was I doing? Trying to destroy one of two people I trusted?

When he turned around, I rubbed my forehead. He didn't deserve the shit I was giving him.

"That was fucking shitty of me. I know you suffered, and you didn't do anything wrong. You had no way of knowing how she'd react."

"Yeah? Well, that's not what she believed. She thought I wanted to hurt her."

His voice was riddled with pain. Another moment of silence passed between us.

"What time are we leaving in the morning?" he finally asked.

"Early. Did you take her phone?"

He hesitated before answering. "Secured safely. Damn it. What are you really afraid of, Randolph? If I had to guess, I'd say it was caring about someone other than yourself. I think you're already falling hard for the girl."

"Then you would be wrong."

"Am I? I think it's something you need to ask yourself. Your need for vengeance isn't against Scarlett. It's against yourself. Maybe if you opened up for once, really trusted someone, you could free yourself from the damn demons eating you alive."

"Nothing can do that."

"Jesus Christ. Have it your way. Destroy her. Take her company. When you do, you will have sealed your fate. When you die, you'll go straight to hell."

After he went inside, I threw my arms back, issuing an angry roar.

It was past time to face certain ugly truths. While he was right on so many levels, what he didn't know was that my father had already sold our souls years ago. It was only a matter of time before the grim reaper came for his payment.

With my blood.

CHAPTER 10

S carlett

"Remember that every opponent has a weakness, Scarlett. When learning exactly what makes them tick, never allow yourself to fall into their web. The second you do, they will have won."

As I swam up from the intense fog, the words burned into the back of my mind, my father's voice lingering in the far reaches of my brain. Exhaling, I shifted before opening my eyes, my body's slow reaction registering, although I wasn't certain why I couldn't seem to move easily.

Then I remembered.

As I jerked my head off the pillow, my natural instincts of survival kicked in. Fuck. I struggled, trying to bite back a series of whimpers. There was no sense in fighting. I was firmly secured, my arms shackled over my head.

Every detail of the night before rushed into my mind like a cyclone, whirling around the remaining fog, barely able to dip into my conscience. At first I couldn't identify the odd noise over my head. Then I realized I was hearing the sound of metal hitting something hard. After taking a deep breath, I stretched my neck, finally able to see the handcuffs that had been placed around my wrists. Even though I knew there was no way of freeing myself, I continued to fight the restraints, bucking hard until I was out of breath.

Damn the assholes.

Fuck them.

A light breeze filtered across my naked skin, creating wave after wave of prickles. However, the sensations had nothing to do with the air temperature. My nerves were on edge, as raw as the blasting images forming in my mind.

I did what I could to control my breathing, blinking several times as the light swallowing most of the room burned into my retinas. The sun was bright, which meant I'd slept through the night. Had the fuckers also given me a sedative? My body tingled, my muscles aching, but not nearly as much as the discomfort encapsulating every inch of my naked bottom.

They'd spanked me.

And fucked me.

And...

My throat constricted, my heart racing. Just the thought of what had occurred only hours before cut through me like a knife. Disgusted, I couldn't seem to get visions of their naked, buff bodies out of the forefront of my mind. They were hot, muscular in all the right places. And I'd enjoyed being treated like some possession, a mere object and nothing more. What was wrong with me?

Anger boiled from deep within my system, pushing my mind to the outer limits of acceptance. I didn't care who heard me as I thumped against the tight bindings. This was outrageous. How could they do this to me?

Because of the wager...

The thought was never far from my mind.

I closed my eyes, counting to five, managing to calm my accelerated nerves. When I opened them again, I scanned the room, fighting back laughter. They'd shoved me into the master bedroom, even leaving the set of French doors cracked. I kicked out, managing to shove the covers further away, leaving me even more exposed.

Breathe and think. You need to get away from them.

I did what I could, trying to remember every detail from the night before. While Trent and Alexander had been fully engaged in the carnal acts, Randolph had remained in his ugly shell. Maybe his conscience had gotten the better of him. I snorted at the thought, resisting calling out. How long was I supposed to remain this way, unable to move? I was nothing but their prisoner, a possession to be toyed with.

While I allowed my thoughts to roam over everything that had happened during the last two days, I could do little to fully make sense of why they'd gone to this extreme.

Other than the possibility that they were facing extreme difficulties in their company. What could that mean? Threats? Coercion? They certainly weren't going to tell me, but it was clear they thought of me as the enemy. I wanted to gloat except

I remained tethered like a prisoner. I was so freaking angry I couldn't stop the murderous thoughts from filtering into my mind.

When I heard someone at the door, I held my breath, prepared to give the jerk the wrath of God.

As Trent walked into the room, the same damn boyish grin on his face as he usually had, I couldn't seem to form words.

He kept the door open as he took long strides toward the bed, peering down at me as if I was the perfect specimen of filet mignon at the local market. When he remained quiet, his eyes never blinking, I lost my patience.

"What the hell are you looking at, asshole? I demand that you get me out of these handcuffs."

As he cocked his head, his eyes twinkled. All three of them found my predicament amusing. "I don't think you're in the position to demand a single thing, Scarlett. However, you have been bound far too long." Very slowly he removed a single small key from his pocket, holding it over my head. I could only concentrate on the way the piece of metal glistened in the morning sun.

"Fuck you." The words just flew out of my mouth.

"Such a bad girl. While I can understand your anger, you should get used to the fact there's nothing you can do about the situation. At least not at this point."

When he leaned over, prepared to unlock the cuffs, I hissed, "Why do you follow Randolph's orders like some hired slave?"

He didn't say anything at first, but he slowed his actions, taking his sweet time to unlock my wrist. When one arm was free, he glared down at me. "I'm not certain why you think Randolph controls me in any way, but that doesn't matter."

"Of course it doesn't. I'm nothing to you." I thought about what Ashley had said regarding her room-mate. It was on the tip of my tongue to ask him about Madisen, but I wasn't ready to show my hand just yet.

Trent lowered his gaze, his eyes piercing mine. There was extreme depth pooling in his irises, the look he gave me yanking me into his world for a few seconds. "You do mean something to us, Scarlett. All three of us."

Every time one of them said my name, I usually cringed, but the softness in his tone, the care in which he'd expressed his sentiment was off-putting. "Then let me go."

"A deal is a deal. You had free will going into that wager. I'm not certain why you thought you could get out of it if you lost."

Of course, he was right. "Because I never lose."

A smile crossed his face. "There's a first time for everything."

"Yeah, like kicking your ass."

The small click as the second handcuff was released made me jump for no other reason than I knew in the back of my mind I should fight the man with everything I had. Sadly, I didn't seem to have the drive and I wasn't certain why. At least my fight or flight survival mode kicked in, allowing me to slam my hands against his chest as he leaned over.

He didn't budge a single inch, instead lowering down ever more until his face was only inches from mine. "I think you need to stop."

"Or what?" My challenge was little more than a whisper.

"Then I'll have to turn you over and spank that rounded bottom of yours all over again."

"Don't try it."

His laugh was heartfelt, subtle yet powerful enough it ticked me off. When I curled my hand, he stopped it before I could lift my arm off the bed, pressing it against the pillows. "I need to ask you a question."

I loathed the way his natural smell, so freaking masculine and inviting, floated all around me, creating the same kind of desire I'd felt the night before. "What?"

"That's what I'm wondering. What do you have against Worth?"

His question managed to catch me off guard. I had to think about how I wanted to answer him. "You mean other than your practices are unscrupulous, even bordering on criminal?"

"That's what I don't get," he said, inhaling deeply then pulling away, daring to turn his back on me and walk toward the open set of doors. "We have a highly revered company. Are we ruthless in going after business? Absolutely, but that's how to make money in this dog-eat-dog industry. You already know that. However, you are wrong that we've ever crossed a line."

I eased into a sitting position, grabbing the sheets in some wayward attempt to cover my body. "You really think that isn't true?"

Trent didn't bother looking at me. "I assure you that no company I'm involved with will ever do anything considered criminal."

"My God. Randolph has brainwashed you." I rubbed my wrists, eyeing the open door to the hallway. Thoughts of racing outside were quickly thwarted by the fact the house was a hell of a long way from a single other building or person.

"You hate the man. I just don't get that."

"What's not to get? He's an asshole who only gives a damn about himself."

He cocked his head. "He has his reasons for being cautious and unforgiving, Scarlett. We all have dirty little secrets and anguish from our past we are required to deal with. I'm certain even someone as virtuous as you has something you'd prefer to keep hidden."

The jab wasn't surprising. Sadly, he was right. I'd gleefully hired the two associates who used to work for Worth, gleaning as much information as possible from them. Maybe that placed me firmly in their category, but Trent was right, the business was dog-eat-dog. However, I was intrigued he would come to Randolph's defense. He'd seemed less than enthused about hunting me down. I'd been able to read that easily in his body language and the way he'd looked at Randolph. "That may be true, but both he and his father have done everything in their power to stop my company from succeeding."

He turned and narrowed his eyes. "Wait a minute. What are you talking about?"

"What am I talking about? You must be kidding me. I thought you'd been in this business with him since he took over."

"Randolph handles certain aspects of business his way without needing approval from anyone else. And to answer your question. I came on board last, almost six months after he took over, three months after Alexander accepted his position as CFO. Tell me what you're talking about. That's a serious accusation."

Of course it was serious. I jerked the sheets around me, fighting with them in order to get off the bed. I backed all the way against the wall, glaring at him with as much hatred as I had in me. "My father helped me start my company when I was barely twenty-two years old and right out of college because he believed in me when no one else would. He gave a damn about my success. That was several months before Randolph's father died under mysterious circumstances, yet during those twelve months, Sampson Worth did everything he could to derail what little I had, nearly shoving my company into the toilet with his false accusations of infringement on patents and theft of his products, which was bullshit. I almost lost everything before I even began."

I could tell my story had caught his attention, even his surprise. He kept his eyes narrowed as he looked at me. Or maybe he was looking right through me. Either way, I didn't give a shit. He was part of the same regime that had nearly driven me into bankruptcy.

"I thought your father was a card shark."

Just the way he issued the statement was like a knife being jammed into my heart. "My father wasn't *just* anything. He was a great man with a big heart. He was a champion card player, winning hundreds of thousands of dollars. He knew people, important people. That's why I was able to start my company. He provided support as well as capital to enable me hit the ground running. Don't you dare belittle my father."

Trent held up his hands, his features softening. "I'm sorry. That was shitty of me, but this game that's being played isn't in either one of our best interests."

"How fascinating of you to say."

"Don't do that, Scarlett. I'm not your enemy."

I laughed, shaking my head. "All three of you are. Don't kid yourself. You think I'm trying to sabotage your business when all I've ever wanted to do was compete fair and square. Can you say the same thing? Can Alexander? I know Randolph certainly can't." Once again, my words troubled him. Maybe he should think about who he was doing business with.

We both remained quiet for at least a full minute. Finally, I was sick of the silence and the unknowing.

"What's going to happen now in this adventurous game of yours?" I couldn't keep the demanding tone out of my voice.

He offered a genuine smile, which also threw me. He had a way of unnerving me more than the other two. I purposely looked away briefly, still shivering from the round of nerves that refused to go away.

"It's not my game, but it is one you accepted. We're going to another destination, one that's also tropical. That's all you need to know."

I rolled my eyes, tugging on the sheet. "Of course. Tropical. I suppose you're going to toss me off a cliff or something at the end of the week."

He dared to laugh, shoving his hands into his pockets as he sauntered forward. "Nothing that dramatic, I assure you."

"And I'm supposed to believe you."

"Look. I realize there's bad blood between our firms, but no matter what you think, Randolph would never do anything improper to you or your company."

"Improper? The club was improper but tolerable. Randolph wants a full takeover. All the signs are there. I can't talk with Mr. Dockett, which could mean he'll move on to his second candidate. My guess that would be Worth. How underhanded of you. Keep me prisoner so I can't go through with my obligations. I hope you can sleep well at night."

"As a matter of fact, I can. You've not a fairy princess in all of this, Scarlett, no matter what you think. You've badmouthed Worth to the press every chance you've had. The press conference was creative, but you have no idea what ramifications you might have caused. You hired two of our employees, which is extremely unscrupulous. You've undercut two other bids by only a small percentage, which I find very interesting."

"What the hell does that mean?"

"That means there's a possibility you have someone supplying corporate information from our firm. How? I don't know because the employees who quit didn't have much insider information. I assure you that I will find out and if that's the truth, I will be the one to report you to the Securities Exchange Commission. Just imagine what will happen to your stock, let alone any consideration of future customers."

I was shocked at what he was insinuating. "Do you really believe that I have to stoop to something so low in order to win contracts? You're out of your mind. That's not me. I have integrity. As far as the two employees you mentioned. From what I learned from both of them, they hated working for Randolph. Notice I say for. They were treated like shit and quit because they couldn't take it any longer. Considering how talented they were, I would have been a fool not to hire them, but I assure you that they did not provide me with any plans for projects in the works by Worth Dynamics." I hated lying, but that had begun with doing so to myself.

A line in the sand had been drawn. I wanted to hate the man, but just watching the way he reacted, I could tell he cared about the company. How had he become friends with Randolph?

The bastard snorted. Goddamn him. I thought about the contracts he was talking about. How the hell did he know what I'd bid in the first place? Jesus. My entire team had worked on those two bid packages. But... One man had suggested both bid amounts. Was that a coincidence? Did someone leak him information to provide to me? I didn't like it. I wouldn't tolerate it. "I don't cheat, Trent, no matter what you think."

"Interesting, but I believe you."

Miracles would never cease, but I wasn't buying his act.

"You know what I find interesting? Some mysterious company with no real past is buying up several shares of our stock. Out of the blue over the past couple of months while we were both vying for the same large contract. I've also had threatening calls. I'm no fool. That sounds like something Randolph would do to scare me into being unable to provide the technology that Mr. Dockett required."

When he stopped short, I was surprised, but more so by the odd look on his face. He purposely looked away then huffed as he shook his head. "I understand and I'm sorry, but even Randolph isn't that relentless."

"Maybe you don't know Randolph as well as you think you do. Just so you know, Prestwood Automation is everything in my world. All that matters to me. I have every dime I have locked up into new automation. Yes, I have a strong work ethic, but I need to. I can't fail." For some reason, I hated admitting it to him.

His silence and the way he was studying me drove me crazy.

"You should get a shower."

"I'm allowed?"

"Of course you're allowed. We're not monsters, no matter what you think." His body seemed stiff as he walked toward the door. "We'll be leaving this morning, so gather your things after you get ready."

"Fine. *Master*."

Trent stopped moving altogether. I guessed I would be chastised for my surly attitude. When he spoke, the softness of his tone was far too disarming. "I'm sorry about whatever Randolph and his father did to you, but I think Randolph had no other choice. Yes, my friend is brutal by nature, something his father taught him, but Randolph is a good man underneath his sometimes repulsive layer of armor. Trust me. I didn't like him at first. And his father was oppressive, requiring Randolph to excel at everything he did or face his wrath." He exhaled, the sound exaggerated and his shoulders slumping. "For what it's worth. What you're doing with Prestwood Automation is something you should be very proud of."

I opened my mouth to retort, spewing whatever horrible words came to my mind, but I couldn't., the softness of his voice countering my need to unload on him. "It's my baby, something I dreamed about for years, never thinking it would come true. I was the nerd in school, enjoying tinkering with electronics, building my first robot at age eight. I know that doesn't matter to you at all and you probably don't believe me."

When he nodded several times, I could tell he was struggling with his emotions as well as what he wanted to say to me.

"I believe every word you've told me, Scarlett. As I said, you should be very proud. Go ahead and shower." His tone had changed, returning to the authoritative, dominating man I'd experienced earlier.

"Fine."

When he shifted enough to be able to turn his head, his heated gaze slowly trailing all the way down the length of me, I shivered to my core.

I stiffened from the way he was looking at me, giving him a defiant look even though my scattered breath forced my back to rise and fall rapidly. I could tell by the way his nostrils flared, his eyes dilating, what he was thinking. Swallowing, I dared not stare at the bulge between his legs, his desire roaring through him even more than the night before.

A sly smile crossed his face, his eyes narrowing. "Be careful tempting me, Scarlett. I'm very hungry this morning."

I continued to hold my head high, refusing to move. Then I smiled, laughing softly.

I should have known better than to challenge him any more than the other two. He took two long strides to get to me, clamping his fist around the edge of the sheet and yanking. As he tore away the thin covering, the light breeze felt like a cold wave hitting me like a sledgehammer. I didn't want to react around him in any way, but I couldn't bite back the whispered moan.

There was something even more barbaric about the way he looked at me, as if he would defy Randolph's wishes, taking me as his own. He slammed his hands on either side of me, lowering his head. "You have no idea how much I've craved you or the kind of thoughts that have nearly driven me mad. You are very special."

A part of me still wanted to lash out at him, but there was something different in the way he was staring at me, as if he wanted no part of the end game of the wager. I remained immensely attracted to him, every nerve standing on end. I had no idea what to say to him. Maybe there was nothing that could be said. We were sworn enemies, which eliminated all other possibilities.

Then why did I continue to feel butterflies around him?

He reached out, fingering my hair, his breathing shallow. "You will also never win at this game."

"Which game is that?" I asked, wrapping one hand around his shirt, using my hold to pull myself closer, even arching my back and tilting my head until our lips were little more than a few centimeters apart.

"The game of cat and mouse." He chuckled before crushing his mouth over mine, sliding one arm around my waist and pulling me onto my toes. His sudden move was unexpected, allowing me to catch a different glimpse of what he was made of.

The explosive heat was also entirely different than before, more powerful and passionate, the taste of him driving me wild. I continued to cling to him even if a portion of my mind had no intention of doing so. When he thrust his tongue inside my mouth, he slipped his hand to my buttocks, squeezing until I winced from discomfort. He was doing nothing more than reminding me that he was also in charge, capable of doing anything he wanted to me.

I slipped one arm around his neck, tangling my fingers in his shaggy hair, surprised just how soft his long strands were. His masculine scent filled my nostrils, keeping me lightheaded, my nipples aching to be sucked and twisted. I wrapped one leg around him as he ground his hips back and forth. He was hard as a rock, his cock throbbing.

As he explored the dark recesses of my mouth, I closed my eyes, allowing myself to pretend that this wasn't just a portion of the game. He was testing me, pushing my limits on purpose and nothing more. I loathed the way my pussy had already leaked, trickling juice down the inside of both thighs.

When he broke the kiss, he kept his tight hold, slowly dragging his tongue along my jawline to the soft skin of my neck just below my ear. When he nipped my earlobe, he issued a gravelly growl, sending another array of shivers all the way down to my toes.

Then he fisted my hair, yanking as he whispered in my ear, "I will take you when I want. Never forget that." When he pulled away, his eyes darted back and forth. "God, you are so damn beautiful."

With that, he walked out of the room, leaving me aching as well as pissed off.

 andolph

Threats.

I'd grown sick of them, enough so I was determined to find out who was behind them, including reaching out to the one man who had the power and influence to find out. He also knew the right kind of people to find out what I was looking for.

While it would be at a hefty price, at this point it was well worth it. And if Scarlett was involved, I would learn that as well. I stared at the email, not bothering to try to find the source. I'd already attempted to go down the trail, the email leading to a dead end. Just like the bogus phone calls. To find out that Trent had received them as well meant the plan was escalating. Then the stock purchases. What the hell was going to be next?

Your time has come. You will lose everything. The sins of the father must be repaid.

I rubbed my forehead, tossing my phone onto the table and walking toward the window. As I stared out at the ocean, hoping it would calm me, I was beginning to rethink my insistence that Scarlett was involved. But I had to know. I had to find out before it was too late.

I'd already fallen in love with her. Maybe I'd always been since the day I first saw her. Half laughing, I placed my hand on the window, enjoying the heat of the sun tickling through my veins. Somewhere in the back of my mind I realized I was a stupid man, determined to make her the bad guy in all of this when in fact, the dark, damning secret my father had left along with his billion-dollar company was to blame. Damn it.

I debated my actions for a little while longer before retrieving my phone and dialing his private number. While I wouldn't necessarily consider Carlos Santiago a close friend, he and I had similar backgrounds, which had allowed us to strike up a friendship of sorts.

"Mr. Worth," Carlos said, his thick Spanish accent even more so over the phone.

Chuckling, I walked out onto the deck. At this point, I didn't want Trent or Alexander to know I'd made the call. "How are you doing, Carlos?"

"Fantastic. I'm currently enjoying a cocktail on my veranda under a glorious blue sky. What can I do for you, my friend? Are you ready for another fantasy to be fulfilled?"

"This time, all I need is information."

"Regarding?"

"The person or entity making anonymous threats to my company. If I'm right, they will attempt a hostile takeover soon. You know people who can find out for me."

He remained quiet for a full twenty seconds. I was risking using a favor, one likely not afforded to me again.

"Fascinating, Randolph. I've heard about your recent troubles, the contract a significant loss," he said quietly. His admittance would have surprised anyone who didn't know Carlos well. He made certain he learned about every member of his club, employing a team of people to learn all their trade as well as private secrets. He wasn't against blackmailing his members if necessary, given his choice of business operations.

I had no doubt what he provided to certain clients was very much against the law.

He'd started the Clubhouse after years of owning casinos and nightclubs, his family's wealth allowing him to become a playboy. They were also considered the most powerful and dangerous mafia family in Spain, something he'd wanted no part of. He'd been smart as well as savvy parlaying his business acumen into providing something every powerful man wanted.

A fantasy without repercussions.

And if he or his operations were fucked with, the person responsible would quietly disappear.

While he knew my proclivities, I also knew his. He'd allowed his guard to fall around me once. That gave me certain privileges, including a favor or two.

"Very little gets by you, Carlos. That's why I'm calling."

"You believe the people responsible are club members?"

"If I had to guess, I would say yes. Regardless, you certainly know people who can try and ascertain what I'm dealing with."

He hesitated again and I could tell he'd walked indoors. "What you ask for, my friend, is costly. It could also be dangerous."

"I don't care about the money at this point, Carlos. I can handle myself if feathers are ruffled. I need to know."

"Very well, my friend, but what you are asking will be difficult. I will see what I can do; however, there are some who can hide behind a thick enough curtain even I am unable to hunt them down."

"All understood. I will give you a lead. I'm certain it has to do with my father."

"Your father." There was a catch in his voice that I hadn't heard before.

"Yes."

"Interesting and that may prove to be helpful. If I find anything, I will only provide it in person. Do you understand?"

"Of course. I'll be arriving in Cancun tomorrow."

"By yourself or are you bringing a special lady friend?" He laughed, knowing my taste in women.

"I have someone with me that I would consider special, although she is from a rival company."

"Of course. I also read about the wager that was made and her creative handling of the media as well. She is quite beautiful and would do well on the circuit if that's what you're intending."

The circuit. The ultimate fantasy, specialized auctions where men could purchase the woman of their dreams, requiring them to do their biddings. I'd refused to participate in something so barbaric. A headache had formed hours earlier, the anguish now pounding in my temples. "I'm uncertain at this point, but I need to know if Scarlett Prestwood is involved. If so, that might influence my decision."

"You're playing a risky game, my friend. Whoever is threatening you might decide to alter their methods, taking something even more important from you. That is, if Scarlett has become your weakness."

"I'm aware of that. See what you can find."

"Yes, I will, Randolph, but keep in mind that my favors come at a price. I will contact you in a couple days one way or the other."

"I appreciate your help." Of course he would remind me again.

"Yes, we shall see."

When I ended the call, I turned to find Trent standing on the deck. While I couldn't tell if he'd overheard the conversation, his expression was something I wasn't used to seeing from him.

Hatred.

When he turned and walked away, I realized that I had the potential to lose everything I cared about.

And it had nothing to do with Worth Dynamics.

* * *

Scarlett

Trent's unassuming ways were just an act. Hissing, I grabbed a few of my things, heading into the bathroom and closing the door. Then I dared lock it, laughing softly after I did. I deserved a little private time.

I turned the shower on as hot as possible, dropping my clothes onto the bathroom counter. Just catching a glimpse of myself in the mirror was troubling enough but the disheveled mess of my hair also made me laugh. I stared at myself for a full minute, forced to realize I was tired of fighting with them. It was childish and could damage my business.

As I hung my head, I realized my skin remained tingling from Trent's rough touch. I pressed two fingers against my lips, still able to taste him. This was ridiculous. The last thing I needed to do was lament over three men I couldn't have and didn't want.

But as I stepped into the shower, I couldn't seem to get my mind off their rugged bodies or the hunger continuing to furrow throughout my body.

I closed the shower door, standing directly under the water. At least the warmth felt good to my skin. Perhaps I'd anticipated that Trent wouldn't be able to leave me alone, but when the cool air hit my back, I bristled for no other reason than the anger I had for my body betrayal. I didn't bother turning around, instead planting my hands on the tile, doing everything I could to control my breathing.

As Trent crowded closer, pushing his cock against my bruised backside, I let out an audible shudder. He nuzzled against my neck before wrapping his hands around my breasts, kneading them roughly.

Panting, I dragged my tongue across my lips, balling my hands as he fingered my nipples, taking his time to roll his index fingers around them several times. Jolts of current shot through both of us leaving me wet and aching.

When he bit down on my neck, his growl became more intense. I realized I was arching my back once again, keeping my hands over my head as if I'd been told to do so. He continued toying with my hardened buds, pinching and twisting until I finally cried out in pain.

His hot breath cascaded across the back of my shoulders as he kicked my legs apart, finally trailing his fingers all the way down the back of my neck and along my spine, slowing down when he crawled them along the crack of my ass before sliding his hand between my thighs.

Then he slid his other hand to my neck, wrapping his long fingers around my throat and squeezing, using enough pressure I took several deep breaths. I wasn't afraid of him, but given his size and strength, he could certainly do anything to me he wanted.

I pressed my palms against the cool tile, the water pounding down over me like a rainfall. As he fingered my clit, I was unable to keep a series of whimpers from escaping my pursed lips. Then he pinched my tender tissue, the slice of anguish forcing me onto my toes.

"If I could, I'd keep you chained to my bed the majority of the time, waiting for my return. Would you like that, little kitten? Would you enjoy pleasuring my every wish?"

I wasn't certain if he expected a real answer, but I remained quiet, still quivering but trying to control my emotions.

He laughed softly, as if he could read my mind. The way he teased me, sliding his fingers up and down the length of my pussy was exciting, almost as much so as the anticipation of what he was going to do to me. When he plunged them deep inside, flexing them open as he thrust hard and fast, I panted as the adrenaline rush powering into me became more intense by the second.

"So damn wet. I could fuck you for hours, shoving my cock deep inside. I think I will." He tightened his hold around my throat as he pushed his cockhead just past my swollen folds. Another burst of electricity shot through me, searing every nerve ending. "You truly are a very bad little girl, though."

A single crack of his hand across my backside was a reminder of just how dominating he could be. For some reason, the sting was more intense, my legs quivering.

"Did you know that water accentuates a good, hard spanking?"

"Now I do," I whispered, closing my eyes and panting.

"Keep your hands on the wall, Scarlett. If you move, I'll be forced to chain you to the showerhead."

The guttural sound to his voice echoed in my ears, the sultry tone sending vibrations all the way down to my toes. I darted a look over my shoulder as he opened the door. While I heard sounds, I had no idea what he was doing.

I found out soon enough as he returned with a nasty-looking bath brush in his hand. After sucking in and holding my breath, I realized my stomach was in knots from just seeing the wooden implement.

Trent twirled it a few times, his eyelids little more than slits. "I think this will work nicely. Don't you?"

I braced for instant pain, shocked when he rubbed the bristles down my spine, taking his time in doing so. Then he rubbed it between my legs, moving down one then up the other. The tingling sensations only increased, the strangest feeling of pleasure tickling my nerve endings.

"You have a gorgeous body, perfect in every way," he murmured as he lowered his head, brushing his lips across the back of my neck. "I could spend hours just exploring every inch of you."

"Then why don't you?"

"Is that a blatant invitation?"

"As I said, I'm not certain you can handle all of me."

He laughed, the deep baritone sliding over me like a feathery blanket. "You are a tempting vixen, but you've yet to learn your place." He pressed the bristles against my swollen pussy and instantly, several shots of electricity pulsed into me.

Whimpering, I clawed the tile, blinking in some crazy effort to focus. There was no chance. He rubbed gently for a few seconds, pushing me closer and closer to an incredible orgasm. As he increased the pressure, I rose onto my toes once again, my body swaying back and forth.

"Good girls are allowed to orgasm."

"I'll never be good."

"You will learn. I promise you." He continued rubbing, moving up and down in a perfect rhythm. "You need to ask permission in order to be allowed to come."

"That's not fair."

"You have no other options, little pet."

Why did his words excite instead of piss me off? Maybe there was no rhyme or reason. I tried to ignore the sensations, but within seconds it was next to impossible. Steam continued to float all around me, making the atmosphere surreal.

I could feel my body bucking against the implement, pushing myself toward a raging orgasm. There was nothing I could do to stop it. A laugh bubbled to the surface of my lips, my pulse rapid. "Can I come?"

"What did you say?" he teased.

"Please. Can I come?"

"Hmmm…"

"Fine. Master. Can I come, Master?"

He breathed across my shoulders before easing his hand around to my breast. "Yes, you may." As he rubbed harder and faster, he pinched my nipple. The combination of pain and pleasure was too much to take.

Seconds later, I threw back my head, trying to keep from screaming as the beautiful wave of ecstasy rolled into me, capturing every ounce of my breath and energy.

"Yes. Yes. Yes. Yes. Yes."

Trent refused to stop, pinching and twisting my hardened bud, but within seconds, he pulled the brush away, leaving me panting and writhing.

The snap of his wrist came quickly, the agony driving into me in an entirely different way than before.

I bit my lower lips, wiggling and kicking out.

"You will stay in position, Scarlett. Don't make me tell you twice."

He smacked me several times in a row, one coming after the other. Every inch of me was on fire, but mostly from the heightened level of arousal, the scent of my desire more intense than ever before.

Heat continued to build across my bottom, the discomfort burning all the way down my legs.

"I can't wait to be inside of you," he growled, lowering his head and biting me on the shoulder.

Even as the spanking continued, I remained in the world of bliss, refusing to believe I was enjoying being disciplined.

But that just might be the truth.

When he rubbed the bristles across one butt cheek then the other, I couldn't stop from making guttural sounds.

After four more smacks in rapid succession, he tossed the bath brush, wrapping his hand around my hair. "Fucking you is one of the greatest pleasures of my life."

Just when I thought he was going to drive his shaft into me, I felt another blast of cold air. Suddenly, we weren't alone. I didn't need to turn my head to know which of the other two had found our little rendezvous. Alexander's scent was unique, rough and tumble just like the man. There was no exchange between then, just an orchestrated change in their positions as if they'd done this before.

When I was sandwiched between them, I couldn't seem to stop shaking. My heart hammered deep inside my chest, leaving echoes in my ears. Alexander remained behind me, brushing his fingers down my arms as Trent cupped both sides of my face. His stare was even more piercing than before, his expression telling me in no uncertain terms he wasn't taking no for an answer.

Not that I wanted to.

The excitement continued to build, my mind reeling from how natural it felt between them. Maybe I was sleep deprived or falling into a mind game, but it was becoming far too easy to let go around them.

And I hated myself because of it.

Trent lifted me off the shower floor, forcing me to wrap my legs around him. I eased my arms over his shoulders, surprised that they hadn't tethered or disciplined me. The fact they both reeked of passion was unexpected, keeping me on edge as if they were planning something else nefarious.

When he slipped his cock inside, taking his time until he was fully seated, there was no holding back a single moan.

Both men issued guttural sounds, Alexander raking his nails down my back as he pressed kisses from one shoulder to the other. My muscles strained to accept the full girth of Trent's cock, the dazzling sensations pumping through me leaving me breathless.

"Tight. You're so fucking tight," he murmured as he pulled out, rolling onto the balls of his feet and slamming into me again.

"I can't wait to fuck you in the ass," Alexander growled. "Open your mouth, pet," he instructed.

When I hesitated, he smacked me on the bottom several times.

"Don't make me tell you again. You follow our orders."

"Yes, Master."

He laughed then shoved his fingers into my open mouth. "Suck on them, little girl. Get them nice and wet for me."

I cinched my eyes shut, obeying him as he pistoned his fingers several times.

"That's it. She can be a good girl," Trent added.

When Alexander finally yanked them away, I bit my lower lip, the anticipation killing me. He wasted no time rimming my asshole with a single finger then plunging it all the way inside.

"Oh. Oh!" The pain was instant, biting yet sensual in some crazy kind of way.

He wiggled it several times before adding a second and third finger. As he pumped hard and fast, I stared into Trent's eyes. For some reason I expected jealousy, but he was content, even happy with the arrangement. At least I had my answer. They *had* done this before.

I wasn't certain whether the realization added to the excitement or continued to fuel the bad boy images that had been in my mind for years. Did it really matter any longer? A series of dancing vibrations gave me the answer. This was sinful, a filthy fall into a mere hint of their darkness. What else would they have in store for me? One solid week. Not even a day had passed. Wherever they were taking me, I had a feeling the experience could change my views.

And quite possibly my life.

"Now, I fuck you in the ass," Alexander growled as he pushed the tip of his cock against my asshole.

Shuddering, my body tensed involuntarily, my blood pumping to the point my face was flushed. Even the hot water and steam had no real effect on me. Just their heated bodies, the possessiveness that they'd presented. They were kings of their domain. I was nothing but a pretty little object to be used and toyed with, taken down from a gilded shelf whenever their needs surfaced.

I had the distinct feeling that would be often as well as brutal.

Alexander crushed his massive hands over my hips, his fingers digging into my skin as Trent jerked me closer, keeping me elevated and immobile. I'd never felt so powerless in my life. While the thought remained uncomfortable, I couldn't help but fall into the extreme pleasure.

Hot breath skipped across the surface of my skin, the scent of both men invigorating. I clenched Trent's shoulder with one hand, his muscular arm with the other. And I continued staring into the man's eyes, trying to capture a full glimpse of his soul. What made him tick? Why was he working with Randolph in any capacity? I wasn't certain he would allow me to know the real reason.

Another secret or perhaps another lie.

As Alexander pushed inside, taking his time driving in an inch at a time, my mouth went dry from the increasing level of pain. I sucked in my breath as anguish took over, pushing my limits to the point my mind was a blur, stars in bright gold and silver flashing in front of my eyes. Nothing would ever be the same after this.

Nothing.

They'd already stripped me of my inhibitions, forcing me to face what I'd kept from myself my entire life. Pleasure. I'd been so determined that I'd lost the most important part of me.

The ability to enjoy.

And to love.

As the ugly word flashed in my mind, I did everything I could to shove it aside. This wasn't about developing anything tangible. What would happen during the remainder of this week was all about control, a desperate need to alter the balance of power. In fact, anything could happen. And afterwards, there would be no returning to normal.

"That's it," Alexander whispered in a guttural tone. "Take all of me."

"Oh, I... So big." The words sounded ridiculous, and I laughed, forced to loll my head on Trent's shoulders. When the man was fully seated inside, I let out an exaggerated sigh until they started using what seemed like a perfect rhythm, one driving into me then the other. Both men crushed their chests against me, ensuring I know my place. And damn if it didn't feel glorious, as if I was always meant to succumb to three brutal men.

Trent lowered his head, issuing beastlike sounds before peppering my cheek and jaw with kisses. I languished in the treatment, their actions as tender as I knew the men could provide. They weren't romantic. There wouldn't be candlelight dinners or walks in parks or art galleries. There would be hard fucking and nothing more, forcing me to submit. The thought was provocative and breathtaking.

No. No! I couldn't think of it that way.

But I did.

As their actions became even more savage in nature, I found it even more difficult to breathe. Then my body betrayed me all over again, an orgasm sweeping through me like a wildfire consuming everything in sight.

"Yes. Yes..." I tossed my head back and forth, wiggling in their hold, my legs aching from the tension.

"Breathe, little pet. Come for us. Come hard." Trent's command was almost inaudible, the hoarse whisper fueling the fire.

The tingling sensations built to an explosive level, pushing me into a frenzied state. As I bucked hard against them, one climax shifted into a blissful tidal wave, pouring over me like the water dousing our bodies. When I let off a high-pitched scream, the two men howled their appreciation.

I was shocked how exhausted the rush of adrenaline could be, making it almost impossible to catch my breath. Now their actions became even more dominating, so brutal that the sound of skin slapping against skin permeated the dense space, overpowering every other noise. Within seconds, I could tell they were close to exploding deep inside of me.

Alexander fisted my hair at the scalp, yanking my head until he was able to look me in the eyes. What he said should have bothered me, but it didn't.

"When we're finished with you, no other man will be acceptable. You will belong to us. Forever." He crushed his mouth against mine, thrusting hard and fast. I clamped my legs around Trent's hips, fearful I would fall, but in the next few seconds, I no longer cared about anything but the amazing ecstasy shared between us.

Their booming roars echoed in the shower, saturating my eardrums just as they exploded, the cum spewed deep inside, filling me with their seed.

Yes, everything had changed between us, but a foreboding settled into my system, and I had no idea why.

I was surprised I'd been allowed to wear clothes or bring a few items with me. While Randolph had insisted that my suitcase be filled with only intimate apparel, I defied him as I planned on doing the entire time. I glared at my reflection one last time in the mirror, promising myself that I would find a way to contact Mr. Dockett. I could steal one of their cell phones if I had to. There was no way I'd lose the contract I'd worked so hard to win.

As I walked downstairs, I was surprised at the quiet in the house. After placing my suitcase on the stairs, I debated running out the front door. That wasn't feasible or intelligent. They would hunt me down, the barren landscape surrounding the property making it easy for them to find me. Then God knows what they would do at that point.

Resigned to going with them, I was determined to find out everything I could about what they were hiding. I wondered when Marjorie would try to get ahold of me. At least she would realize something was off, or so I hoped. I couldn't wait to learn what she found. I moved through the house, finally hearing voices coming from a partially cracked door. As I inched closer, I held my breath, trying to remain silent.

"What the hell are you getting at?" Randolph snarled.

"What I'm trying to tell you is that Scarlett has nothing to do with the stock purchases or the threats. She's been receiving them herself, shares of her company suddenly being purchased by what she called a mysterious company," Trent answered, his tone more dominating than ever.

I slunk back, pressing my hand against my mouth. Was it possible someone was threatening them as well? What was the point? To rid the robotics world of the top two companies? Yes, that could be the case. If someone was successful in forcing not one but two takeovers, they would control such a massive empire that no one could challenge them.

"Trent is right. We need to explore other options," Alexander insisted.

The loud thudding noise pushed a sound from my lips even though I squelched it immediately.

"Scarlett is behind this. I'm positive and we will find out who she's working with. Period," Randolph huffed. "If the two of you don't like it, then get the fuck out. I'll handle her from here."

"Her? Goddamn it, Randolph. Whatever is going on with you had better stop. You need to get control!" Trent hissed. "She's a good person, better than most, and I will not be a part of destroying her."

"Then leave," Randolph demanded.

"Not a fucking chance."

The quiet settling between the three men was palpable, sending shivers down my spine. Something tragic had occurred in Randolph's life. What? What had made him into such a brutal, angry man?

"This is going to stop, gentlemen," Alexander stated in an even tone. "We made a deal and we're keeping it. If Scarlett knows anything, we will find that out. If not…"

I was surprised he didn't finish his sentence.

"Scarlett isn't the enemy, Randolph. Whatever you're hiding is the real issue. And you will come clean or plan on buying me out."

"Bring Scarlett to me. It's time we leave," Randolph demanded.

When I heard footsteps, I rushed away, trying to understand what I'd just heard, my thoughts returning to the threats I'd received. What in the hell was going on and why did I have the distinct feeling all four of us were pawns in some vicious game?

 *andolph*

"Did you enjoy fucking her?" I asked as I looked up from her computer, still thinking about the earlier call I'd made.

"Do you enjoy going through her things?" Alexander countered.

"This is just business. What you did was very personal."

He snorted as he walked closer. "I think you just might be jealous."

"And you'd be wrong. Again." Although hearing their passion had bothered me more than I'd wanted to admit. I'd spent one night around the vivacious woman, and not only did I remain hungry, but I was also incapable of getting her out of my mind.

Or from under my skin.

Carlos' warning had also remained festering like a disease. I had to trust the man, which is something I never did.

"I'm going to repeat an earlier question, Randolph," Alexander said with almost no inflection in his voice.

"Why not?" I said, half laughing as I eyed the open door. Trent had left our tedious meeting to bring her to me, our flight leaving in less than two hours, the airport far enough away we needed to leave immediately. I could tell something had been on Trent's mind. All he'd done during the meeting was stare at me, refusing to say anything.

I closed her laptop, unable to find anything of use, including on Southport Industries. She had no secret plans to coerce a takeover. She'd also seemed surprised that Michael Wentworth had changed his mind, bringing his business to her firm after placing all her efforts in securing Dockett's business.

That didn't mean she was totally innocent, but I was beginning to believe she was being played along with the rest of us. Why? The dark instinct I'd always had continued to enflame the gasoline ready to spark at any time. If Carlos was unable to secure any decent information, then I knew things would get very ugly, even damning.

"What the fuck is wrong with you?"

"Why should anything be wrong?" I asked, giving him a hard look.

He closed the distance, his fury riding his face. "Are you prepared to fuck up all your father left you with some need for vengeance when you have no idea who the hell is behind the threats? Do you really want to hurt someone who you clearly care about? I've seen the way you look at Scarlett, the longing you feel. I've only seen you this way one other time and even then, you fucked it up with your steadfast conviction to take over the world. Or was that all about your father's influence?"

Was he joking? Did he really think I gave a damn about Scarlett other than longing to fuck her again and again? Snorting, I glared at him the same way my father had once done to me, acting as if my question meant nothing to me.

Yet the fact he was bringing up my past further fueled my anger. I couldn't afford to care about anyone, especially not now.

But the attempt at lying to myself was failing. The yin and yang of my emotions were all over the place. How could a single woman appear to change my entire attitude?

And my world?

"Don't mention her name to me, Alexander, if you know what's good for you."

Laughing, he stared at me incredulously. "What are you going to do, Randolph? Use violence? Is that what we've been reduced to in our tumultuous relationship?"

"Need I remind you that you seemed excited about what you called my 'dirty idea' with regard to Scarlett."

"Enjoying her company because of winning that stupid wager is similar to what we used to do in the past, Randolph, when we were still in college. Sure, I enjoyed the hell out of the thought of getting to spend time with Scarlett, indulging in fulfilling my sadistic needs, but I don't like the game of chess you're playing."

"You mean poker, don't you? Did you find anything else to incriminate my father on your witch hunt?"

He remained where he was, refusing to budge. This time, I was the one who backed down, skirting around him and walking toward the window. The trouble was my feelings only increased with every passing hour, even though it didn't make any sense. I'd wanted her for so long that my desire had pushed past the limit of self-control, more so than when I'd first met her. It was my father who'd insisted I stay away and that showing her any sign of affection was akin to highlighting a weakness. I'd subscribed to his methodology, refusing to get close to anyone.

Including the one woman who'd shown me attention years before. I'd pushed her aside, pretending I didn't care. The look on her face as she'd walked out my door for the last time would never stop from haunting me. At least Cherise had found someone to treat her much better than I ever had. And I'd gotten praise from my father for shoving her out of my life. Damn my father for interfering in my life even now.

The fact Alexander hadn't answered me meant he sensed I was hiding something significant and was waiting for me to confess.

The awkward silence was something I wasn't used to with my best friend. "Since you mentioned our college days, do you remember all the plans we'd made with regard to business?" I'd always had good memories of the times spent in college. Even my father hadn't attempted to shove them out of my life. In fact, just before... Just before he'd died, he'd encouraged me to take them on as partners. That had shocked the hell out of me.

"Of course I do. You convinced both Trent and me to consider coming to work with you. Not sure how that happened since I was determined to build a company of my own." Alexander shook his head. "But you were persuasive, foregoing the usual extracurricular activities in order to secure straight A's."

"And I don't regret it. Besides, we did have some fun," I mused as I turned to face him. His expression finally softened.

"Yeah, we did. The three of us together hunting down beautiful women. That's part of the reason Worth has exceeded what your father had planned for you."

"Do you really want that now, sharing a woman together for an extended period of time?"

Alexander shifted his attention toward the door before answering. "I wasn't certain at first, but Scarlett is perfect. She's everything all three of us said we wanted."

"Times change. People change."

"I don't think so. I can see it in your eyes. You've been in love with her for years. You might as well admit it."

I remained quiet for a few seconds, my mouth watering from the thought of holding her in my arms. I almost laughed as the simplistic need. "Let it go, Alex. We have a plane to catch."

"Right. You really think she's behind the threats," he said almost in passing.

"I'm not certain any longer, Alex. Since you keep insisting that I'm hiding something from you, I'll tell you this. My father made a hell of a lot of mistakes and bad decisions when he started to get older. Yes, he did get into some financial trouble, but I'm not certain why or how, just that whoever it was made certain his repayment had significant interest. I found that out by snooping, not because he trusted me enough to tell me anything about his precious company that he'd promised to me. One thing was certain. He was damn good at hiding whatever private life he had outside of the family."

"You never told me this before."

"No, because he did what he could to erase a good portion of his past, even instructing his accountant to doctor the books. So, yes, I knew that there was something off about a portion of his past. I had to force the retired man to provide the ugly information. It was clear to me my father had been placed into a level of duress he couldn't handle, doing everything he could to get a hefty loan to repay his debts."

"Let me guess. He couldn't find a bank to loan him the money."

"No, but he obviously found a way. It's funny. I always wondered why my father retired five years earlier than his great plan, basically forcing me to take the helm at twenty-three. Let's face it. I wasn't ready for the responsibility, but he kept pushing up until the day he died."

"Jesus Christ. What are you trying to say?"

I walked closer, making certain no one else could hear what I was saying. "I think whatever my father got involved in was very dangerous, perhaps even criminal, but that started years before, when I was ten or eleven. He got mixed up with some people and if I had to guess, I'd say it was because he owed them money. I also think he did their biddings."

"Meaning what?"

"Meaning I think my father was capable of murder."

"Whoa. What?"

I nodded several times. "I can't prove it and my mother refuses to talk about what she calls the most horrible time in her marriage, but my gut tells me he was threatened by these individuals. I don't know. Maybe I'm making too much out of this."

"And maybe you're not."

"Yeah, maybe not." I allowed my mind to return to the ugly time before, loathing that I'd shoved the memory into a black box for far too long.

Alexander didn't seem as stunned as I thought he'd be. "How did your father die? You never told me. In fact, it's been a dirty little secret all these years."

The embarrassment I'd felt from years before rushed into the forefront of my mind, the dirty little secret something my mother had forced me to promise would never be shared with anyone, including my best friends. Before I had a chance to respond, Trent and Scarlett entered the room. As always happened, the moment she walked into any space, my attention was drawn to her and not only because of her beauty but also by her sophistication and grace under fire.

I'd never seen her losing her cool or expressing her anger.

Except with me.

If she'd provided the truth to Trent and she was being threatened, then whoever had captured my father's soul meant to take control of the industry. My instinct told me they'd eliminate anyone who'd dared to get in their way.

Just like they'd done with my father.

Only the person responsible for destroying his life hadn't been the one to pull the trigger.

* * *

Alexander

Revelations.

Secrets.

The combination haunted me, everything Randolph had told me never far from my mind. What I'd learned wasn't exactly what I'd expected, but it explained my friend's odd behavior over the last few years. Jesus. Maybe money was still owed from all those years ago.

I studied Scarlett, observing her facial expressions during the trip. She'd said almost nothing during the nine-hour flight. In fact, all four of us had remained quiet, Randolph going over the financials, including those I'd found regarding the past. Trent had been handling the engineering department's emails while I'd spent time attempting to delve into finding more about the corporate entity who'd purchased our stock. I had a name. Big fucking deal. While Southbound Industries had filed with the SEC as required, there was little about them on any of the supporting documentation or in my research of traditional sources find the registered agent or the principles of the company. Whoever was responsible had been very careful keeping their identity private.

That had led me into contacting an old buddy of mine who worked for the Securities Exchange Commission, but Jack had other qualifications as well. That included resources he'd never identified that allowed him to discover information about anyone, no matter how secretive they attempted at being.

While Southbound had paid normal prices for the shares, my gut told me that if this was an attempt at a hostile takeover, they would eventually go to some of the shareholders, trying to coerce them into selling for a premium price.

Or simply coercing them under duress, which is what I was leaning toward given what Randolph had admitted. So I'd kept digging.

What I'd learned just before landing had confirmed we were facing a takeover, although so far not in the traditional ways I'd seen and read about. Southport was damn good at hiding their identity, more so than any other firm Jack had encountered. However, he had determined the company had only been in operation for four months, one month longer than the first purchase of our stock. He'd also found an offshore bank account that was locked down tight. Even the physical address they'd used had turned out to be an abandoned warehouse in Jersey, the owner also listed in Southport's limited documentation.

That had led me to the previous owner, the one who'd sold it to Southport. While shell companies were used all the time, between what Jack had found and what I'd been able to discover, the picture was grim. The previous owner of the building couldn't remember a thing about the transaction, his reluctance to talk to me for more than two minutes a clear indication he was afraid. Perhaps even more curious, Scarlett had watched me the entire time I'd been on the phone.

Given her insistence that she was experiencing the same situation with regard to her stock, I'd also checked her claims. She hadn't been lying, unless she owned Southbound, which there was no indication of. Several smaller purchases had been made of her stock in recent weeks, but nothing alarming.

"Where are we, Disneyland?" she asked after the jet came to a complete stop.

"Cancun," Randolph told her, which seemed to surprise her.

She turned her head in my direction, studying me intently just like she'd done before.

"You're going to be a very good girl when we get off this flight. Do you understand?" Randolph asked as he rose from his seat.

"Why, yes, *Master*."

There was a change in her demeanor, but not because her defiance had returned, but because of the difference in the look in her eyes. I couldn't determine what kind of emotion she was holding inside.

"Come on," Trent said as he unfastened Scarlett's seatbelt, pulling her onto her feet.

"Did you bring my laptop?" she asked, slowly turning her head in Randolph's direction. "I'm certain you couldn't get to all my files. I'm not stupid enough to keep them out in the open. You'll need my fingerprint to unlock them."

Randolph chuckled under his breath. "Yes, I brought it and I would appreciate your assistance."

"Why, of course. Anything for my… keepers."

I shot Randolph a look, barely able to keep from hissing. I loathed the game, wanting nothing more than to abandon the trip altogether. His determination to come to Cancun meant he'd contacted Carlos already. I didn't like the mafia prince, his sadistic needs bordering on heinous. He wasn't the kind of man you crossed under any circumstances.

As we walked off the plane, the sun was just beginning to set, leaving the area enshrouded in shadows. While I usually adored coming to any place tropical, I wasn't in the mood to pretend I was having a good time. In fact, it was reckless to remain. We needed to return to our home base, doing everything we could to protect the stock base while discovering the person behind the takeover.

Then I'd have no problem doing everything in my power to help crush the enemy. I walked down the stairs in front of her, waiting on the tarmac until both Randolph and Trent made their way out of the plane, pulling them aside.

"Stay right there, Scarlett," I instructed after she'd walked several feet ahead.

"Where, oh where could I go?" she asked far too sweetly.

As Randolph flanked my side, he kept his eyes on her. "What did you find in that long search, the phone call you made?"

"It's not all about what I found," I answered. "It's what my buddy found. Southbound is a dummy corporation behind the stock purchases, but from what Jack was able to determine, the company purchased stocks from two companies and no others."

"Let me guess," Trent piped in. "Worth and Prestwood."

"Yes, which is pretty telling that whoever is after us also has plans on taking down Scarlett's company as well." I shifted my gaze toward Randolph, able to see his eyes in the waning light. He wasn't ready to buy her innocence just yet.

"No coincidences," Randolph mused.

"I don't like this bullshit," Trent hissed. "Scarlett could be the one really hurt in all of this."

"I agree with him, Randolph. People like this have a reason they don't want to be identified. They purchased an entire building just to pull off the act, but the person they bought it from is terrified of talking. At this point, we've reached a dead end. We're here in a freaking tropical location when we should be in Pittsburg hunting down this fucker. What the hell is wrong with you that you can't see that?"

Randolph exhaled, his eyes never leaving her. "If I can't find what I need in the next couple of days, then we'll return."

"You mean your meeting with Carlos Santiago?" Trent snarled. "What exactly do you hope to find, buddy? Whatever it is, if you're planning on terrifying her by going to one of his illustrious dark events, I won't allow it. I suggest you keep that in mind."

"I'll do what's necessary in order to keep my company protected, including whatever is necessary with regard to Scarlett."

My company. The bastard actually had the nerve to use that phrase after all the work both Trent and I had done over the years. I turned my gaze toward Scarlett, watching as she shifted back and forth from one foot to the other as if she was humming a tune to herself, enjoying the warm air and myriad colorful hues dancing across the horizon.

And I was angry.

Enraged.

Appalled.

But something or someone had to get through to Randolph.

Only I wasn't certain I cared enough to try to intervene again. What was the point? He'd fallen deep into a rabbit hole, refusing to face whatever truths had been holding him back. Until he did, he'd continue to be an angry man.

Exhaling, I looked away. "I don't know what's happened to you, Randolph, but Carlos Santiago can't provide what you need in your life. Only you can do that, but you'll be forced to face whatever demon has been haunting you since your father's mysterious death. The young man I met in college would never play games or hide behind his past. The man I considered a friend would stop at nothing to get answers, not resorting to anyone else's help. Whatever is going on with you, you need to get your shit straight or I'll be happy to sell my shares of stock to the highest bidder. Imagine that."

When I walked away, I half expected Randolph to tackle me to the pavement. When he didn't, that confirmed what I'd suspected.

That he'd was indeed in love with Scarlett.

And that his father had killed himself out of guilt and shame.

Whatever his father had done, his sins had been forced on all four of us. If that was the case, danger had already found us. It was only a matter of time before everything came to a head. And sadly, my gut told me someone else was going to lose their life in the process.

Scarlett

Cancun. I'd never been to this portion of Mexico before and while I had to admit the atmosphere was amazing, I continued to think about what I'd heard earlier that morning. It had become clear to me that Randolph was hiding something tragic that had occurred from everyone, including himself, and it was eating him alive. Was someone using that secret against him, or did it have more to do with his dead father? One thing was certain. Randolph would never tell me since I was considered public enemy number one.

The flight had been exhausting, mostly because I'd remained on edge the entire time, uncertain what the men were going to do. At least they'd kept to themselves, almost acting as if I was nothing but a typical passenger on their impressive jet. Nothing was making any sense, but I couldn't get over the uneasy feeling that all four of us were in danger.

That had been magnified by overhearing a portion of a phone call Alexander had on the plane. Why was he asking about who'd purchased a building?

As I sipped my margarita, I tried everything I could to ignore all three of them. The tension between us was horrible, enough so I couldn't relax. At least the band had started playing, the dancefloor already crowded with vacationers enjoying every moment of the tropical setting. If only I was here under different pretenses. If only I could learn what Randolph was hiding but it was obvious that he trusted no one.

"You ate very little at dinner," Randolph said.

"I wasn't very hungry." My answer was laced with venom. "That's what happens with you take someone against their will."

Alexander chuckled. "You are truly a spitfire."

"You need to eat." Trent leaned over, placing his hand on my leg. For about a million reasons, I bristled, unable to breathe, but I was locked in a moment of arousal just like I'd been before. Memories of time spent with him in the shower had been special, entirely different than I'd expected. Both he and Alexander had a softer side, one they hadn't let me to see up to this point.

"As I said, I'm not hungry." I licked around the rim of the glass collecting salt, inching as far toward the edge of my chair as possible. He didn't deserve my nastiness. All my hatred and anger were now centered directly on Randolph.

"Then how about a dance?" Trent didn't wait long enough for me to answer, rising to his feet and taking the glass out of my hand. Every action he took was deliberate, including the way he placed the drink on the table before clasping his fingers around mine. I had no choice in the matter, allowing him to lead me to the dancefloor.

As he took me into his arms, his hold firm, I pressed my hand against his chest in some effort to gain a little space between us.

Trent cocked his head, studying me for a few seconds. His concerned expression allowed me to breathe a little easier. While I hated to admit it, being in his arms felt good. Natural.

"I won't allow Randolph to hurt you. Alexander won't either."

"Hurt me? In what way? Taking my company or spanking me for some insane infraction?"

Chuckling, he flashed a smile. "Both, although you do have a naughty as hell side."

"Why should I believe you?" I asked, biting back a moan as he brushed his hand down my back.

"You need to learn to trust me. I don't want anything to happen to you ever," Trent pulled me closer and the heat between our two bodies was explosive. I enjoyed just being in his arms for a few seconds before easing my head back, locking eyes with his.

"Trust isn't easy for me, especially when the livelihood of my company is involved. Plus, you've given me no reason to trust you, other than you haven't been a complete asshole like Randolph, accusing me of sabotaging your company."

"As I told you before, I believe you, but you aren't innocent."

"I'm sorry. I guess I believed I had no other choice. Fight fire with fire."

He looked away for a few seconds. "You learned from our tactics. While I don't blame you, that's not what you're made of."

He was right.

"Why doesn't Randolph believe me? What is that man hiding that's burning a hole in his soul? If he has one." Sighing, I looked out over the crowd, unable to catch sight of the other two.

"He's a complicated man, Scarlett, but I know how much he cares about you."

I laughed, rolling my eyes. "No, he doesn't. I assure you that he absolutely hates me and that's fine. Why are we here in this place?" I asked as I slid my hand over his shoulder. If I was going to glean any information, it would be from Trent. Of that I had no doubt.

"Randolph owns the villa we're staying in. It's secure and private."

"That's not why. I overheard the conversation you and Alexander had with him. I know about the Clubhouse."

His eyes opened wide at first. Then he laughed softly, shaking his head. "Before or after you accepted the wager?"

"Before."

"Interesting. What exactly did you find?" he asked, a sly smile sliding across his face. He didn't miss a beat, the dance becoming more sensual than before.

"Very little. Even the private investigator I hired couldn't discover anything worthwhile, including who or what owns the establishment."

Trent lowered his head. "All you had to do was ask. However, then you already know that membership is exclusive and kept private at the owner's insistence. He finds out and provides fantasies for his members, for a hefty price of course."

"That's not just it. There's more."

"What are you getting at?"

"I don't know but I am going to find out. My assistant, Ashley mentioned her roommate was invited to attend one of these fantasies. I assume that means she participated. From what Ashley said, when her roommate returned, she was shaken to the point she refused to talk about what happened."

"I'm sorry to hear that. Not all of the fantasies are about whips and chains, if that's what you're thinking."

I kept my eyes on his, trying to figure out if he was holding back. He seemed genuine, enough so I decided to trust him with what could be a damaging question. "I think you know Ashley's roommate, a girl by the name of Madisen." I watched as he narrowed his eyes, the dim lighting of the dancefloor allowing me to see a complete change in his demeanor. When he tried to pull away, I refused to allow him. "You dated her. If I had to guess, I'd say you forced her to participate in one of those fantasies."

"Let it go, Scarlett."

"No, I'm not going to. You want me to trust you. Then why can't you do the same? What fantasy did you force her to endure? Did you break her like you want to do with me?"

Trent reared back, releasing his hold. "I didn't force her to endure anything. Yes, I introduced Madisen to my lifestyle, which she seemed to crave learning about. However, it wasn't the life she wanted, but she realized that at an awkward time. We'll leave it at that. Yes, I cared about her, but she wasn't the right woman. Indulging in the kind of fantasies as provided by the owner of the Clubhouse isn't for the faint of heart. However, I didn't harm her on purpose, if that's what you're thinking. I might be brutal in my methods of business, but when I care for someone, I will stop at nothing to keep them safe. That is a promise I make to you."

"Do you have plans on sharing one of your fantasies with me?" I couldn't resist asking. While the man seemed sincere, I wasn't willing to buy everything he said at a hundred percent.

"No. That's not what this is about."

This. Whatever 'this' was no longer made any sense. What had started out as two companies refusing to back down to the other had been changed by a sinful wager.

Even in the dim lighting, I could see utter sincerity in his eyes, but there was something else. Love. Was it possible he'd fallen in love with me? Blinking, I looked away, but he cupped the side of my face, forcing me to look him in the eyes. When he lowered his head, pressing his lips against mine, I fisted his shirt with both hands, moving onto my tiptoes.

Revenge was a funny thing and also something not for the faint of heart to enter into. I'd heard it said many times that there was a fine line between love and hate. Up until this point, I'd balked against the thought. And now?

Now I was no longer certain how I felt.

And that terrified me most of all.

 _andolph_

I'd been surprised by Carlos' call as well as the odd tone in his voice. He'd insisted that we meet in the early morning hours, which indicated whatever he'd found was time sensitive. What I wanted now was a better understanding of the threats Scarlett had received. It was time to end the charade portion of the game. If she lied to me, I'd know it without question.

Then I'd punish her mercilessly and without hesitation. My fingers itched with the desire to do so.

However, that would need to wait, at least for now. After our return, I'd given both Alexander and Trent their choice of weapons to carry. At this point, we couldn't be too cautious. Whoever was behind the threats would escalate their actions. Of that I had no doubt. If the asshole dared try to attack us, they would pay a hefty price.

"You summoned me?" she asked from the doorway.

After shoving the weapon into my desk drawer, I turned to face her, the drink remaining in my hand. "Yes. Come in."

After lifting her gaze from my desk, she glanced around my office, allowing her disdain for my decorating style to cross her face. When she approached, she did so cautiously, keeping her distance in front of my desk. "Did I do something wrong at dinner?" she asked.

Exhaling, I moved toward the bar, pouring her a glass of cognac. I remained quiet as I approached, studying her intently. She seemed uncomfortable by my gaze. After offering her the glass, I waited as she debated whether or not to toss the liquid into my face. Maybe that's exactly what I deserved.

Pulling away, she moved around me and toward the set of French doors overlooking the ocean. "Am I allowed to go outside?"

The question startled me for no reason. "Of course. You're not a prisoner here."

"I'm not?" She threw a look over her shoulder before opening one of the doors, immediately heading outside.

I refilled my drink, thinking about how to talk to her. With her. I wasn't good at small talk, yet I couldn't stand the adversarial tension that had been between us for days. Hell, what was I talking about? Months. Years. And there'd been no reason to consider her an enemy that long ago other than advice from my father. What a fool I'd been.

She'd always been a sight to behold, but more so these past couple of years. I stood in the doorway, admiring the view. Even though I adored the setting of the villa, the serenity afforded me because of the money I'd spent, the location paled in comparison to the woman standing in front of me. The fact my cock ached, pinching against my trousers was an indication of my raging desire. However, that didn't mean nearly as much as the way my heart thumped in my chest, complete with burning sensations.

I'd seen the way men had looked at her at the restaurant and I'd wanted to fight them off like some lovesick warrior. Maybe she would have enjoyed that, a grown man fighting for her hand. She remained tense as she always did around me. Tonight, I wanted to change that.

"Is this really your villa?" she asked in such a quiet voice, which was totally unlike her.

"Yes. I own several residences in different countries but this one is my favorite." Trent had made me aware that she'd done everything in her power to learn about our membership in the Clubhouse. She'd gone to great lengths to find dirt on all three of us.

"I never know when you're being serious or playing the game."

"I'm tired of playing the game, Scarlett."

She chuckled softly, as if she couldn't believe in anything I said.

I moved closer, still finding it difficult to talk with her. When I placed my hand against the small of her back, she sucked in her breath.

"What are you doing, Randolph? It's clear you hate me."

"I don't hate you. It's quite the opposite."

"Then what the hell are you trying to do, destroy all I've worked for? Is winning the only thing that matters in your life?" She pulled away, even though I could tell she was shivering from my touch.

"It's not about winning, Scarlett. It's about being the best."

"And you think you are. Don't you?"

Even in the dim lighting, I could see such rebellion on her face. Goddamn, how I wanted nothing more than to take her right here and right now. "Yes, I've thought so for a long time."

"You're unbelievable, Randolph. I'm curious. Do you remember the first time we met?"

"That's not something I could forget, Scarlett." How could I? She had been dressed in a bright red suit, the color accentuating her gorgeous copper locks. I'd been struck by her sense of worth and her ability to take the heat from my father.

And I'd made a vow to myself on that day that I would own her.

Then my father had forbidden me from giving a damn about anyone. Yes, I had been a damn fool.

That stopped here. She kept her distance away from me, not bothering to look me in the eyes again.

"Against everything you've taught me with your ruthless actions, I'm about to allow you to see a weakness. I'm certain you'll use it against me at some point. The day we met is one I'll never forget either. You see, I was very much looking forward to the meeting. I looked up to you and your father. I'd read the article in whatever that magazine was highlighting the accomplishments Worth Dynamics had made over the past year, all the awards you'd won, and I made a promise to myself that I would be there one day. Me, the girl who was shunned early in the industry. All boys club. That's what I was told."

There was so much angst in her voice.

"Anyway, I modeled my company after Worth because I believed it was run with a high level of integrity. On that gorgeous, sunny day I'd changed clothes three times to ensure that I would be taken seriously. Do you remember the very first thing your father said after bothering to shake my hand?"

"My father could be an asshole. In fact, he was most of the time." A part of me hated to admit that about my father, but another felt damn good in doing so.

"But you don't remember." She finally snapped her head in my direction, inching closer. "He said that I'd never make it in what he called his world and that I should just not bother to try."

"As I said, he was an asshole, including to me."

"Interesting. You're just like him."

She was right. I'd turned into a carbon copy of the man I respected yet hated. "My father was wrong and I'm sorry you had to deal with that."

"But you agreed with him."

"I was an arrogant young man who thought he had the world in the palm of his hand." Little did I accept at the time my father had already turned to a darker side, doing anything in his power to excel and to claim what he'd boasted more than once belonged to him.

"You did and you still do. It's unfortunate you don't care about anything or anyone."

I crowded her space, drinking in her exotic perfume. She was my fix, the drug that my soul needed in order to survive. "That's not true at all, at least not any longer."

"Then why the game?"

Laughing, I wasn't certain how to answer. "Because I hate to lose, especially to someone as amazing as you. And as beautiful." As I brushed strands of hair from her face, she narrowed her eyes.

"Who are you, Randolph? Do you even know any longer?"

"I didn't until a sinfully lovely woman kicked me in the ass."

She pressed her hand against my chest. "Then tell me the truth. What is going on? Your partners are very worried about the threats, but you don't seem bothered in the least."

I continued my actions, hating to break the quietness that had settled between us. However, she deserved the truth that I knew at this point. I reluctantly eased away, leaning over the railing. There was only a single explanation that made any sense regarding his change in behavior. I should have put two and two together years before. "I've been threatened from the day after I took the reins from my father. There will always been men and women who fail to understand that success takes hard work, preferring the easier path of stealing what doesn't belong to them, defiling a man and his company just because he's on top. As I said, my father was an asshole; however, he was an astute businessman. At least until he faltered."

"Meaning what?"

"While I don't know for certain, I think he got involved heavily with gambling and lost most of the time. He once told me gambling was a way to ease the tension that he felt one hundred percent of the time. He lost control. Then he borrowed money from the wrong people."

"Are you serious?" she asked as she moved closer. The warmth of her body next to me was just as comforting as it was arousing.

"I'm very serious."

"Wait a minute. You think the person your father owed money to is coming after you because of money still owed to them? That doesn't make any sense. It's been years since your father's death."

"No, it doesn't, but I can't think of any other explanation."

"Then they are the ones purchasing the stock as well as threatening you?"

"Yes, and I'm actively trying to find out who that is."

"Whether you care to believe me or not, an unknown entity is also purchasing my company's stock and I wasn't lying when I said I've been threatened."

"Tell me about the threats. What was said exactly?"

Scarlett closed her eyes, her nose wrinkling. "At first it was something like 'I'm watching you.' I honestly thought you'd sent them, but after sending a nasty reply, it came back as undeliverable. The second was 'watch your back.' The last one came on the day Mr. Dockett made his decision. The asshole said it was my last warning to stay away from Worth."

"That spurred you on."

"Maybe," she whispered. "The last threat was different, personal. I'll never forget the last words the asshole said. The sins of the fathers will never be repaid."

Growling, I fisted my hand, doing everything I could to keep my rage at bay.

"You've heard that before," she murmured.

"Yes, but the phrasing was different."

"Then you believe me?"

Someone had targeted both companies on purpose, using the fact we'd sparred in the past to overshadow their threats.

"I believe you, Scarlett. What I can't figure out is why this person is playing a game with both of us. You had nothing to do with my father, no matter that you had a single meeting with him." I laughed bitterly.

"What are they trying to accomplish?"

I took several deep breaths, finding it impossible to ignore the draw I felt to her, the longing to hold her in my arms. It was overwhelming as well as unexpected. "Finishing what was started years ago."

"What happened, Randolph? I know you're hiding something that's been eating you alive for years."

"I'm not certain it matters."

"Maybe it does to me."

As I gazed into her eyes, even the shadows and clouds forming a dense blanket around her couldn't hide the conviction in her eyes. She was determined to break through my defenses, as if she was capable of dragging out the goodness in me. Sadly, I wasn't certain I had any left.

Or if I ever had.

"My father killed himself, Scarlett. I found him in his office. He'd shot himself in the head. There was no note, no indication of why he'd made that horrific decision, but I knew in my gut the reason he'd resorted to something so drastic. He couldn't take the guilt of almost destroying our family, let alone his company. His legacy. But I know he kept other burning secrets, the kind that had eaten at what was left of his soul. That's why we're in danger."

She cupped my chin, the touch of her fingers searing every nerve ending. "My God. I am so sorry. There is an incredible man fighting to break free of the chains your father placed on you. I can see your beautiful soul crying out for freedom. You don't have to live behind whatever horrible deeds your father did while he was alive. Don't allow them or his memory to haunt you. Whoever is seeking revenge doesn't know what you're made of."

The woman was ripping through a good portion of my armor, desperate to find out why she remained attracted to a monster. I didn't want to break the bad news to her that I was a carbon copy of my father. I dragged her closer, keeping my arms firmly planted on her hips. "You don't understand anything about me."

"That's where you're wrong, Randolph. I saw the real man years ago."

I couldn't stand it any longer, the desire and angst building to a point of no return. I captured her mouth, pulling her onto her tiptoes. She felt so damn good in my arms, as if she was always destined to belong to me. I raked my fingers up and down her back, grinding my hips back and forth. Nothing could stop me from tasting her.

Taking her.

Fucking her.

She belonged to me. Mine!

My mind was a blur as I thrust my tongue inside, savoring the sweet flavor as I explored the dark recesses of her mouth. I was no longer the bastard who'd challenged every move she made. That was no longer important. All I cared about was consuming her.

Protecting her.

As the kiss exploded with passion, she wrapped her long fingers around my hair, moaning into the moment of intimacy. My cock ached to the point I could barely breathe, my balls tight as drums. I had to be inside of her, driving my shaft all the way into her womb. And I wanted nothing more than to fill her with my seed.

She undulated against me, clinging to me as if I was her lifeline. I'd never felt so exhilarated in my life, the electricity shooting through me one of the most incredible experiences there could possibly be. I'd been shut down for so long that I was breathless, my heart thudding to the point my breathing was shallow. God, I wanted this woman, every inch of her.

And nothing would stop me from taking what I wanted.

When I broke the kiss, a series of growls erupted from the depths of my being. Huffing, I gripped her jaw, nipping her lower lip before lowering my head and dragging my tongue down the length of her neck.

"Mmm..." she purred, closing her eyes, her lips parted.

"I want you," I whispered. "And I will have you." I pushed her away, wrapping my hands around portions of her dress and yanking it over her head.

Her laugh was instantaneous as well as nervous, but she yanked at my shirt, not bothering to unbutton a single one, simply ripping it apart. "You look better without clothes," she whispered, rolling the material over my shoulders.

After the shirt fell to the deck, I cupped her breasts in my hands, rolling my thumbs back and forth across her already hardened nipples. My hunger was off the charts, enough so I lowered my head, taking a tender bud into my mouth, sucking on her sweet flesh. I could do this for hours, indulging in memorizing every inch of her body. But I knew I wouldn't be able to last that long, my needs only increasing with every passing second.

She slid her hand down my chest, crawling her fingers as she dug them into my skin. I was on fire, flames licking at my insides. When she wrapped her hand around my cloth-covered cock, I let off an intense roar, the wind taking it toward the tumultuous sky.

Then I shoved my hand between her legs, taking raspy breaths as I realized she was soaking wet. Within seconds, I yanked at the thin elastic keeping her delicious pussy covered, tossing her panties aside.

Purring, she fought with my belt, her chest rising and falling rapidly as she struggled to unfasten it. When she finally freed my cock, she brushed the tip of a single finger across my sensitive slit.

"Fuck. I want you." My words were gruff, too harsh for the delicate flower standing in front of me, but I wasn't certain I cared. This was about fulfilling our combined needs, satisfying the desire we'd felt for far too long. After tonight, there was no turning back. I would never be able to let her go.

Her sweet laughter was like music I'd never heard before and the way she undressed me only added fuel to the fire. I'd never been so fully aroused, every sensation as if feeling it for the first time. Only seconds after I was fully undressed did I wrap my arms around her, yanking her into the air.

Scarlett gripped my shoulders, sliding her legs around my hips, pursing her luscious lips until I drove the entire length of my cock deep inside.

"Oh!" Her scream was guttural, matching the rumble erupting from my chest. Her muscles immediately clamped around my shaft, the softness of her warm pussy driving me toward madness.

I pumped long and hard, keeping her aloft and rolling onto the balls of my feet as I fucked her like some crazed animal. I breathed in her scent, savoring the intense fragrance as it floated into every cell and muscle.

Her breathing ragged, she dug her fingers into my skin, tossing her head back and forth. Together we were like a wildfire blazing in the darkness, the hunger exploding into something else altogether. Maybe this woman could soothe the demons, keeping their monstrous actions at bay.

But I would never be able to get enough of her, needing more and more as time went on. My vision was clouded, my mind a blur. All I could think about was this moment.

And fulfilling our needs.

"So wet," I managed to mutter as I rolled my index finger down the crack of her ass. A smile never left her face as I shifted her around, pushing her hard against the railing. The light breeze had increased, wind now whipping against us. A single crack of thunder indicated a storm was close, but I couldn't care less.

When lightning flashed across the sky, her body jerked, a series of moans pushing past her voluptuous lips.

"Don't worry. I'll protect you." The words were easy to say, the sentiment heartfelt. In the few moments, she'd freed the part of me she'd realized was chained, bringing my soul into the light.

As the rain started to fall, cascading down over our heated bodies, she lowered her head, lolling it against my shoulder. Together, we were as one. One man. One woman. One desperate need.

I thrust with wild abandon, no longer giving a damn about what we were facing. No one was going to interfere. No one would ever tear us apart.

God help them if they tried.

As the rain picked up in intensity, her breathing became labored. I could tell she was close to coming.

"Come for me, baby. Let go. Just let go."

It was as if my words had given her permission, her body instantly becoming tense. As a powerful orgasm rushed into her system, I threw my head back, enjoying the pelting water dousing our bodies. Her scream of ecstasy made me smile even as several growls rushed from my throat. I refused to stop, driving hard and fast, pushing her into another climax.

"Oh. Oh. Oh!" she cried, bucking hard against me.

When she reared back seconds later, she pressed her forehead against mine. Just listening to her scattered breathing filled my heart.

I loved her. There was no possibility of ignoring what I'd felt for so long.

Tomorrow was the beginning of a new chapter of my life. Damn all those attempting to make me pay for my father's sins.

She pushed her hands against me, tossing her hair against my chest as she clenched her pussy muscles on purpose. And in the next few seconds, I knew there was no way of holding back.

My body shaking, I continued plunging deep within her until I could take it no more. As I erupted deep inside of her, I stared at the electrifying storm.

The game was coming to a close. The players would be identified.

Then the hunt would begin.

And I would enjoy crushing them.

As our breathing started to slow, she nuzzled against my neck, murmuring words I couldn't understand. I gathered her into my arms, taking her inside and up the stairs. After grabbing a towel from the bathroom, I eased her onto her feet, taking the time to dry every inch of her body, rubbing her long locks of hair. And all the while, she kept her eyes on mine, still searching my soul.

Still seeking answers.

I only hoped I'd be able to provide them.

When she took the towel from my hands, rubbing my chest and arms, a strong foreboding shook my system. They would use her against me. Somehow. Some way.

Scarlett backed away, turning once and holding out her hand. There was no way to resist her. None. I intertwined our fingers, allowing her to pull me into the bedroom. She yanked back the covers without saying a word, slowly crawling onto the sheets.

As the storm raged on, I eased beside her, kneeling on the bed and taking my time gaze down, memorizing every inch of her body. She had the kind of curves that all men preferred, luscious and feminine, yet there was a hardness about her, as if up to this point, she'd never been treated well by a man.

And I'd followed suit, acting like a Neanderthal, pushing her away every chance I had.

Her touch had been so soft against my rough skin, brushing her fingers along the curve of my arm as if she had all the time in the day to explore. I loved the elegant curve of her throat, the way her pulse ticked when she was furious with me, which had been every meeting, every moment shared. What I adored most was the soft valley of her breasts. Sighing, I lay down, trying to relieve my tension.

When she pulled the sheets over both of us, my body stiffened. Then she placed her hand over my heart, rubbing her face against my arm. I wanted to explore every inch with my lips before rolling on top of her once again, enjoying the way she writhed beneath me.

My cock stirred, already prepared to take her again, until I realized she'd trusted me enough to fall asleep.

Trust.

Something so hard for both of us, but vital if we were going to get through this ordeal. As I closed my eyes, she murmured in her slumber, the words more chilling than anything I'd ever heard.

"I love you."

The palatial estate where Carlos lived was more like a fortress. I'd been there once, the sweeping views and long, roving driveway that was lined with palm trees providing just a taste of the dazzling architecture and expensive toys hidden behind fortified concrete block walls disguised as Dryvit.

I had to pass through a guarded entrance, the men behind the steel bars holding AK-47s. Then there were the two hulking men who'd frisked me, making certain I hadn't bothered to try to sneak a gun onto the estate. I certainly wasn't that stupid, although I'd slipped my Glock under the seat before leaving the villa.

After the brutes had given the okay, another soldier escorted me toward Carlos' office, knocking once then glaring at me before walking away.

"Come," Carlos said from behind the massive wooden doors.

As I walked inside, he approached, a genuine smile crossing his face.

"Welcome, my friend. It's good to see you." He held out his hand, using his other to grasp my arm as I clasped my fingers around his.

"You as well. I was surprised to receive your call that quickly."

"I could tell discovering the information was important to you. I conveyed that to my people." He finally let go of my hand, moving toward an ornate buffet table, the entire surface covered with breakfast foods and various juices.

"And I appreciate that."

"Would you like something to eat or drink?"

I was surprised he was offering. When I said nothing, he shifted in order to gaze in my direction, a coffee cup in his hand.

"I'm fine."

"A man who doesn't accept such hospitality is a man who cannot be trusted. At least that's what my grandmother used to say."

Laughing, I walked closer. "Coffee then. Just black."

"A simple man, although I know your tastes are varied, especially given the woman you are so interested in." He poured a second cup, a mischievous look on his face as he handed it to me. "Is she as amazing as your eyes divulge?"

"Nothing gets by you. Does it, Carlos?"

"Absolutely not. That's how I've survived all these years. Come. Let's go into my courtyard. We'll be more comfortable there." He didn't wait for me to answer, moving quickly through an open set of

French doors, immediately sitting in the middle of an outdoor couch.

I sat on one of the chairs, able to see the lagoon-style pool from where I was sitting, as well as the six women who were laughing and playing in the water, all of them without swimsuits.

"Yes, they are beautiful creatures. Too bad I haven't been able to find the right one," he said casually.

While I usually enjoyed his banter, I'd remained wide awake all night, my instinct telling me that danger was encroaching. My patience was waning.

"Finding the right one isn't easy, Carlos. Women are complicated in their desires."

"Yes," he said. "I agree with you. If you believe this woman is perfect for you, heed my advice and don't allow her to get away."

His words surprised me.

He took another sip of coffee then placed the cup on the coffee table, leaning over. "You were right to be concerned."

"As I suspected. What did you find?"

He took a deep breath, turning his gaze toward the frolicking women for a few seconds. "Things are not always as they seem, my friend. Even those we trust the most, including our family, often betray us."

What the hell was he trying to get at? "I am well aware that my father had an alternative life."

Chuckling, his dark eyes flashed. "You were always formidable, Randolph, refusing to take no for an answer. I respect that in a man, which is one reason that I granted you your wish."

My wish. He made this out like one of his fantasies. "As I said, Carlos, I very much appreciate your help. I wouldn't have asked if I hadn't exhausted all other methods. Do you know who's attempting to take over my company?"

"Yes, I do. However, what I'm about to tell you will be disturbing for you."

I took a deep breath, leaning forward and sliding the cup across the table before resting my elbows on my knees, placing my flexed fingers together. "Carlos. You've spent a great of time making sure that every member of your secret club meets your criteria. You are well aware what I am capable of and what I can handle. I mean no disrespect, but I don't need anyone to soft-sell the truth. That solves nothing when everything my father worked for, what I've slaved over is being threatened. I will stop at nothing to ensure that those responsible will face my wrath."

A smile slowly crossed his face as he gave me a nod of respect. "Very well. First. Were you aware that your father was a member of this club?"

Chuckling softly, I closed my eyes. "Nothing will surprise me about my father's life."

His eyes darkened more than I thought possible, his smile waning. "Does the name Rizzo Valenti mean anything to you?"

"Only from what I've read online. A mob boss from New York?"

"He and his ancestors have controlled the Northeast for decades. They are powerful and they are vicious. And as you can imagine, they have many enemies who've challenged them over the years. Only one was successful in hurting the organization."

"Killing the patriarch."

"Yes, the killer managed to avoid Rizzo's soldiers, killing him with a single muffled shot while the man went to the toilet in a crowded restaurant."

I folded my hands together, exhaling. "Did anyone claim responsibility?"

"Yes, but mostly in their actions as they attempted to muscle in, taking over the Valenti territory. There was much bloodshed, my friend, as Luciano Gambini made his presence known. Rizzo's soldiers were able to keep Gambini from taking over, but the war between the families goes on to this day. Rizzo's soldiers hunted for the gunman, which they never found since no one on the street dared go against Gambini. His methods of inflicting his wrath were and still are… savage in nature."

"A fascinating story, Carlos, but if you don't mind, please get to the point."

"Patience, my friend. That is a virtue that you must learn. Before Rizzo's death, he gave his soldiers explicit instructions that would ensure his heirs had a kingdom to rule in case something should ever happen to him."

"Rizzo's children."

"Yes," Carlos stated, chuckling softly. "You see, the children were incapable of taking over his empire at the time, the preteens a product of the man marrying a very young second wife. However, the sins of the father are often placed on the shoulders of his offspring."

Bristling, I cocked my head. "An interesting choice of words, Carlos. They happen to be similar to ones I've received in several recent threats."

He narrowed his eyes, obviously irritated that I would consider accusing him of anything. "Be careful, Randolph. You are treading on thin ice."

"If there's one thing my father taught me that I will never forget, it's that I should never avoid the ice."

After a few seconds, his nostrils flared. "You have balls, my friend. Huge ones. Another reason I like you. What I'm trying to tell you is that Rizzo's children are all grown up and they are seeking revenge against all those who had anything to do with their father's death."

"Why are you telling me this?"

"Because your father was almost four million dollars in debt to Luciano Gambini for gambling in the man's casinos. The interest rate was eating him alive."

"Old news, Carlos. I know he took money from the company in order to pay that debt."

"That may be, but Luciano gave him an alternative, which it would appear your father took instead of draining his company funds."

"Which was?"

As Carlos reached for his coffee, the memory I'd lived with for over ten years came crashing down. But as he finished the rest of the story, the images became more intense.

The bloodstains.

The threats.

The brutal beating.

My father had succumbed to the darkness.

He'd become a hitman for the Gambini crime family.

* * *

Goddamn it.

I tossed the phone on the passenger seat, continuing to curse under my breath. The approaching storm had killed the reception. As I glared at the swirling black clouds, the first strike of lightning flashed across the sky. I'd never felt more on edge in my life.

All four of us were being toyed with by three powerful mafia princes, the bastards enjoying every second of making us sweat. Now that I knew who was responsible for the entire dark game, we would become the hunters, destroying everything near and dear to them.

My father had once told me he knew I was capable of murder. Well, he certainly knew what he was talking about. I yanked the weapon from the glove compartment, pressing down on the accelerator as I placed it on the seat beside me. I'd be forced to wait to make a call to our pilot until my return to the house, but as soon as it was possible, we would be returning to Pittsburg. We were far too exposed at the villa.

I veered around a steep corner, the tires screeching. My blood pressure was increasing, my heart racing fast enough it pulsed in my throat. I would do everything in my power to keep Scarlett safe. Jesus. Another crack of lightning flashed as thunder rumbled all around me. Rain had already started falling, making the faded lines on the dark and curvy road all but impossible to see.

As my thoughts drifted to what I should say to Scarlett or to my two partners for that matter, I noticed a pair of headlights behind me. The fucker was coming way too fast. It was probably a tourist who didn't know the road. Snarling, I twisted my hand around the steering wheel, furious that I'd allowed any of us to be fucked with.

When the driver continued creeping closer, my instinct kicked in. We'd been found. The game was almost over. I snapped my other hand around the steering wheel, doing everything I could to stay on the road. All I could think about was getting back to Scarlett. I continuously glanced into the mirror, finally able to catch a glimpse inside with the help of a series of lightning bolts.

The driver appeared to be the only one inside. I'd driven the damn stretch of road only once before, Carlos' estate perched far above the beaches, miles of land surrounding it. Anyone could have followed me, hiding in the lush terrain waiting for my departure. If I could get to the main road, I might be able to turn the tables. There was nothing else for me to do. I kept the pedal pressed to the floor, but the asshole was gaining quickly.

Shit. Shit!

After yanking my weapon into my lap, I was forced to slow in order to make the turn. That's the moment the unknown asshole decided to ram the back of my vehicle. When I stomped on the brakes, the momentum threw me into a three-sixty. The second I skidded to a stop, the motherfucker decided to come at me again. I threw a look over my shoulder, realizing a hundred foot drop-off was too close for comfort.

I wasted no time, jamming my foot down on the gas and lifting my weapon, a different flash catching my eye.

Pop! Pop!

As the force of the bullet threw me back against the seat, I lost control.

And all I could think about was Scarlett.

CHAPTER 14

 lexander

Storms.

I'd enjoyed them for as long as I could remember, especially the morning after, Mother Nature using the squalls to cleanse the earth. I had a feeling the approaching storm would be violent, the wind already whipping through the sand, the water turbulent. I stood in the doorway of the living room, studying Scarlett. She'd followed the rules, remaining on the property but moving to the very edge of the stone patio, staring out at the nearby ocean.

Just seeing the way the wind whipped through her copper locks, the odd lighting adding a shimmer was enough to keep my heartrate high. I'd sensed she'd grown closer to Randolph. While that's exactly what I'd wanted initially, I was no longer certain it was in her best interest to be involved with any of us.

Even though I wanted her more than I could dare admit to the others. I glanced at my watch, shaking my head as I realized Randolph had been gone for over almost two hours, heading out to visit with Carlos. While I didn't trust the Spaniard, his connections could help us find some answers. Sleep had evaded me the night before, my senses on high alert.

At least he'd provided weapons before leaving, the Glock positioned just under the waistband of my trousers. After watching her for a few more minutes, I walked outside, slowly heading in her direction, the rumble of thunder in the distance.

She didn't stiffen as normal, even when she darted her head toward me. "You look relaxed," she said breathlessly.

Her statement made me laugh. "I'm anything but relaxed."

"I understand. Where did Randolph go?"

"To a meeting."

"With this person who owns the Clubhouse. Right?"

"Yes, but not for the reason you might be thinking. Besides, I'm not in favor of taking you to one of the events." I glanced at the sky, the clouds already becoming darker. Something about this storm bothered me.

"Are you certain he's not developing another level to this game?"

I had to laugh. She still didn't trust us, which I couldn't blame her for. "The game has taken a different turn. I doubt we'll be continuing."

"Does that mean I won?"

"Maybe this round." I had no idea why there was sadness lacing my voice.

Scarlett turned to face me, her arms folded. "Then who is this man and why is meeting with him so important?"

"He's someone who can find answers. That's exactly what we need at this point."

"About who's threatening our companies."

I nodded as I walked closer, brushing hair from her eyes. At least she didn't flinch from my touch. "Yes. I think it's become very clear that there's another game being played. It can't continue."

"I agree with you. Can I ask his name?"

I debated telling her but at this point, I didn't see any reason not to. "His name is Carlos Santiago. He knows certain people who can help us." That is if the man was willing to do so. He didn't take kindly to favors being asked. I knew that personally. I'd used up the only one he would ever provide, the man keeping me from being arrested after a fantasy had gone very wrong. I gritted my teeth, doing what I could to push aside the ugly memory.

There was a flash in her eyes as if she recognized the name. "His father is a powerful mafioso in Spain. Right?"

I couldn't help but laugh by seeing her expression. "You've investigated everyone."

"I enjoy reading about true crime but yes, the key to success is knowledge."

"You fascinate me, Scarlett. You have such tenacity and verve for life. I used to be that way, but after a while, long hours change everything."

"Then don't allow it to a moment longer. Life is far too short." Her soft lilt drove a stake straight through my heart. I hated what we'd already put her through.

When she touched my arm, I couldn't hold back a growl. "Be careful, Scarlett. I'm not a good man. I think you've already realized that."

"And I think all three of you are hiding behind your power. Maybe it just takes the right woman."

"As I said, be very careful. I could change your life forever."

Scarlett took a deep breath, darting a glance at the ocean. "What if I wouldn't mind? What if I need something different in my life? All I've ever done is work."

I pulled her into my arms, wrapping my hand around her neck. "Woman. What I could do to you now and for weeks to come."

She pressed her hands against my chest, clutching my shirt and tilting her head. "Just weeks?"

There was such an intensity about her today as well as a letting go, which surprised the hell out of me. I pulled her even closer, pressing my lips against hers. As I brushed them back and forth, she shuddered audibly, darting out her tongue and swirling the tip around my lips. The taste of her was even more disturbing than before, my desire roaring to the surface. I wasn't a patient man by any means and on this day, my entire body ached to take her right here and right now.

Unable to hold back, I crushed my mouth over hers, thrusting my tongue inside. Nothing else seemed to matter around us as I held her in my arms, allowing myself to enjoy the moment. She moaned into the kiss, the sultry sounds echoing in my ears. Everything about her reeked of passion, bringing out the darkness deep inside of me. She reminded me that I hadn't enjoyed living in a very long time. That needed to change. After all, she was right.

Life was far too damn short.

When I broke the kiss, I smoothed down her hair, sensing a slight tension had returned between us. I backed away, giving her space. I wanted more than the game. Trent was right.

It was time to settle down, to savor aspects of living I'd forgotten.

She exhaled, slowly turning her head toward the water. "I always loved the ocean, even though I only got to see one a couple of times while I lived with my parents. My father was just too busy to take us on vacation. I think he would have liked this place."

"He's no longer alive?"

"No. He's been dead for a couple of years."

"I'm sorry," I said quietly. There was a difference about her, as if she was more content than before. The sky was lit up as lightning flashed in the distance.

"I've come to terms with what happened to him. Sometimes it's hard since he was my rock, the one who encouraged me to follow my dreams. I could crush the person responsible for his death."

"Do you mind if I ask what happened?"

She seemed flushed after I asked the question, her lower lip quivering. "He was murdered coming out of a casino doing what he loved."

My jaw clenched. There were too many coincidences about who he was and how he died. "There's nothing worse than losing someone you love. It takes away a piece of your heart."

"I know but I'm a survivor. My father taught me to be very strong." She narrowed her eyes, pressing two fingers over her mouth for a few seconds. "You lost someone. Didn't you?"

"Haven't we all?"

When she inched even closer, the surge of electricity was exactly as before, pushing me into another realm. While I wanted to devour her, my job was to provide protection at this point. I only hoped Randolph was successful in finding decent information. I didn't like being in a foreign country given the circumstances.

"But you lost someone that was very special to you. I can see it in your eyes." She was shivering, but I doubted it was only from the chill of the wind.

The near tragedy was never far from my mind, one of the reasons I'd forgone indulging in another fantasy. "What happened is in my past."

"But it affects you today."

"Yes, it does. The past shapes everything about our future."

"Let's just say that a fantasy went too far, allowing someone who trusted me to be hurt. I can never allow that to happen again."

"Then don't."

The two words were so simple.

And I hated that I couldn't share the entire story with her. "I need to make a few phone calls. You will remain right here. Correct?"

"Where could I go? Look at the gorgeous beach that I have all to myself. Why would I go anywhere?"

"Don't get caught in the rain," I said with a commanding voice.

"Maybe rain will wash away my sins."

As I backed away, I realized that when I'd shut down my heart two years before, promising I'd never care about anyone again, I'd lost a part of myself. Somehow, Scarlett had awakened not only the hunger but the need to share an entirely different portion of my life.

Only at this point, I was no longer certain if that was possible.

She continued looking at me until I turned around and for some reason, I had a bad feeling swirling in the back of my mind.

The danger wasn't just coming from another source. The real threat was coming from within, our hunger for power stripping away a portion of our humanity.

One or the other just might get us killed.

After walking inside, I stood by the window for a full two minutes before walking away, heading toward the office. I found Trent inside, obviously angry about something, glaring at the laptop.

"What the hell is going on?" I demanded, trying to drag my thoughts away from Scarlett.

"I just received notification that additional stocks changed hands. The share was much larger than before. In addition, I can't get ahold of two of our major stockholders. One is on vacation and out of range, at least according to his secretary. The other has... disappeared. How does a fucking millionaire disappear?"

"Easily, Trent. What's bothering you even more?"

"Everything is bothering me, Alexander, for God's sake. We need to get a handle on this and Randolph had decided to trust a man like Carlos. So, I decided to take matters into my own hands and warn as many of the larger stockholders that a storm is brewing."

The storm wasn't just brewing. It was already here.

"Just take a look at what I'm talking about," he barked.

"What the hell are you talking about?" I huffed as I took long strides toward the computer and swiveled it around. "Shit."

"And you damn well know who just purchased it. This is getting out of hand."

I took a deep breath. "And the stockholder?"

"Jack Marshall. He was good friends with Sampson, helping him find seed money. He's held onto his shares since the day Sampson took them public. He left for his office this morning and never arrived."

I hissed at the several red flags that had been raised. "You're right. We need to make contact with as many as possible."

Trent slammed his hand on the desk. "What in God's name is going on, Alex?"

"We will find out. Somehow."

A full hour had passed. Fortunately, only Jack was still unattainable, but at least the others had been warned they would be approached. So far, none of the ones we talked to had been. However, it was only a matter of time until they were.

What bothered me even more is that Randolph should have gotten back by now. Two phone calls had resulted in dead air given the storm. It was raining fucking cats and dogs outside, the sky almost completely black.

"I don't like this," Trent said as he stared out the window.

"Yeah, I know. I'm going to make certain Scarlett is settled. And I'm going to check all the locks as well as the security system."

"You're that worried?"

"I've had a bad feeling for hours. We no longer have control of the game that's being played. If Randolph's father was involved with criminal activity, owing money to God knows who, then they will want it back."

"Now?" Trent huffed.

"Right now," Randolph said as he entered the room. He glanced from one of us to the other. There was a haunted look in his eyes, and I could swear he'd aged by several years.

He was also bleeding.

"What the hell happened?" Trent snarled. "We need to get you to a hospital."

"I had a special surprise waiting after I left Carlos' estate," Randolph said. "Fortunately, it's just a flesh wound."

"And the assailant?" I asked under my breath. Things were getting out of control.

"Let's just say he's swimming with the fishes," Randolph said, laughing darkly. "I need to call the pilot. We're getting out of here right now. I know exactly what we're dealing with."

"Then talk. Whoever that asshole was, you know he's not alone." I no longer cared how demanding my tone of voice sounded. I refused to be caught in the middle of this bullshit any longer.

He moved closer, although his actions were stiff. "No, I would guess you're right. My father made a deal with a devil named Luciano Gambini, a kingpin who was attempting to take over New Jersey and other territory from another powerful mafioso family. Gambini also owed several casinos, one of them a location my father went to gamble, losing millions of dollars. A special deal was offered to him. To have his debts erased, all he had to do was kill a rival mafia leader. And he did."

"What?" Trent exclaimed, tossing me a glance. "Why the hell would he resort to something that drastic?"

"Because he was pressured, my mother's life threatened if he didn't. Because he owed a significant amount of money. And because he felt he had no other choice. That's why he took his own life just before I took over the company, because he couldn't face what had occurred all those years before and what he'd done to our family."

I tried to absorb what he was telling me, but certain aspects didn't make a damn bit of sense.

"Wait a minute. Who is seeking revenge after all this time? I don't understand, Randolph," I huffed.

"The sons of the man my father killed are seeking revenge. Somehow, they finally found out my father was the shooter. They've spent over two years hunting down everyone involved. And exterminating them."

I'd never seen Randolph fail at anything nor had I seen him admit a single weakness. Today, he seemed like a beaten man. "Jesus. That's why an attempt was made on your life."

"Likely since it would seem they are moving into the final stages of their game. The Valenti children want to destroy everything my father touched, including his business. "

"What about your mother?" Trent asked.

"She's living in Washington State, but I will need to warn her." Randolph pulled off his jacket, tossing the bloody garment away. "I need to see Scarlett."

"Scarlett is fine," I told him. "Finish the story."

"It would seem the Valenti brothers are trying to go legitimate, at least according to Carlos. However, another soldier will attempt to end my life as well as anyone I care about," Randolph sneered, his resolve kicking in. He yanked his weapon into his hand, removing the safety. "I will kill the bastards before I allow that to happen."

"Take it easy, Randolph," I encouraged.

"Fuck this. We need to make certain Scarlett remains by our sides at all times." Trent walked toward the door.

"Agreed, but there's more," Randolph said. "You need to fully understand the ramifications of what we've done and the danger we've placed Scarlett in."

As he told the last of the story, my blood boiled, my heart racing.

"Sins of the father," he whispered.

"Damn your games, Randolph. No more." I stormed out of the room, jogging down the stairs to the living room. There's no way she would have remained outside. When I couldn't find her anywhere on the first floor, I threw open the door, hissing from the whipping wind as I moved onto the deck. My gut told me something was wrong. I scanned the area, taking deep breaths. Then I rushed back inside. "Scarlett. Where are you?"

"What's wrong?" Trent asked, Randolph flanking his side.

"I can't find her," I barked, racing toward the stairs, taking them two at a time. "Scarlett! Don't do this." Every room was empty. By the time I headed toward the third floor, Randolph had already beaten me to it, coming out of one of the rooms, raking his hands through his hair.

"Where the hell is she?" he demanded.

"She was outside before the storm rolled in." I bolted down the stairs, flying outside and onto the beach.

"I thought you said she was fine. Find her," Randolph yelled as he took off in one direction.

"He's losing it," Trent snarled.

"Yeah? Well, maybe the man has a right to. We need to find her."

I took off jogging, heading in the opposite direction, barely able to control my breathing, seeing anything almost impossible from the swirling sand, but something caught my attention. There was something strange about the sand. What I found was horrifying.

"Scarlett," I whispered as I yanked one of her shoes from the wet sand.

"What the hell?" Trent appeared from behind me, yanking the shoe out of my hand.

As the wind howled all around us, I threw back my head and roared. Scarlett was gone, taken and I had a terrible feeling I'd never see her again.

* * *

Scarlett

Bzzzz...

The sound. A rumble. A…

Shifting, I tried to open my eyes but the second I did, pain slammed against my head, the agony enough I had to fight to keep from retching. Everything was foggy, like I'd been shoved inside a vacuum. What the hell had happened?

I issued a single moan, my throat so dry and tight the sound was garbled. Everything in my body hurt.

My legs.

My arms.

My head.

A dream. This had to be a horrible dream.

"She's awake." The voice was foreign to me, unrecognizable, but it jolted me into consciousness.

"That's to be expected. We'll be back in la-la land in a few." The deep laugh held a tone of evil intent.

A second voice. Panic settled in and I forced myself to open my eyes, ignoring the agony. There was nothing but darkness all around me. I shifted again, finally realizing my wrists and ankles had been tied. Oh, my God. No. No. Struggling, another moan escaped my mouth.

Suddenly, a bright light was flashed into my eyes, forcing me to wince. I flopped from one side to the other, fighting with whatever was keeping me from moving.

"Just calm the fuck down. I don't want to be forced to gag you, but I honestly don't give a shit at this point."

The first asshole was talking to me. I glanced away, trying to remember anything about what had happened. I'd defied orders, taking a walk on the beach. The storm had come on fast and I was heading back. Then... Someone approached from behind and...

Something was stuck into my arm. They'd drugged me.

Oh, God. Oh, God!

I took gasping breaths, refusing to cry. That wouldn't do me any good.

"What are you going to do with me?" My mouth was like cotton. I wasn't entirely certain the words made any sense.

"Whatever we're told."

Who the hell were these two goons?

"Who are you? Where are you taking me?"

"Can you shut the bitch up?" the second guy asked. He was obviously in front. That's when I realized I was in a vehicle. The engine rumbled beneath me.

"Don't call her a bitch. The three princes wouldn't like it," the first asshole said.

Princes? That's what I'd called the men of Worth. A sick feeling pooled in my stomach.

"I don't give a shit. I don't want to listen to her babbling the rest of the trip."

Trip. That meant I'd been taken away from Cancun. By boat? By plane? It was dark outside, which meant I'd been out for an extended period of time. Or maybe days had passed.

Finally, the jerk pulled the light away. I tried to move, realizing my back was against hard steel. I was trapped in a van. Shivering, I fought to keep from crying, hating the series of emotions racing through me.

Terror.

Anger.

Confusion.

Pain.

Who the hell were they?

"Let me go, you bastards. I don't know who you are, but you have no right to keep me." Why was I bothering to argue for my freedom? That was never going to happen, yet I refused to give up.

A hand was wrapped around my throat within seconds. As something sharp was pressed against my throat, I whimpered.

"Just shut the hell up and you'll be alright," the first asshole said under his breath. Maybe he didn't want his buddy to hear him give a damn about me. "I don't want to cut you."

No, he didn't give a shit.

Oh, God. Oh...

"Can I have... some water?" Now my damn teeth were chattering.

He snuffed then pulled the knife away. "Yeah, I guess that'll be alright. Just don't try anything stupid. I haven't cut a woman in days."

If he was trying to terrify me, it was working. I leaned my head against the van, praying Alexander, Trent, or Randolph knew I'd been kidnapped. Then a horrible thought shifted into my system. What if they were the ones to blame? Would they do this to me? No, they wouldn't. This was... this wasn't just part of the game. Was it?

"Here. Drink it nice and slow." The asshole's gruff hand grabbed my jaw, squeezing until I opened my mouth. As water was poured inside, I sucked down some, collecting more then spitting it into his face.

"Jesus."

The hard slap against my face and jaw was excruciating, my head slamming against the floor as I went down with a hard thud.

"Just knock her out again," the second asshole said.

"Yeah. I think I'm going to do that. Don't worry, little pet. This is only a fantasy."

As the needle was jammed into my arm, I could see their faces inside my mind. The three men I thought I cared about.

The same three men I thought might be falling in love with me.

But it was all just a game.

A freaking, horrible… game.

CHAPTER 15

 andolph

"Who needs the dark ambiance of night when nightmares can collapse you in broad daylight?"

Kaulab Basu

Nightmares.

I'd had them for years on and off, the kind that always forced me awake from my deep slumber drenched in sweat. Sadly, the images that had fractured my mind were ones that could come true. I slammed my hand on the surface of my desk, trying to shake the sickening feeling that I'd never see Scarlett again. Snorting, I closed my eyes. That *we'd* never see her again. Both Trent and Alexander were fueled only by the anger ravaging their systems.

It had been two days since her disappearance. Since her abduction. I knew the names of the monsters who'd taken her, the three assholes seeking revenge for something that had occurred over a damn decade before.

Only they'd disappeared from the face of the earth.

However, I refused to allow the fuckers to hide from us. We would find them.

"Son, I'll give you one last piece of advice before you take the helm."

I studied my father's thin face, allowing my gaze to fall to his frail body. He'd aged so much over the last two years as if the life had been sucked out of him. "Okay. What is that, Father?"

"You must be prepared to do anything in order to survive."

"I'm not sure what that means."

He smiled, the light I'd no longer seen in his eyes shining for a few seconds before returning to a dull emptiness.

"You'll know, my boy. You will know without question. Don't follow your heart. Follow your instinct."

That's where my father had been wrong. If he had followed his heart, his world wouldn't have crumbled around him. And he wouldn't have taken his own life. Maybe in his sick mind he thought he was protecting his family. Thank God my mother was safe, heeding my encouragement to go stay with an aunt I'd rarely seen for a couple of weeks.

At least I'd taken out one of the assholes. The thought made my mouth water. Maybe everyone was capable of crossing the thin line of right versus wrong if necessary. How had we been found? There'd been too many opportunities from the pilot to one of our assistants. There was no way of knowing.

Another threat had been made and I had no doubt in the dark reaches of my mind that it was the final one. Half laughing, I stared at the screen before pushing my computer away. The email from a bogus account was nothing more than an invitation. If I accepted, they would put a bullet in my brain.

Two more major stockholders had disappeared. Even worse had been the phone call I'd received early in the morning. Jack was dead, his bullet-ridden body found along the banks of a river. They wanted a clear warning sent. Sadly, Jack had sold his stock prior to his murder. The Valenti family now owned fourteen percent. It was only a matter of time before the others were forced into doing the same thing. Then we'd be fucked.

There was no knock on the door, no announcement of entrance. Just the two men I trusted the most coming through my office door.

"Did you see the news this morning?" Alexander asked.

I glanced at him, not bothering to answer.

"There was a horrific fire in one of the Gambini casinos. Several people had died, including one of the sons who ran the place. It would seem the Valenti family was cleaning house."

Cleaning house. They'd waited, collecting evidence and eliminating low level players over the past few years. While there might not be any rhyme or reason to their extended wait, I didn't care. What the hell did any of it matter any longer? Money meant nothing. My possessions meant nothing.

I'd give them all away to ensure Scarlett's safety.

But in my heart, I knew that was an unlikely possibility.

They would kill her for no other reason than the fact we loved her.

Love.

Jesus.

"They are finalizing their plans," I said after a few seconds, heading toward my laptop.

"Meaning what?" Alexander asked.

A smile crossed my face as I shifted the computer in their direction. After reading the email, Alexander bristled.

"Time to die? Really? And an address?" he asked, mocking the few words on the screen.

"It would appear we no longer have to be on a wild goose chase." I was surprised how hungry I was for the taste of blood.

"This is getting outrageous," Trent snarled, planting his hands on my desk and glaring at the screen. The look in his eyes likely matched my own. Haunted. Enraged.

Murderous.

I would kill the motherfuckers with my bare hands.

"It would seem Carlos doesn't need to provide another favor," Alexander growled, obvious disdain in his voice. He looked haggard as if he hadn't slept since her disappearance.

Little did they know the hefty sum I'd already paid to employ his men in our search and rescue mission. Even then, Carlos had made certain I understand in frank terms that I would owe him and one day he would collect. I didn't give a shit. They could keep the money. It meant little to me any longer.

"Yes, it would seem that way," I hissed. We couldn't go to law enforcement. As soon as the Valentis noticed a police presence, they'd kill Scarlett.

Trent shook his head, his eyes boring into mine. "This is a trap."

"Of course it is, but she'll be there. They will want to make certain we understand their power, taking something valuable away from us." My tone was flat, as if there was nothing left inside of me. But there was. It was called rage.

"Let's go through the damn details again," Alexander suggested.

"We've been over it a thousand times," I retorted. "I'm not certain it will help any longer."

"Do it again." Alexander cocked his head, his chest heaving.

I rubbed my eyes, taking scattered breaths. "My father made some bad investments, hedging his losses by believing he would win two lucrative contracts. But the patents hadn't come through and he lost both. That sent him into a spiral. What had once been a hobby of gambling for recreation turned into attempting to win back what he'd lost. Only he was a horrible poker player, even though one of his good friends tried to teach him everything he knew."

A good friend. A man who knew the industry and the pitfalls. A knot formed in my stomach.

Trent exhaled, fisting his hands. He'd fallen the hardest for Scarlett and I had no doubt he would never forgive me for initiating the game. I bit back a laugh. Had I known the goddamn circumstances, I would never have been so fucking stupid. Or was I just like my father?

"Go on," Alexander said through clenched teeth.

Trent continued to glare at me, his question terse. "How the hell did your damn father get mixed up with the Gambini family in the first place?"

"He was gambling in their casino and asked for a line of credit. But he couldn't make up the difference. They made him an offer of how he could get out of his debt, but he fought that demon for weeks until he felt he had no other choice. I don't know any additional details, for fuck's sake. I'm going off what Carlos told me."

"And what you learned the night your father returned after murdering a human being." Alexander half smiled.

"Fine," I snapped, jerking away from the desk. "Yes, I snooped in his damn office after he went to clean off the blood. I found the promissory note he'd been forced to sign from the casino, but I didn't understand the true meaning. I just knew he owed a hell of a lot of money. I thought he'd been beaten because of it and nothing more."

Fuck. The tension was so damn high.

"Are you certain about that?" Alexander asked quietly.

I closed my eyes, my mind a damn blur of images and words my father had said. "I'm not certain of anything except that Scarlett is being held against her will because of me. Because of me."

The silence was almost deafening.

"Because of all three of us," Trent finally said. "We agreed to the wager."

"If this is a trap, we don't have any backup," Alexander stated after a full two minutes had passed.

"No, but we also have no other choice." I moved closer, staring him in the eyes.

My buddies were right. This was a trap, a maze so complicated that no one could solve it. We were all playing a dangerous game. However, it was time to risk the entire hand.

This time we couldn't lose.

"We make a visit to the location. After that, we claim what belongs to us," I said with more conviction than I believed.

"And after that?" Trent asked, lifting his head as his eyes darted back and forth.

"Then we eliminate our problem."

My father had been the one to tell me that everyone could cross the line, the thin mark of good versus evil. He'd laughed after sharing that with me, patting me on the shoulder and reminding me to be a good boy always and the world would fall at my feet. I'd learned that wasn't entirely the case, that I had to have a thick skin, no emotions and no care for anyone else. If and when I did, I would lose sight of my goal.

I'd been indoctrinated into his world, enjoying all the spoils of the win. The price had been devastating.

"We will save her," Trent murmured. "It doesn't matter what needs to be done. Do you hear me?"

"Agreed," Alexander said gruffly.

As Alexander turned his heated gaze in my direction, neither one of us needed words. All three of us would cross that thin line, becoming capable of doing anything necessary in order to get her back.

In order to bring her home.

If selling our souls to the devil meant saving her life, then so be it.

* * *

Scarlett

Cold.

I was so cold my teeth were chattering. I remained curled in a ball, the small cot providing little in the way of comfort. At least I had a thin blanket, a flat pillow, but that was the only comfort I'd been allowed. Why had this happened to me? Why had I been taken? I had no way of knowing how long I'd been in this ugly room, but at least two or three full days. Three days of being tormented with ugly words. Three days of nasty soldiers leering at me. Where had I been taken? I'd say the cement floors and ceiling indicated some kind of warehouse, but I wasn't certain of anything any longer. Whoever had captured me had turned it into a glorified cage.

This couldn't be a fantasy.

If so, the men involved with the Clubhouse were sick, demented individuals. I threw back the scratchy cover, stretching my aching legs then placing them on the frigid, hard floor as I stared down at the chain wrapped around both my wrists. Then I followed the thick piece of steel with my eyes, wincing when I realized it was attached to the wall with a thick eyebolt. I was going nowhere. The assholes had even removed my shoes. I rubbed my arms before attempting to stand, swaying several times in my attempt to get my balance. The bare bulb hanging from the ceiling did little to light the area, but enough I was forced to realize I'd been placed in prison-like confinement.

The only noise I heard was the churning of some apparatus, maybe a heating and cooling unit over my head. I remained shaken to my core, trying to keep from losing my shit. That wouldn't do me any good. In my haze, I remembered two men who'd dragged me from the beach, forcing a dark hood over my head.

But almost everything was foggy after that.

Except for the sound of their voices.

Those I would never forget.

A fantasy.

They'd called me a pet, just like... just like Randolph, Alexander, and Trent had done on numerous occasions. Bile formed in my throat from the thought that they were behind my abduction. Where the hell was I? Why would they do this to me?

I inched toward the window, rising onto my toes to try to see out of the dirty surface. All I was able to catch a glimpse of was gray sky and what appeared to be the side of the building I was in. If only I could remember any other details, but it was impossible.

Shrinking back, I backed against the cement wall, struggling with so many emotions. I'd allowed myself to trust the three men who'd won me in a wager. I'd opened a portion of my heart to them, asking for almost nothing in return but the truth. And they'd lied and used me. A single tear slipped past my lashes, trickling down the side of my face. I'd never felt such agony before, and it was all internally. I'd been so strong all my life, but I felt a part of me fading away, no longer certain of the bright future I'd planned for myself.

No one was coming to save me. No one would ever care that I was missing.

I slid down the wall, holding my head in my hands, fighting the sobs building in my chest. The building seemed to be alive, creaking and shifting beneath my feet. Somewhere water was trickling, escaping its prison in a way I couldn't escape mine. I was envious of a natural element, which almost made me laugh. Maybe I was already starting to lose my mind, days and nights meshing together.

This is just a game. It'll be over soon.

I wasn't certain I could trust my little voice any longer.

Then I heard a clattering noise, the sound of metal being clanged. Someone was coming through the steel door. As I jerked my head up, I took several shallow breaths, lightheaded from fear.

Then the door opened.

The soldiers were coming again to dump what little food and water they allowed me. I bristled, wanting nothing more than to find a way to escape. Maybe I could find a way to play a game of my own.

Then they walked inside.

Three men, only they weren't soldiers. I knew exactly who they were, the cowards finally showing their faces.

Three bastards.

Three… monsters.

"Hello, little pet. How do you like your new home?"

The voice was dark and husky, the three sons of bitches remaining in the shadows. But seconds later, they gave up their charade, moving under the ugly light. I moved to a standing position, keeping my head held high even though I was shaking like a leaf.

All three were carrying weapons, and as I glared from one to the other, a strange moment of sheer joy swept through me.

I'd been wrong.

I'd never seen their ugly, horrible faces before.

A moment of elation swept through me. Was it possible the three men I'd fallen so hard for might still be alive? Maybe they would rescue me after all.

Or maybe they were already dead.

"Who are you?" I managed, my throat so tight I had difficulty breathing. "Why am I here?"

"I guess you deserve to know that," the first man said. "I'm Mario Valenti. The two men behind me are my brothers Gio and Salvatore. As far as why you're here. You were just a delicious part of a game."

"A game? Why?" Why did their names ring a bell to me?

"Because you are part of the reason our father was murdered in cold blood."

"I... I don't understand." I glared at Mario, trying to put the pieces of the puzzle together.

Gio chuckled as he inched closer, darting his gaze down the length of me. "Your father was an excellent card player, but a terrible teacher. Unfortunately, he was unable to teach Randolph Worth's father how to keep a straight face. So he lost time and time again."

"I don't understand." What the hell were they talking about? I thought about what Randolph had said days before. His father had lost money, a lot of money.

Gambling. Was it possible he'd sought advice from my dad? Nothing made any sense. Then I remembered why I knew their names. A mafia war between two families. I'd read about the two crime syndicates years before, the blood that had been shed over the murder of... Oh, my God.

"Because of Sampson Worth's losses, he was allowed to pay back his debt another way, by murdering our father."

As small pieces of the puzzle started to fall together, I lunged forward, the horror of facing my past almost too much to bear. "You murdered my father because he couldn't teach Sampson how to play well enough to win. You're crazy. You're disgusting." This was insane. They'd harbored the need for revenge for years. Years!

All three of them laughed, Mario answering. "Yes, we did, but that was just the beginning of the game. And, sweet Scarlett, you're our greatest prize."

Trent

Romance.

My mother had been the great romantic, indulging in novel after novel in her mental search for the perfect romance while my father had worked sixteen-hour days as a surgeon. I'd never thought of myself as amorous, my first taste of a kink club becoming an indulgence I couldn't avoid. But everything had changed over the last few days. I'd actually seen myself as I'd described to Alexander, able to settle down, perhaps even consider raising a family.

But the only person who could fit into what many considered to be a self-indulgent life was Scarlett.

My insides continued to churn at the thought of losing her, although even if we managed to save her, it was doubtful she would ever consider becoming a fourth in our jaded friendship, let alone a family. However, I could still dream like some wayward boy with a crush.

All three of us remained on edge, the drive to the location without incident, but then again, we knew it would be. This was all another layer of their charade, grandstanding as they gained more and more power. From what little I remembered reading about the family years before, the Consigliere, a close friend and confidant of Rizzo Valenti had protected the boys after the patriarch's death. If I had to guess, I'd say he'd groomed the boys into becoming just like their father.

Why the game had been concocted we might never know, but the end of the charade involved an entirely different level of destruction.

Including taking something precious from us.

Scarlett.

The sky was gray, the air chilly, and the building in front of us had seen better days.

We were powerful men, the kind of people considered vile and ruthless. However, what we were facing wasn't the kind of challenge we'd fought and won before. The world of robotics wasn't traditionally dangerous, yet here we were prepared to enter what appeared to be an abandoned building in search of someone we cared about.

However, our world wasn't without danger, the need for protection often necessary. That included all three of us keeping weapons in strategic locations in the offices, our vehicles, and our homes. My father had taught me to shoot when I'd reached the ripe old age of twelve. At least he'd taught me the importance of how to handle a weapon when necessary. And what few people knew is that all of us had been required to brandish one more than once.

This was an entirely different situation.

Everything had changed for us, retaliation weighing heavily on our minds.

I stood in front of the other two, staring up at the building. The Valenti family had purchased several warehouses in Pennsylvania, New Jersey, and New York over the course of several months. If Carlos had provided decent information, the crime syndicate was planning on using them for drug running, expanding their operations into other states.

I couldn't give a shit what they did for their livelihood. All I cared about was saving Scarlett. No matter the outcome, she didn't deserve what she was facing. We were in the industrial section of the city, only blocks away from Club Velvet. There were cars lining every street, abandoned parking lots used for the half dozen bars that had sprung up over the last few years.

We said nothing as we entered the building, the side door unlocked as we knew it would be.

Randolph entered first, remaining silent as he moved through the downstairs, Alexander and I trailing behind him. We found nothing of use other than stacks of chemicals known for use in processing heroin. In another location, I could swear

I heard water dripping, the slow and easy manner the trickles were splashing against the floor only adding to the rage churning in my stomach.

The only other noise was the scuttling of rats, several racing away from our presence. Hissing, I scanned the area, motioning toward the set of stairs near the back wall. All three of us remained silent as we headed toward them.

The second and third floors were empty. The fuckers were baiting us.

"Get to the roof. There's no other place," Randolph snarled.

He bounded up the last remaining stairs, both Alexander and I following closely behind. As we burst through the door leading to the roof, a sick sense of dread rushed into my mind.

Then we heard a woman's cry.

Scarlett…

 *carlett*

As soon as I got off a single shot, the gun was knocked out of my hand, the booming sound I'd just heard echoing in my ears. I was tossed to the ground, Mario pinning my arms over my head. I struggled with him, doing everything I could to kick as I pitched my body back and forth.

Pop! Pop! Pop!

Pop! Pop! Pop!

Gunshots peppered all around me, but I was unable to see anything. What the hell was happening?

"No, you don't, sweetheart," Mario's growl sounded in my ears and seconds later, he managed to jerk me to my feet. "Oh, look. Your saviors are trying to rescue you. Too bad that's not going to happen. They will die here today, just like we wanted. Won't it be nice for you to see all three of them take their last breaths? Or will you die first? I haven't decided yet."

My God. This had just been another part of the game.

I managed to pummel my fists against him, but he swung me around like a ragdoll, forcing me to face the carnage.

"No! No!" I caught sight of Alexander's face just before he was shot, that he seemed to fall in slow motion. Where was Trent? What the hell had happened to Randolph? When I noticed Trent wrestling with one of the soldiers, I sucked in my breath.

Mario pulled me closer, dragging me toward the edge of the building.

"Let go of me!" I hissed, darting my eyes back and forth.

Pop!

The single shot came from where Trent was positioned, both men now on the ground. *Please, God. Don't let him be dead. Please.*

Hissing, Mario pressed the barrel of his weapon against the side of my neck.

Trent rose to his feet, a gun planted in both hands. When he noticed I was being held, he jerked to a stop. "Let her go, you son of a bitch."

Mario laughed, enjoying every second of this. Trent gave me an imploring look and I could almost read his mind, his expression one of anguish as well as rage.

Where was Randolph? My mind was a blur, my vision foggy as tears continued to fall. Every part of me was shaking.

When Mario jerked me another foot I yelped, managing to wiggle enough I pulled out of his grasp, but not for long, his arm slapping around my throat.

"You will be punished for that, little pet."

"Not so fast, Mario."

Randolph.

His voice was like sweet music, the tone dark and laced with anger. I managed a slight smile from seeing his face, his handsome, chiseled face. I continued scanning the area, realizing that the other two captors had disappeared. Alexander was still lying on the ground. No. No! He couldn't be dead. He couldn't be. They had to be surrounded. The Valentis wouldn't allow any of us to leave alive.

At least two of the three soldiers were down, but there was a third, the one I'd managed to knock out after the asshole had bought my cries of help. I'd taken what I knew would be my one chance to get away, grabbing his keys and unlocking my chains then racing away from the sounds of the other guards and onto the roof. But he would be back. So would others.

"Well, well. You finally arrived," Mario said as he continued to hold me. "We thought you'd never follow our directions." When Gio and Salvatore flanked Trent and Randolph's sides, I bit back a whimper.

The handsome men I'd fallen in love with weren't killers. They weren't…

"They're dangerous men, Scarlett, capable of doing anything."

As Marjorie's words floated into my mind, I realized all I could do was pray she was right.

"You will let her go, Mario. Your revenge is meant for me alone," Randolph stated with no inflection in his voice.

"Quite the contrary. Our little pet's father was intricately involved. But you already know that. Don't you?" Mario asked, laughing as if this was nothing but a joke.

Randolph cocked his head, a sneer crossing his face, but he said nothing.

"Yes, Carlos. And you thought you could trust him. Tsk. Tsk. You failed again. You will pay the price for what your father did. Sins of the father and all. But first, you're going to suffer." When Mario dragged me closer to the edge, everything seemed to fall into slow motion.

With guns pointed at both Trent and Randolph, I knew there was nothing they could do. When I was dragged onto the ledge, I closed my eyes, and all I could think about was how much I loved the three men who'd come to my rescue. If only things could be different. If only…

"Say goodbye, little pet," Mario whispered before kissing my cheek. When he shifted, prepared to toss me off the edge, I dug my fingers into his arm.

Then I heard another bellowing cry.

Alexander. He lunged forward, lifting his weapon.

As shots were fired, Mario growled, pushing me even further. And the look in his eyes was pure evil.

With another slight shove, I lost my footing, my hold on Mario's arm slipping. As I started to fall, I kept images of the three men I adored in the front of my mind.

Pop! Pop! Pop! Pop!

Just seconds before I was shaken free of the monster holding me, a pair of hands grabbed my wrists and Mario was jerked away from me. He was bleeding from the mouth, gurgling as he continued to claw at my arm. Then he was knocked away by Trent's weapon. A single cry erupted from my lips, tears sliding down both cheeks. They'd saved me. They'd...

"Hold on, baby. Just hold on."

All time stopped as I locked eyes with Randolph as he eased me over the ledge.

Suddenly, my other two heroes were leaning over, all three men pulling me to safety. Randolph tumbled backwards, cradling me in his arms.

"You're safe now. You're safe," Alexander muttered, wrapping his fingers around mine.

"And nothing will ever happen to you again," Trent added.

My mind was a blur, my heart aching.

Revenge.

Wealth.

Power.

Love.

They were all powerful, but only one mattered. I'd finally found the missing piece of my heart. But would it ever be enough to ease the pain?

* * *

One week later

A tropical island.

All three of my saviors had insisted that they take me away, allowing me time to heal. All four of us needed that time, the events of only a week before still creating nightmares. I stood on the deck of another gorgeous villa, this one owned by Alexander, but my heart remained heavy even though the time we'd spent together had been amazing.

Passionate.

Fulfilling.

Relaxing.

Romantic, which had surprised me the most.

But I couldn't stop thinking about what had occurred, my father dying because he and Sampson Worth had been friends.

Alexander had been shot, but the bullet had gone straight through his shoulder. I found it difficult to get over the fact he could have been killed. I shuddered as visions of being on that roof entered my mind. Maybe one day I could finally sleep without horrible nightmares.

Maybe.

All three men had experienced painful pasts, not just because of business. All three had cared for someone individually, only to destroy their relationships with their sadistic needs. Even though they'd found talking about their experiences difficult, they'd opened up more than I ever would have imagined, sharing both the good and the bad times in their pasts.

In turn, I'd done the same thing. Confessing our sins and our sadness had seemed to make us closer.

And we'd laughed.

And we'd indulged in wine, food, and delicious fucking.

An electric boost shot through every cell in my body just thinking about the heated passion.

When I felt a presence behind me, I knew instantly who it was. Randolph. He'd hovered over me even more than the others, ensuring I had everything I needed. That was his way of asking for forgiveness, although it wasn't necessary.

He had been responsible for saving my life after all.

As he remained quiet, flanking my side but keeping his distance, I could tell how troubled he was.

"You're going to laugh, but that's just fine. When I was a little boy, I wanted to be a fireman," he said after a few seconds.

"Why would I laugh? I thought I was going to be a princess in a castle, protected by a warrior. You would have been so good fighting fires, saving people's lives. You saved mine."

The half-smile on his face saddened me. "I'm no hero, Scarlett. Don't try and make me one. I placed your life in danger."

"You had no idea, Randolph."

"You know that's not true." As he turned his head toward me, I shuddered all the way to my core. I'd been able to read his feelings from the day I met him, mostly contempt yet sparked with lust. Today, it was entirely different. As if he'd decided to become a different man.

As if he couldn't live without me.

"What I know is that you risked your own life to find me. I also know is that you could have killed every man on that rooftop, but you injured them instead. That tells me so much about you."

"That I couldn't do what was necessary?" He laughed bitterly.

I inched closer, every part of me tingling. "No, that you really couldn't cross that line. You aren't your father. You're a strong, resilient, brilliant, and some-times pigheaded leader."

He burst into full laughter, the sadness disappearing. "I'll take that. And you're a spitfire vixen with a heart of gold and a determination to make life exactly the way you want it to be. I admire that more than you know."

Why was the man so entirely intoxicating? Why could I see spending the rest of my life with all three of them?

"Do you know what my father told me after my statement about what I wanted to be when I grew up?"

I was terrified to ask.

"That he would disown me if I did." He shook his head, fisting one hand. "What a crock of shit."

"I'm so sorry," I said quietly.

"Don't be. I honestly would have made a lousy fireman anyway." He laughed again, darting another look in my direction. "I finally made my peace with who he was, but I'll never be able to forgive him."

"Don't harbor hatred, Randolph. Live your life the way you want to, no matter what that means to anyone else."

He turned to face me, sliding his arms around my waist. "I plan on it, but I want you involved."

"Involved? That sounds like business and I'm not sure where I want to take Prestwood."

"I'd love to share business tactics with you, even merge our companies, but that's not what I'm talking about."

"Then what are you talking about?"

When his nostrils flared, all I had to do was shift my gaze to his throbbing cock to know. "I want you. All of you. So do Alexander and Trent. You are the only thing that matters in this life."

His words were stunning, both thrilling and terrifying me. As he closed the distance, I became lightheaded.

"Hmmm... Are you certain?" I crawled my hand along his chest then dragged a single finger across the seam of his mouth.

Growling, he nipped my finger, sucking gently for several seconds. "I've never been more certain of anything in my life."

When he pulled me onto my tiptoes, I drank in his amazing exotic scent and was almost instantly intoxicated. He did that to me, just like the others. I adored all three of them. No, I loved them deeply. As he lowered his head, capturing my mouth, I fell into the moment of passion. We'd made love several times, the four of indulging in our deep passions, but there was something missing between us, and I wasn't certain what that was. However, I knew it would eventually pry us apart.

And I wasn't certain I could tolerate the heartache. It would crush me.

He held me tightly and I sensed both Alexander and Trent had approached. When I felt their hands rubbing up and down my back, I tingled all over, my nipples aching.

Randolph refused to let me go, dominating my tongue as he took his time with the kiss.

When Trent cleared his throat, he finally pulled away, growling as if he was angry at being interrupted, but I knew better. The three of them were more playful than I thought they could be, which had given me moments of sheer joy.

Being with them had also challenged everything I'd ever wanted.

"It's time for Scarlett's spanking," Alexander said in his usual husky voice.

"Wait a minute. I haven't misbehaved this entire time," I objected.

"Yes, you have but I'm talking about leaving the villa in Cancun and taking a walk. That was totally against the rules." Trent gave me a stern look.

"Oh, that," I mused.

"Yes, that," Randolph huffed. "You know what happens when you break the rules."

Frowning, I did my best to pout, although I knew it wouldn't do me any good.

When Alexander tugged on my dress, yanking it over my head, all I could do was moan.

"Now, you can remove those sexy little panties of yours or I'll do it," Trent added, winking to the others.

"Oh, no, you don't. I know how you would do that," I teased, still pursing my lips as I slowly slid my thong past my hips. I darted a glance over my shoulder, glaring at the beach. While the villa was in a private area, that didn't mean people couldn't walk on the beach, capturing a close up and personal view of me being spanked. I felt heat rise on my face, moaning when Alexander pushed me against the railing.

"Now, if you're a very good girl and stay in position, we might be lenient," he said.

I gave him a mischievous look. Of course I couldn't stay in position. As I gripped the railing, staring out at the beautiful turquoise ocean, I thought about what the future might be like.

The first hard crack of Trent's hand brought me out of my little fantasy.

"Ouch. That hurt."

"Spankings are supposed to hurt. Remember?" he asked before giving me four in rapid succession. He continued, smacking me several times, leaving me breathless and panting.

While there was pain, it was nothing in comparison to the sadness encroaching my heart. Sometimes love wasn't enough to erase the fears or self-doubts. What all four of us had been through was something I would never forget. The events had changed me. Not just for a little while but forever. I was no longer interested in destroying their company or their reputation. The fight had been knocked out of me. That wasn't something I could accept.

Sighing, I closed my eyes.

That's the moment I realized that I would always love them, but I couldn't be their fourth. I couldn't give up that much of myself. After our return to

Pittsburg, I would do everything in my power never to see them again.

And that alone would break my heart.

* * *

Two weeks later

Alexander

Retaliation.

I knew that Randolph remained hellbent on finishing the nightmare mostly because of Scarlett's decision to return to her life alone. He'd yet to discuss how he felt, other than in terms of anger, but my gut told me this wasn't a battle he wanted to fight.

"Any word on the Valenti brothers?" Trent asked. He'd been tasked to drive all three of us, the ride laced with utter silence up to this point.

Randolph remained quiet, staring out the passenger window. I shot him a look over my shoulder, shaking my head. "From what I know, only Mario remains in the hospital. There have been no additional threats and no recent stock purchases. The DA called me yesterday. It would seem the Valenti family is under investigation for extortion attempts, wire fraud, stock manipulation, and murder. I doubt they'd bother continuing with their plan of revenge."

"They'll return one day. That's the way a mafia family works," Randolph stated, although there was no emotion in his voice.

Trent and I shot glances at each other.

"Since when are you such an expert?" I asked, more as a dare.

"Since I was forced into the life because of my father," he answered, hissing afterwards.

"You need to let it go or it'll continue eating you alive," Trent offered.

Randolph growled, the sound filling the dense space. "You don't get to tell me what I can and can't do."

I wasn't shocked at the fact he raised his voice or used his commanding tone. That meant he wasn't completely dead inside.

"You're right," Trent answered for both of us.

The tension remained although I could tell Randolph's mind was spinning out of control.

"Steven Dockett called for a second time. He wants to set up a meeting," I said in passing.

"Why in the *fuck* did she give up that contract?" Randolph demanded.

"I can't answer that, my friend. Scarlett won't return my calls. Her assistant told me she's taking a leave of absence."

"She's a fool. She'll never regain her footing because of this," he added.

"I don't think that's what she wants any longer." Trent's voice seemed more haunted than it should be.

We were all affected by the loss of such an incredible woman, a beautiful relationship that had been so unexpected, but there was nothing we could do but honor her wishes.

As the house came into view, every muscle in my body tensed. The Clubhouse was in session. We'd received an invite but had no intentions of participating in whatever kinky event Carlos had provided. This was all about business.

"Whatever happens today, you know this means we will never be invited to another event again," Randolph said after Trent parked.

"I'm no longer interested in being a member," Trent answered, immediately throwing open his door.

"I second that," I huffed, smiling as I tossed a look Randolph's way.

"Then let's do this."

The estate was packed with members as I'd suspected it would be, various rooms closed off for private use. We headed toward the lounge, immediately noticing Carlos preening at the bar. When he noticed us, he smiled as if he'd expected us.

Randolph approached first, keeping a smile on his face. "We need to talk." He motioned toward the bartender, more relaxed than I thought he'd be. "Bourbon. Neat."

"We can arrange that," Carlos answered. I could tell he'd glanced subtly at the two men who stood guard at the door. Perhaps he was concerned about our arrival.

He should be.

"Robert will bring you to my office after you've gotten a drink," he said, moving between us. He stopped long enough to shift his head over his shoulder, locking eyes will each one of us before moving on. The smile he wore told me he knew exactly why we'd accepted the invitation.

After selecting our drinks, we took our time before approaching Robert. The man said nothing as he led us down a long hallway, opening one of the double doors.

Carlos stood at his window, staring out at his expansive lawn.

"I'm glad to see the three of you survived," he said after a few seconds.

"Are you?" Randolph asked. "This might be my opinion, but I think you were hoping the Valenti brothers would succeed in eliminating us."

He snorted, taking a sip of whatever drink he had in his hand. "Then you don't know me very well. I do enjoy a good game of chess."

Randolph walked closer, taking his time in doing so. "And you obviously didn't know what we were made of. I learned from my father that when a man is pushed up against a wall, he'll either come out fighting or he'll be eliminated. We chose to come out fighting in order to protect everything that's important to us."

"You mean the woman," Carlos said, half laughing.

"Yes." Randolph's simple answer gave me a smile.

"I applaud you, my friend. You've finally come to your senses," Carlos half whispered as he turned to face us. "Why have you come to see me?"

Randolph gave both Trent and me a glance before continuing. "Because the game is over. Forever. We are well aware that the Valenti brothers are current members and that you're very close to the family. In fact, you've been good friends with the Consigliere your entire life."

Carlos took a deep breath, finally nodding.

"While the taste for blood remains in my system," Randolph continued, "I'm going to treat this as a business transaction and nothing more. Therefore, after today, the three of us are no longer members."

"And in turn?" Carlos asked, acting as if Randolph's statement didn't bother him.

"And in turn," I stated as I walked closer, "you will call off the Valentis' plan of revenge, helping them understand that it wouldn't be in their best interest. In addition, they will resell the stock they own in Worth Dynamics as well as in Prestwood Automation."

"It's that simple," Trent added.

The silence in the room was interesting, and I had to admit being in this kind of control was exciting, an adrenaline rush flowing through me.

Carlos took a deep breath, finally nodding. "Very well. You have a deal. However, if you break our agreement, you will suffer in ways you cannot comprehend."

"Likewise, Carlos. As I said. You have no idea who we are and what we're capable of." Randolph still wore the smile on his face, and I could tell he was more relaxed than before.

Randolph polished off his drink first, placing the glass on Carlos' expensive desk. Trent and I followed suit, finally heading for the door.

"One last piece of advice, *señor*. Don't allow Scarlett to get away from you. You will regret it for the rest of your life."

Carlos' words were as haunting as they were aggravating.

But he was right.

Only we couldn't have the one thing that made us whole.

The woman all three of us had fallen in love with.

* * *

Scarlett

"I understand, Mr. Wentworth. And yes, I hope we can do business in the future. I'm just taking some time to restructure my company." I rubbed my eyes as the man blabbered on about what we could have done together. I knew exactly what I was giving up, but I needed time.

Marjorie remained in front of me, pacing like a lion. I knew she didn't agree with my decisions, but I owned the company.

"Thank you again and I wish you luck in your endeavors." As I ended the call, I closed my eyes for a few seconds, still able to envision the last night I'd spent on a beautiful tropical island.

"What are you doing?" Marjorie demanded.

"Changing."

"By giving up two lucrative contracts? You must be out of your mind."

I took a deep breath, trying to think of how to explain it to her. "I love this company and the people who work with me, but it's not enough any longer. I

413

need more. When you reminded me that I used to have integrity, but I'd managed to lose it somehow, it struck a nerve. I'm going to find that woman again somehow. Some way."

"Did you know that the stock that was recently purchased was sold again?"

That I did not know. "To whom?"

"The people who owned it before. It's the craziest thing."

Somehow, I knew Randolph had made that happen. My heart fluttered at the thought. "That's great but it doesn't change my mind."

She inched closer, shaking her head. "Then I'm going to give you one piece of advice. Take this from an older woman who made decisions she regrets. Don't continue to push them out of your life. You're in love, Scarlett. I can see it in your eyes and in everything you do. They gave you something that this business has never been able to. Peace of mind. Whatever it takes, find your way back to them. Move out of your comfort zone if that's what it takes. That's what you need in your life, and you know it."

I was shocked she'd give me that advice. Sighing, I knew the demons inside my head would never leave me alone if I didn't make some peace with my heart.

"Maybe you're right," I finally said.

"I'm always right. Think about it and call me when you have your head on straight." She laughed as she walked toward my office door, giving me a motherly look before leaving.

How many nights had I gone without sleep? How many dreams had I experienced? Shit. Shit!

I walked from one side of my office to the other then couldn't take it any longer. I moved toward the computer, allowing my fingers to fly on the keyboard. Then I made a call.

"Hi. This is Scarlett Prestwood. You don't know me, but I need your help. Desperately. And I'm willing to pay whatever you need."

* * *

One week later

Randolph

"What the hell is this?" I barked as I glanced at the invitation.

Alexander chuckled. "We got one too. I don't know. Some special event at Club Velvet. I think we should go."

"No way. I couldn't care less about some kink club," I retorted, tossing the invitation on my desk. Although I had to admit I was intrigued.

"I agree with Alexander. We've been working twenty-hour days getting everything ready for Dockett. We need a night out," Trent piped in.

Growling, I hated everything about the thought. "No fucking way."

"Well, I think I'll go. Why not? Maybe it will give me some inspiration," Alexander tossed out.

"I agree with you," Trent said, giving me a stern look. "You need to get your head out of your ass, Randolph."

Snorting, I lifted my middle finger just for the hell of it. I refused to go. Kink clubs meant nothing to me any longer. Hell, little did. I was empty inside, unable to sleep or eat. At least business was on the uptick. As if that mattered any longer.

"Have fun," I commented, walking around my desk and sitting down. Today was just like every other one.

All business and nothing that mattered to me any longer.

I'd lost the woman I loved.

Forever.

After they left, I fingered the invitation, glaring down at it. I'd never given up on anything in my life. Why now? I didn't have all the answers. What I did know is that I would never care for anyone else again. That was my promise to myself.

The bastards managed to drag me to the club. I wasn't entirely certain how it happened. We even had a damn table right in front of the stage. I fingered my drink, glaring at the sparkling lights swimming across the platform and groaned. Why the hell did I feel so uncomfortable in my own skin?

"The place is packed," Trent mused, sitting back in his chair.

"Maybe a celebrity is about to make her debut," Alexander suggested.

"As if I give a shit." My answer was curt and to the point.

As the lights dimmed, I glanced at the crowd. There were more politicians and corporate moguls in the audience than usual. For some reason, that disgusted me. I tried to relax as the club owner stepped onto the stage.

"What the hell is he doing?" I mumbled.

When a spotlight was placed directly over his head, I rolled my eyes.

"Good evening, ladies and gentlemen. Tonight is a very special night. We have an ingénue ready to perform her debut act."

"Christ," I mumbled. This I didn't need.

"And because of that, we need three members from the audience to help with her act," he continued. He smiled and looked out at the audience, walking to the other side of the stage.

"This should be interesting," Trent said, half laughing.

Yeah, or boring as hell. Why did I waste my time?

When the owner returned in front of our table, my hackles were raised.

"I think the three of you are perfect. Why don't you gentlemen come up on stage?" he asked as he pointed toward us.

The crowd began to cheer.

Not a fucking chance in hell I was going on stage.

I started to wave it off as Alexander leaned toward me. "Why not? This could be fun," he said."

"Are you kidding me?" I snarled.

"Come on. What's it going to hurt?" Trent moved to his feet.

I hesitated for a few seconds then finally gave in. Fuck it. Why not? Maybe it would be a diversion that would do me some good.

As the three of us moved on stage, the curtains remained closed.

"Thank you for participating," the owner said as he led us to a table full of implements. "You're going to provide our lovely temptress with the punishment she needs for being a very naughty girl. Your pleasure, gentlemen."

As he backed away, allowing us time to choose, I grumbled under my breath. This was grandstanding and nothing more. I selected a tawse, barely interested in what was about to happen.

The curtains finally opened, revealing a lovely woman in a sheer gown and an intricate mask. As she walked toward us, I had to admit she was an incredible vision, but she wasn't the woman I cared about so nothing would matter.

She inched closer, dancing around the three of us for several seconds before kneeling, lowering her head.

I took a deep inhale and almost instantly, I was thrown into an utterly intoxicated state. I knew the incredible exotic perfume, the scent deliciously overpowering, electrifying every cell in my body. My heart started to race, and I glanced at the other two men. They sensed the same thing.

She remained in position, obviously waiting for our instructions.

"Rise," I commanded, barely able to think clearly.

When she did, she kept her head down. I lifted her chin with a single finger, my chest heaving as I struggled to breathe. Then I ripped off her mask.

A smile crossed Scarlett's face, her eyes lighting up like I'd never seen them before.

"What are you doing?" I whispered, cupping her jaw, rubbing my thumb across her lips.

"Pleasuring my three masters, men I've fallen in love with," she answered. A single tear slipped past her long eyelashes and for a few seconds, I was breathless. Then I gathered her into my arms, crushing her against me.

"My God. I thought we'd lost you forever," I managed, drowning out the cheers from the audience.

"Never," she managed, pushing away and reaching for Alexander and Trent.

"She is one mischievous woman," Trent struggled to say.

"She needs a hard spanking," Alexander managed.

"Yes, she does," I whispered. "And we're going to give it to her whenever she needs for the rest of her life. I love you, Scarlett. I've always loved you. Now you belong to us." As I lowered my head, pressing my lips against hers, the past horrors slipped away, leaving only the promise of the future.

Maybe I had crossed that thin line, but I'd learned that love was the only tangible thing that mattered.

Not money.

Not fancy toys.

Not power.

Just the love of an incredible, amazing, naughty woman.

"Come, sweet Scarlett. We're going to teach you how to obey."

The End

AFTERWORD

Stormy Night Publications would like to thank you
for your interest in our books.

If you liked this book (or even if you didn't), we
would really appreciate you leaving a review on the
site where you purchased it. Reviews provide useful
feedback for us and our authors, and this feedback
(both positive comments and constructive criticism)
allows us to work even harder to make sure we
provide the content our customers want to read.

If you would like to check out more books from
Stormy Night Publications, if you want to learn
more about our company, or if you would like to
join our mailing list, please visit our website at:

http://www.stormynightpublications.com

Men like me.

I could romance her. I could seduce her and then carry her gently to my bed.

But that can wait. Tonight I'm going to wring one ruthless climax after another from her quivering body with her bottom burning from my belt and her throat sore from screaming.

She will know she is mine before she even knows she is my bride.

Savage Prince

Gillian's father may be a powerful Irish mob boss, but he owes a blood debt to my family, and when I came to collect I didn't ask permission before taking his daughter as payment.

It was not up to him… or to her.

I will make her my bride, but I am not the kind of man who will wait until our wedding night to bare her and claim what belongs to me. She will walk down the aisle wet, well-used, and sore.

Her dress will hide the marks from my belt that taught her the consequences of disobeying her husband, but nothing will hide her blushes as her arousal drips down her thighs with each step.

By the time she says her vows she will already be mine.

I didn't choose to go with him, but it wasn't up to me. That's why I'm naked, wet, and sore in an opulent Swiss chalet with my bottom still burning from the belt of the infuriatingly sexy mafia boss who brought me here, punished me when I fought him, and then savagely made me his.

We'll return when things are safe in New Orleans, but I won't be going back to my old home.

I belong to him now, and he plans to keep me.

King's Possession

Her father had to be taught what happens when you cross a King, but that isn't why Genevieve Rossi is sore, well-used, and waiting for me to claim her in the only way I haven't already.

She's sore because she thought she could embarrass me in public without being punished.

She's well-used because after I spanked her I wanted more, and I take what I want.

She's waiting for me in my bed because she's my bride, and tonight is our wedding night.

I'm not going to be gentle with her, but when she wakes up tomorrow morning wet and blushing her cheeks won't be crimson because of the shameful things I did to her naked, quivering body.

It will be because she begged for all of them.

King's Toy

Vincenzo King thought I knew something about a man who betrayed him, but that isn't why I'm on my way to New Orleans well-used and sore with my backside still burning from his belt.

When he bared and punished me maybe it was just business, but what came after was not.

It was savage, it was shameful, and it was very, very personal.

I'm his toy now, and not the kind you keep in its box on the shelf.

He's going to play rough with me.

He's going to get me all wet and dirty.

Then he's going to do it all again tomorrow.

King's Demands

Julieta Morales hoped to escape an unwanted marriage, but the moment she got into my car her fate was sealed. She will have a husband, but it won't be the cartel boss her father chose for her.

It will be me.

But I'm not the kind of man who takes his bride gently amid rose petals on her wedding night. She'll learn to satisfy her King's demands with her bottom burning and her hair held in my fist.

She'll promise obedience when she speaks her vows, but she'll be mastered long before then.

King's Temptation

I didn't think I needed Dimitri Kristoff's protection, but it wasn't up to me. With a kingpin from a rival family coming after me, he took charge, took off his belt, and then took what he wanted.

He knows I'm not used to doing as I'm told. He just doesn't care.

The stripes seared across my bare bottom left me sore and sorry, but it was what came after that truly left me shaken. The princess of the King family shouldn't be on her knees for anyone, let alone this Bratva brute who has decided to claim for himself what he was meant to safeguard.

Nobody gave me to him, but I'm his anyway.

Now he's going to make sure I know it.

Forced to Cooperate

Willow Church is not the first person who tried to put a bullet in me. She's just the first I let live. Now she will pay the price in the most shameful way imaginable. The stripes from my belt will teach her to obey, but what happens to her sore, red bottom after that will teach the real lesson.

She will be used mercilessly, over and over, and every brutal climax will remind her of the humiliating truth: she never even had a chance against me. Her body always knew its master.

Claimed as Revenge

Valencia Rivera became mine the moment her father broke the agreement he made with me. She thought she had a say in the matter, but my belt across her beautiful bottom taught her otherwise and a night spent screaming her surrender into the sheets left her in no doubt she belongs to me.

Using her hard and often will not be all it takes to tame her properly, but it will be a good start...

Made to Beg

Sierra Fox showed up at my door to ask for my protection, and I gave it to her... for a price. She belongs to me now, and I'm going to use her beautiful body as thoroughly as I please. The only thing for her to decide is how sore her cute little bottom will be when I'm through claiming her.

She came to me begging for help, but as her moans and screams grow louder with every brutal climax, we both know it won't be long before she begs me for something far more shameful.

he pleased, then showed up at my house the next day, stripped me bare, and spanked me until I was begging him to take me even more roughly and shamefully.

Now, with his enemies likely to be coming after me in order to get to him, all I can do is hope he's as good at keeping me safe as he is at keeping me blushing, sore, and thoroughly satisfied.

Dangerous

I knew Erik Chenault was dangerous the moment I saw him. Everything about him should have warned me away, from the scar on his face to the fact that mobsters call him Blade. But I was drawn like a moth to a flame, and I ended up burnt... and blushing, sore, and thoroughly used.

Now he's taken it upon himself to protect me from men like the ones we both tried to leave in our past. He's going to make me his whether I like it or not... but I think I'm going to like it.

Prey

Within moments of setting eyes on Sophia Waters, I was certain of two things. She was going to learn what happens to bad girls who cheat at cards, and I was going to be the one to teach her.

But there was one thing I didn't know as I reddened that cute little bottom and then took her long and hard and oh so shamefully: I wasn't the only one who didn't come here for a game of cards.

I came to kill a man. It turns out she came to protect him.

Nobody keeps me from my target, but I'm in no rush. Not when I'm enjoying this game of cat and mouse so much. I'll even let her catch me one day, and as she screams my name with each brutal climax she'll finally realize the truth. She was never the hunter. She was always the prey.

Given

Stephanie Michaelson was given to me, and she is mine. The sooner she learns that, the less often her cute little bottom will end up well-punished and sore as she is reminded of her place.

But even as she promises obedience with tears running down her cheeks, I know it isn't the sting of my belt that will truly tame her. It is what comes next that will leave her in no doubt she belongs to me. That part will be long, hard, and shameful... and I will make her beg for all of it.

Dangerous Stranger

I came to Spain hoping to start a new life away from dangerous men, but then I met Rafael Santiago. Now I'm not just caught up in the affairs of a mafia boss, I'm being forced into his car.

When I saw something I shouldn't have, Rafael took me captive, stripped me bare, and punished me until he felt certain I'd told him everything I knew about his organization... which was nothing at all. Then he offered me his protection in return for the right to use me as he pleases.

Now that I belong to him, his plans for me are more shameful than I could have ever imagined.

Indebted

After her father stole from me, I could have left Alessandra Toro in jail for a crime she didn't commit. But I have plans for her. A deal with the judge—the kind only a man like me can arrange—made her my captive, and she will pay her father's debt with her beautiful body.

She will try to run, of course, but it won't be the law that comes after her. It will be me.

The sting of my belt across her quivering bare bottom will teach Alessandra the price of defiance, but it is the far more shameful penance that follows which will truly tame her.

Taken

When Winter O'Brien was given to me, she thought she had a say in the matter. She was wrong.

She is my bride. Mine to claim, mine to punish, and mine to use as shamefully as I please. The sting of my belt on her bare bottom will teach her to obey, but obedience is just the beginning.

I will demand so much more.

Bratva's Captive

I told Chloe Kingstrom that getting close to me would be dangerous, and she should keep her distance. The moment she disobeyed and followed me into that bar, she became mine.

Now my enemies are after her, but it's not what they would do to her she should worry about.

It's what I'm going to do to her.

My belt across her bare backside will teach her obedience, but what comes after will be different.

She's going to blush, beg, and scream with every climax as she's ravaged more thoroughly than she can imagine. Then I'm going to flip her over and claim her in an even more shameful way.

If she's a good girl, I might even let her enjoy it.

Hunted

Hope Gracen was just another target to be tracked down... until I caught her.

When I discovered I'd been lied to, I carried her off.

She'll tell me the truth with her bottom still burning from my belt, but that isn't why she's here.

I took her to protect her. I'm keeping her because she's mine.

Theirs as Payment

Until mere moments ago, I was a doctor heading home after my shift at the hospital. But that was before I was forced into the back seat of an SUV, then bared and spanked for trying to escape.

Now I'm just leverage for the Cabello brothers to use against my father, but it isn't the thought of being held hostage by these brutes that has my heart racing and my whole body quivering.

It is the way they're looking at me...

Like they're about to tear my clothes off and take turns mounting me like wild beasts.

Like they're going to share me, using me in ways more shameful than I can even imagine.

Like they own me.

I fought as he bared me and begged as he spanked me, but it didn't matter. All I could do was moan, scream, and climax helplessly for him as he took everything he wanted from me.

By the time I signed the contract, I was already his.

Unseemly Entanglement

I was warned about Frederick Duvall. I was told he was dangerous. But I never suspected that meeting the billionaire advertising mogul to discuss a business proposition would end with me bent over a table with my dress up and my panties down for a shameful lesson in obedience.

That should have been it. I should have told him what he could do with his offer and his money.

But I didn't.

I could say it was because two million dollars is a lot of cash, but as I stand before him naked, bound, and awaiting the sting of his cane for daring to displease him, I know that's not the truth.

I'm not here because he pays me. I'm here because he owns me.

BOOKS OF THE CLUB DARKNESS SERIES

Bent to His Will

Even the most powerful men in the world know better than to cross me, but Autumn Sutherland thought she could spy on me in my own club and get away with it. Now she must be punished.

She tried to expose me, so she will be exposed. Bare, bound, and helplessly on display, she'll beg for mercy as my strap lashes her quivering bottom and my crop leaves its burning welts on her most intimate spots. Then she'll scream my name as she takes every inch of me, long and hard.

When I am done with her, she won't just be sore and shamefully broken. She will be mine.

Broken by His Hand

Sophia Russo tried to keep away from me, but just thinking about what I would do to her left her panties drenched. She tried to hide it, but I didn't let her. I tore those soaked panties off, spanked her bare little bottom until she had no doubt who owns her, and then took her long and hard.

She begged and screamed as she came for me over and over, but she didn't learn her lesson…

She didn't just come back for more. She thought she could disobey me and get away with it.

This time I'm not just going to punish her. I'm going to break her.

Bound by His Command

Willow danced for the rich and powerful at the world's most exclusive club... until tonight.

Tonight I told her she belongs to me now, and no other man will touch her again.

Tonight I ripped her soaked panties from her beautiful body and taught her to obey with my belt.

Tonight I took her as mine, and I won't be giving her up.

Now they're going to share me, and they're not going to be gentle about it.

burning bottom raised high, and my hair held tightly in his fist as he took me long and hard and taught me the kind of shameful lesson only a man like Scorpion could teach.

She was begging for a taste of my belt. She got much more than that.

Getting so tipsy she thought she could be sassy with me in my own bar earned Caroline a spanking, but it was trying to make off with my truck that sealed the deal. She'll feel my belt across her bare backside, then she'll scream my name as she takes every single inch of me.

This naughty girl needs to be put in her place, and I'm going to enjoy every moment of it.

Mustang

I tried to tell him how to run his ranch. Then he took off his belt.

When I heard a rumor about his ranch, I confronted Mustang about it. I thought I could go toe to toe with the big, tough former Marine, but I ended up blushing, sore, and very thoroughly used.

I told her it was going to hurt. I meant it.

Danni Brexton is a hot little number with a sharp tongue and a chip on her shoulder. She's the kind of trouble that needs to be ridden hard and put away wet, but only after a taste of my belt.

It will take more than just a firm hand and a burning bottom to tame this sassy spitfire, but I plan to keep her safe, sound, and screaming my name in bed whether she likes it or not. By the time I'm through with her, there won't be a shadow of a doubt in her mind that she belongs to me.

Nash

When he caught me on his property, he didn't call the police. He just took off his belt.

Nash caught me breaking into his shed while on the run from the mob, and when he demanded answers and obedience I gave him neither. Then he took off his belt and taught me in the most shameful way possible what happens to naughty girls who play games with a big, rough Marine.

She's mine to protect. That doesn't mean I'm going to be gentle with her.

Michelle doesn't just need a place to hide out. She needs a man who will bare her bottom and spank her until she is sore and sobbing whenever she puts herself at risk with reckless defiance, then shove her face into the sheets and make her scream his name with every savage climax.

She'll get all of that from me, and much, much more.

Austin

I offered this brute a ride. I ended up the one being ridden.

The first time I saw Austin, he was hitchhiking. I stopped to give him a lift, but I didn't end up taking this big, rough former Marine wherever he was heading. He was far too busy taking me.

She thought she was in charge. Then I took off my belt.

When Francesca Montgomery pulled up beside me, I didn't know who she was, but I knew what she needed and I gave it to her. Long, hard, and thoroughly, until she was screaming my name as she climaxed over and over with her quivering bare bottom still sporting the marks from my belt.

But someone wants to hurt her, and when someone tries to hurt what's mine, I take it personally.

By the time I am finished with her, the evidence of her body's surrender will be mingled with my seed as it drips down her bare thighs. But she will be more than just sore and utterly spent.

She will be mine.

Alpha's Mate

I didn't ask Nicolina to be my mate. It was not up to her. An alpha takes what belongs to him.

She will plead for mercy as she is bared and punished for daring to run from me, but her screams as she is claimed and rutted will be those of helpless climax as her body surrenders to its master.

She is mine, and I'm going to make sure she knows it.

Claimed by the Beasts

Though she has done her best to run from it, Scarlet Dumane cannot escape what is in store for her. She has known for years that she is destined to belong not just to one savage beast, but to three, and now the time has come for her to be claimed. Soon her mates will own every inch of her beautiful body, and she will be shared and used as roughly and as often as they please.

Scarlet hid from the disturbing truth about herself, her family, and her town for as long as she could, but now her grandmother's death has finally brought her back home to the bayous of Louisiana and at last she must face her fate, no matter how shameful and terrifying.

She will be a queen, but her mates will be her masters, and defiance will be thoroughly punished. Yet even when she is stripped bare and spanked until she is sobbing, her need for them only grows, and every blush, moan, and quivering climax binds her to them more tightly. But with enemies lurking in the shadows, can she trust her mates to protect her from both man and beast?

Millionaire Daddy

Dominick Asbury is not just a handsome millionaire whose deep voice makes Jenna's tummy flutter whenever they are together, nor is he merely the first man bold enough to strip her bare and spank her hard and thoroughly whenever she has been naughty. He is much more than that.

He is her daddy.

He is the one who punishes her when she's been a bad girl, and he is the one who takes her in his arms afterwards and brings her to one climax after another until she is utterly spent and satisfied.

But something shady is going on behind the scenes at Dominick's company, and when Jenna draws the wrong conclusion from a poorly written article about him and creates an embarrassing public scene, will she end up not only costing them both their jobs but losing her daddy as well?

Conquering Their Mate

For years the Cenzans have cast a menacing eye on Earth, but it still came as a shock to be captured, stripped bare, and claimed as a mate by their leader and his most trusted warriors.

It infuriates me to be punished for the slightest defiance and forced to submit to these alien brutes, but as I'm led naked through the corridors of their ship, my well-punished bare bottom and my helpless arousal both fully on display, I cannot help wondering how long it will be until I'm kneeling at the feet of my mates and begging them take me as shamefully as they please.

Captured and Kept

Since her career was knocked off track in retaliation for her efforts to expose a sinister plot by high-ranking government officials, reporter Danielle Carver has been stuck writing puff pieces in a small town in Oregon. Desperate for a serious story, she sets out to investigate the rumors she's been hearing about mysterious men living in the mountains nearby. But when she secretly follows them back to their remote cabin, the ruggedly handsome beasts don't take kindly to her snooping around, and Dani soon finds herself stripped bare for a painful, humiliating spanking.

Their rough dominance arouses her deeply, and before long she is blushing crimson as they take turns using her beautiful body as thoroughly and shamefully as they please. But when Dani uncovers the true reason for their presence in the area, will more than just her career be at risk?

Taming His Brat

It's been years since Cooper Dawson left her small Texas hometown, but after her stubborn defiance gets her fired from two jobs in a row, she knows something definitely needs to change. What she doesn't expect, however, is for her sharp tongue and arrogant attitude to land her over the knee of a stern, ruggedly sexy cowboy for a painful, embarrassing, and very public spanking.

Rex Sullivan cannot deny being smitten by Cooper, and the fact that she is in desperate need of his belt across her bare backside only makes the war-hardened ex-Marine more determined to tame the beautiful, fiery redhead. It isn't long before she's screaming his name as he shows her just how hard and roughly a cowboy can ride a headstrong filly. But Rex and Cooper both have secrets, and when the demons of their past rear their ugly heads, will their romance be torn apart?

Capturing Their Mate

I thought the Cenzan invaders could never find me here, but I was wrong. Three of the alien brutes came to take me, and before I ever set foot aboard their ship I had already been stripped bare, spanked thoroughly, and claimed more shamefully then I would have ever thought possible.

They have decided that a public example must be made of me, and I will be punished and used in the most humiliating ways imaginable as a warning to anyone who might dare to defy them. But I am no ordinary breeder, and the secrets hidden in my past could change their world… or end it.

Rogue

Tracking down cyborgs is my job, but this time I'm the one being hunted. This rogue machine has spent most of his life locked up, and now that he's on the loose he has plans for me…

He isn't just going to strip me, punish me, and use me. He will take me longer and harder than any human ever could, claiming me so thoroughly that I will be left in no doubt who owns me.

No matter how shamefully I beg and plead, my body will be ravaged again and again with pleasure so intense it terrifies me to even imagine, because that is what he was built to do.

Roughneck

When I took a job on an oil rig to escape my scheming stepfather's efforts to set me up with one of his business cronies, I knew I'd be working with rugged men. What I didn't expect is to find myself bent over a desk, my cheeks soaked with tears and my bare thighs wet for a very different reason, as my well-punished bottom is thoroughly used by a stern, infuriatingly sexy roughneck.

Even though I should have known better than to get sassy with a firm-handed cowboy, let alone a tough-as-nails former Marine, there's no denying that learning the hard way was every bit as hot as it was shameful. But a sore, welted backside is just the start of his plans for me, and no matter how much I blush to admit it, I know I'm going to take everything he gives me and beg for more.

Hunting Their Mate

As far as I'm concerned, the Cenzans will always be the enemy, and there can be no peace while they remain on our planet. I planned to make them pay for invading our world, but I was hunted down and captured by two of their warriors with the help of a battle-hardened former Marine. Now I'm the one who is going to pay, as the three of them punish me, shame me, and share me.

Though the thought of a fellow human taking the side of these alien brutes enrages me, that is far from the worst of it. With every searing stroke of the strap that lands across my bare bottom, with every savage thrust as I am claimed over and over, and with every screaming climax, it is made more clear that it is my own quivering, thoroughly used body which has truly betrayed me.

Primitive

I was sent to this world to help build a new Earth, but I was shocked by what I found here. The men of this planet are not just primitive savages. They are predators, and I am now their prey…

The government lied to all of us. Not all of the creatures who hunted and captured me are aliens. Some of them were human once, specimens transformed in labs into little more than feral beasts.

I fought, but I was thrown over a shoulder and carried off. I ran, but I was caught and punished. Now they are going to claim me, share me, and use me so roughly that when the last screaming climax has been wrung from my naked, helpless body, I wonder if I'll still know my own name.

Harvest

The Centurions conquered Earth long before I was born, but they did not come for our land or our resources. They came for mates, women deemed suitable for breeding. Women like me.

Three of the alien brutes decided to claim me, and when I defied them, they made a public example of me, punishing me so thoroughly and shamefully I might never stop blushing.

But now, as my virgin body is used in every way possible, I'm not sure I want them to stop…

Torched

I work alongside firefighters, so I know how to handle musclebound roughnecks, but Blaise Tompkins is in a league of his own. The night we met, I threw a glass of wine in his face, then ended up shoved against the wall with my panties on the floor and my arousal dripping down my thighs, screaming out climax after shameful climax with my well-punished bottom still burning.

I've got a series of arsons to get to the bottom of, and finding out that the infuriatingly sexy brute who spanked me like a naughty little girl will be helping me with the investigation seemed like the last thing I needed, until somebody hurled a rock through my window in an effort to scare me away from the case. Now having a big, strong man around doesn't seem like such a bad idea…

Fertile

The men who hunt me were always brutes, but now lust makes them barely more than beasts.

When they catch me, I know what comes next.

I will fight, but my need to be bred is just as strong as theirs is to breed. When they strip me, punish me, and use me the way I'm meant to be used, my screams will be the screams of climax.

Hostage

I knew going after one of the most powerful mafia bosses in the world would be dangerous, but I didn't anticipate being dragged from my apartment already sore, sorry, and shamefully used.

My captors don't just plan to teach me a lesson and then let me go. They plan to share me, punish me, and claim me so ruthlessly I'll be screaming my submission into the sheets long before they're through with me. They took me as a hostage, but they'll keep me as theirs.

Defiled

I was born to rule, but for her sake I am banished, forced to wander the Earth among mortals. Her virgin body will pay the price for my protection, and it will be a shameful price indeed.

Stripped, punished, and ravaged over and over, she will scream with every savage climax.

She will be defiled, but before I am done with her she will beg to be mine.

Kept

On the run from corrupt men determined to silence me, I sought refuge in his cabin. I ate his food, drank his whiskey, and slept in his bed. But then the big bad bear came home and I learned the hard way that sometimes Goldilocks ends up with her cute little bottom well-used and sore.

He stripped me, spanked me, and ravaged me in the most shameful way possible, but then this rugged brute did something no one else ever has before. He made it clear he plans to keep me...

Auctioned

Twenty years ago the Malzeons saved us when we were at the brink of self-annihilation, but there was a price for their intervention. They demanded humans as servants... and as pets.

Only criminals were supposed to be offered to the aliens for their use, but when I defied Earth's government, asking questions that no one else would dare to ask, I was sold to them at auction.

I was bought by two of their most powerful commanders, rivals who nonetheless plan to share me. I am their property now, and they intend to tame me, train me, and enjoy me thoroughly.

But I have information they need, a secret guarded so zealously that discovering it cost me my freedom, and if they do not act quickly enough both of our worlds will soon be in grave danger.

Hard Ride

When I snuck into Montana Cobalt's house, I was looking for help learning to ride like him, but what I got was his belt across my bare backside. Then with tears still running down my cheeks and arousal dripping onto my thighs, the big brute taught me a much more shameful lesson.

Montana has agreed to train me, but not just for the rodeo. He's going to break me in and put me through my paces, and then he's going to show me what it means to be ridden rough and dirty.

Carnal

For centuries my kind have hidden our feral nature, our brute strength, and our carnal instincts. But this human female is my mate, and nothing will keep me from claiming and ravaging her.

She is mine to tame and protect, and if my belt doesn't teach her to obey then she'll learn in a much more shameful fashion. Either way, her surrender will be as complete as it is inevitable.

Bounty

After I went undercover to take down a mob boss and ended up betrayed, framed, and on the run, Harper Rollins tried to bring me in. But instead of collecting a bounty, she earned herself a hard spanking and then an even rougher lesson that left her cute bottom sore in a very different way.

She's not one to give up without a fight, but that's fine by me. It just means I'll have plenty more chances to welt her beautiful backside and then make her scream her surrender into the sheets.

Beast

Primitive, irresistible need compelled him to claim me, but it was more than mere instinct that drove this alien beast to punish me for my defiance and then ravage me thoroughly and savagely. Every screaming climax was a brand marking me as his, ensuring I never forget who I belong to.

He's strong enough to take what he wants from me, but that's not why I surrendered so easily as he stripped me bare, pushed me up against the wall, and made me his so roughly and shamefully.

It wasn't fear that forced me to submit. It was need.

Gladiator

Xander didn't just win me in the arena. The alien brute claimed me there too, with my punished bottom still burning and my screams of climax almost drowned out by the roar of the crowd.

Almost…

Victory earned him freedom and the right to take me as his mate, but making me truly his will mean more than just spanking me into shameful surrender and then rutting me like a wild beast. Before he carries me off as his prize, the dark truth that brought me here must be exposed at last.

Big Rig

Alexis Harding is used to telling men exactly what she thinks, but she's never had a roughneck like me as a boss before. On my rig, I make the rules and sassy little girls get stripped bare, bent over my desk, and taught their place, first with my belt and then in a much more shameful way.

She'll be sore and sorry long before I'm done with her, but the arousal glistening on her thighs reveals the truth she would rather keep hidden. She needs it rough, and that's how she'll get it.

Warriors

I knew this was a primitive planet when I landed, but nothing could have prepared me for the rough beasts who inhabit it. The sting of their prince's firm hand on my bare bottom taught me my place in his world, but it was what came after that truly demonstrated his mastery over me.

This alien brute has granted me his protection and his help with my mission, but the price was my total submission to both his shameful demands and those of his second in command as well.

But it isn't the savage way they make use of my quivering body that terrifies me the most. What leaves me trembling is the thought that I may never leave this place... because I won't want to.

Owned

With a ruthless, corrupt billionaire after me, Crockett, Dylan, and Wade are just the men I need. Rough men who know how to keep a woman safe... and how to make her scream their names.

But the Hell's Fury MC doesn't do charity work, and their help will come at a price.

A shameful price...

They aren't just going to bare me, punish me, and then do whatever they want with me.

They're going to make me beg for it.

Seized

Delaney Archer got herself mixed up with someone who crossed us, and now she's going to find out just how roughly and shamefully three bad men like us can make use of her beautiful body.

She can plead for mercy, but it won't stop us from stripping her bare and spanking her until she's sore, sobbing, and soaking wet. Our feisty little captive is going to take everything we give her, and she'll be screaming our names with every savage climax long before we're done with her.

Cruel Masters

I thought I understood the risks of going undercover to report on billionaires flaunting their power, but these men didn't send lawyers after me. They're going to deal with me themselves.

Now I'm naked aboard their private plane, my backside already burning from one of their belts, and these three infuriatingly sexy bastards have only just gotten started teaching me my place.

I'm not just going to be punished, shamed, and shared. I'm going to be mastered.

Hard Men

My father's will left his company to me, but the three roughnecks who ran it for him have other ideas. They're owed a debt and they mean to collect on it, but it's not money these brutes want.

It's me.

In return for protection from my father's enemies, I will be theirs to share. But these are hard men, and they don't just intend to punish my defiance and use me as shamefully as they please.

They plan to master me completely.

Rough Ride

As I hear the leather slide through the loops of his pants, I know what comes next. Jake Travers is going to blister my backside. Then he's going to ride me the way only a rodeo champion can.

Plenty of men who thought they could put me in my place have learned the hard way that I was more than they could handle, and when Jake showed up I was sure he would be no different.

I was wrong.

When I pushed him, he bared and spanked me in front of a bar full of people.

I should have let it go at that, but I couldn't.

That's why he's taking off his belt…

Primal Instinct

Ruger Jameson can buy anything he wants, but that's not the reason I'm his to use as he pleases.

He's a former Army Ranger accustomed to having his orders followed, but that's not why I obey him.

He saved my life after our plane crashed, but I'm not on my knees just to thank him properly.

I'm his because my body knows its master.

I do as I'm told because he blisters my bare backside every time I dare to do otherwise.

I'm at his feet because I belong to him and I plan to show it in the most shameful way possible.

PIPER STONE LINKS

You can keep up with Piper Stone via her newsletter, her website, her Twitter account, her Facebook page, and her Goodreads profile, using the following links:

http://eepurl.com/c2QvLz

https://darkdangerousdelicious.wordpress.com/

https://twitter.com/piperstone01

https://www.facebook.com/Piper-Stone-573573166169730/

https://www.goodreads.com/author/show/15754494.Piper_Stone

Made in the USA
Middletown, DE
01 May 2023

29806228R00265